W9-DIW-752

Lone Rider from Texas

Also by Peter Dawson
in Large Print:

Angel Peak
Treachery at Rock Point
Ghost Brand of the Wishbones
Claiming of the Deerfoot

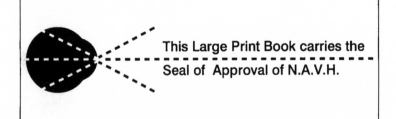

This Large Print Book carries the
Seal of Approval of N.A.V.H.

Lone Rider from Texas

Western Stories

Peter Dawson

Thorndike Press • Waterville, Maine

Published in 2002 by arrangement with Golden West Literary Agency.

Thorndike Press Large Print Western Series.

The tree indicium is a trademark of Thorndike Press.

The text of this Large Print edition is unabridged.
Other aspects of the book may vary from the original edition.

Set in 16 pt. Plantin by Christina S. Huff.

Printed in the United States on permanent paper.

Library of Congress Cataloging-in-Publication Data

Dawson, Peter, 1907–
      Lone rider from Texas : western stories / Peter Dawson.
        p. cm.
      Contents: Manhunt in Malpais — Lawman of Latigo
Wells — The boom-camp terror — A renegade guards the
gold stage — Bushwhack heritage — This one good eye —
Lone rider from Texas.
      ISBN 0-7838-8949-6 (lg. print : hc : alk. paper)
      1. Western stories. 2. Large type books. I. Title.
PS3507.A848 L66 2002
      813′.54—dc21
                                                    2001039378

Table of Contents

Manhunt in Malpais

Jonathan Glidden published all of his fiction under the *nom de plume* Peter Dawson, a name given him by his agent, Marguerite E. Harper, inspired, she said, by the name of a Scotch whisky she liked. "Manhunt in Malpais," as Jon Glidden titled this short novel, was completed late in June, 1938. His agent sent it to Jack Burr at Street & Smith's *Western Story Magazine* on July 14, 1938. The weekly magazine was usually bought ahead for about three months. Burr bought this short novel on October 11, 1938, paying the author $162 upon publication. It was first published in the issue dated February 4, 1939. In 1929 at the University of Illinois, Jon had met Dorothy Steele, and they were married the next year. She was the model for several of his heroines, including Helen Bond in this story.

I

"GUNPOWDER WELCOME"

At Willow, fully sixty miles along Bill Legell's back trail, the hostler at a livery barn had looked at him sharply when he had asked the quickest way to Malpais. The hostler's glance had run over Legell's tall frame, taken in his unshaven face and the two tied-down Colts at his thighs.

"Quickest way to Malpais? That depends." It was evidently the six-guns and the way they were worn that decided him, for he went on: "You could take the road in, but that way you'd waste twenty miles. Your best bet is the pass between them two highest peaks. It's shorter . . . and there's less company."

This last, the hint that the trail through the pass was little traveled, had decided Bill Legell. He wasn't anxious to advertise his coming. Last night, after making camp, he'd transferred his U.S. deputy marshal badge from his shirt pocket to the inside of the sweatband in his Stetson.

Today, riding up into the high pass through the Wigwams, across the boulder fields and down the far side, he'd had the faintly marked trail entirely to himself. Now, halfway the length of a high-walled cañon that emptied onto the grama-grass plain below, he was idly wondering what he'd find in Malpais, why it was that the hostler had directed him to take this out-of-the-way trail into the country.

The commissioner's instructions had been brief, rather ominous. "We know now who killed Fred Sims. The gent's name is Bond . . . Ed Bond. You'll find him runnin' a spread in the hills above Malpais. Go down there and get him. From what I hear, it won't be easy. There's trouble in Malpais. Keep clear of it, but don't let it stop you."

The quiet remoteness of this cañon, the absence of any fresh sign along it, and Bill Legell's thoughts as to what faced him must have dulled his wariness. For as he rounded a bend of the cañon, putting his roan into the gravelly bottom of the wash to skirt a high, finger outcropping, he didn't notice the two riders ahead until his roan lifted its ears and nickered. That sign brought Bill's glance up, sent his right hand instinctively toward holster.

His hand hung above gun butt a fraction of a second, then, along with his left, lifted to the level of his ears. He was staring into the bores of two Colt .45s. The faces of the men behind the guns were set uncompromisingly, their eyes bright with hostility.

"Go ahead, stranger. Make your try," drawled the tallest of the two, a lean-faced 'puncher whose thin lips were etched with a mirthless smile and whose keen blue eyes were granite hard. He waited a moment for his words to carry, then added tauntingly: "Don't tell me that one of Bruce Tonkin's hardcases is losin' his guts against Ed Bond."

"Who's Bruce Tonkin?" Bill Legell queried, more to play for time than out of curiosity. The stunning realization that he was face to face with the man he was hunting didn't show in his expression.

"He's like the rest, Ed," the second rider, a much older man, said to his companion. "Let's get it over with." He jerked his six-gun a bare inch in a menacing gesture.

Came a sharp call from above Bill Legell. "Easy, Grubstake. We aren't killers . . . yet."

The tenor of that voice, its musical quality, brought Bill Legell's glance swinging upward. What he saw perched at the crest of the outcropping, twenty feet above, was the figure of a girl with clear blue eyes looking down at him over the sights of a Winchester. Her outfit was a blue denim split skirt and a bright yellow blouse. She wore no hat over her dark chestnut hair, and Bill momentarily doubted that she could accurately sight her weapon in the full glare of

10

the sun. Then he changed his mind, for the round hole of the rifle's barrel was lined squarely at him and the eyes behind it were steady.

"Watch him while I get his irons, Grubstake," said Bond. He climbed out of his saddle and crossed the twenty feet that separated him from Bill Legell.

"You've got a thing or two wrong here," Bill protested, his hands still up. "This is my first time in the country. I don't know your man Tonkin and don't want to know him. Can't a man ride through and . . . ?"

The girl's low-pitched, scornful laughter cut in on his speech. "Not through here, stranger," she said. "There's a road to Malpais. It's used by everyone but outlaws and the guns Bruce Tonkin has been bringing in. You're one or the other."

"Let me do it, Miss Helen," Grubstake, the oldster with a hay-colored, longhorn mustache, said stridently. "The only way to beat Tonkin is to cut down his men as they come. There's a hundred cutbacks within half a mile we could cave in over him."

"Get his guns, Ed," the girl said shortly, ignoring Grubstake's plea. And with that, the tall 'puncher stepped in alongside the roan and gingerly lifted Bill's right-hand Colt from leather.

11

When Grubstake looked upward, Bill permitted himself a quick glance above at the girl. For a split second she took her eyes from him, looking across at Grubstake. And in that brief moment Bill kicked his left boot from stirrup and rolled out of his saddle. Ed, his back halfway turned as he stepped away, was caught with his six-gun lowered. Bill landed solidly against his shoulder, his right hand stabbing down to wrench loose the Colt from Ed's grasp. Ed fell to his knees, and Bill rolled free and was coming to his feet, swinging up the weapon, when the shot cut loose.

It was the girl's rifle from above that exploded, and at the exact instant its sharp *crack* sounded out Bill Legell felt a searing pain burn across the hunched muscles at the small of his back. It caused him to whirl away from Ed. Grubstake fired, the throaty roar of the Colt pluming a spurt of dust from the sand at Bill's feet. Then, before he could turn, Ed's weight crashed into him from behind.

Bill fell forward, trying to swing his six-gun around, but Ed beat it down in one quick stroke of his arm. As Bill hit the hard-packed sand and felt the air sough out of his lungs, he looked back over his shoulder in time to see Ed's fist swing in a short, hard blow. He tried to dodge, couldn't, and the driving punch hit solidly behind his ear, blotting out his senses in a wave of blood-red light.

Hours later the cut of a rawhide lariat against the smarting flesh of Bill Legell's wrists jerked him back to consciousness. He steadied his wobbling head, opened his eyes, and found himself staring through darkness along the dimly lit length of an unfamiliar street. The next moment he heard a shout, and a man came out of the shadows of the awninged plank walk up ahead and ran toward him. Bill Legell became vaguely aware of several things in the moments that followed. He was tied securely into his own saddle, his arms were bound behind him, and the pain of the bullet burn along the small of his back set a sharp throb coursing up his muscles at each stride that the roan took. A heavy weight dragged at his chest. He didn't know why the man running toward him was shouting; he didn't know why other shouts joined the first; nor why he soon became the center of a milling crowd.

The thing that interested him most was that two men caught the nervous roan's reins and held the animal while three more reached up and untied the length of rawhide so that he could move his arms. As he bent forward in the saddle, the weight sagged off his chest, and he looked down to see his twin belts and his two holstered six-guns hanging there. Others saw that now in the dim light, and a low mutter of laughter ran back through the crowd to be immediately silenced by a shout from the outer fringe.

"Make room up there. Let me through."

Glancing in the direction of that voice, Bill saw the crowd give way, and a frail-bodied old man wearing a sheriff's five-pointed star pushed his way into the open space around the roan. The old-timer threw up his hands, commanding silence.

"Clear the street!" he shouted.

But at that moment one of the men who had helped free Bill stepped into the stirrup and unpinned a white piece of paper from Bill's shirt front.

"Get this, gents!" he yelled, ignoring the sheriff's command. "It's from that little hellion out at the Circle B. It says . . . 'This is a sample of what will happen to any more of your hired law dogs riding through High Pass, Tonkin.' It's signed . . . 'Helen Bond.' "

For a long moment dead silence held the crowd. Then a wave of mixed protest and laughter cut loose. Bill Legell, looking down and only half understanding the meaning of the note, saw the sheriff step across and

14

snatch the paper from the man's hand. The lawman's eyes scanned the message, and then his gnarled fist crumpled it and threw it at his feet.

His gesture brought some laughs, mostly guarded ones. But one onlooker, standing at the inner edge of the circle, put all caution aside and made no pretense at checking his loud guffaw. He was a middle-aged man, heavily built and with a jowled, round face tanned to the color of saddle leather. His outfit was shabby but clean, except for the soiled, floppy-brimmed black Stetson he wore.

"Pack that in your pipe and smoke it, Tonkin!" he called mockingly. Someone behind tried to nudge him and warn him, but at that moment he stepped out into the cleared space, his stride so unsteady as to make it at once obvious that he was drunk. He came on toward the sheriff, finally stopping a stride away with feet spread wide to brace his unwieldy body. He raised a hand and wagged a forefinger almost in the sheriff's face.

"This is only the beginnin'!" he crowed. "Wait'll them Bonds finish with the rest of your. . . ."

"Miles, you're drunk." The lawman's face had gradually turned from beet-red to gray. He had the look of a man wanting to kill, yet hesitating in the face of the mixed emotions of the crowd. "Someone get him and put him to bed."

Evidently Miles had friends, for three men stepped out and laid hands on him, dragging him away from the sheriff and through the crowd. The drunk had more to say, half-formed, incoherent sentences sprinkled plentifully with profanity. But finally one of the men with him had the good sense to clamp a hand over his mouth and choke off his words.

"Barker! Rabbit!" the sheriff called. "Get out here and give a hand. This stranger's got blood all over his back. The rest of you clear out *pronto*."

Ten men left the circle of onlookers as it widened and scattered, hesitantly obeying the lawman's command. As they sauntered forward to stand at each side of the sheriff and silently regard the breaking up of the crowd, Bill Legell had a good look at them. Each wore a deputy sheriff's badge, yet in the way they wore their guns and in the cold merciless stare on at least the taller one's face, they boldly proclaimed themselves for what they were — men of the killer breed.

When the street had nearly cleared, the pair turned and helped the sheriff untie

Bill's boots from the cinch and lift his stiff frame down out of the saddle. He found that he could stand on his feet — although none too certainly — by spreading his feet and reaching up to take a hold on the saddle horn. He shook his arms from the grasp of the two deputies.

"Nice welcome your country gives a stranger," he said shortly. He made no effort to take the edge of sarcasm from his voice.

The sheriff handed him his belts and guns, and Bill buckled them on. "I'm Bruce Tonkin," the lawman announced.

"You're the man I'm lookin' for," Bill said, eying the sheriff coldly. The pounding ache in his head and the searing pain of the wound along his back made it hard to check his temper.

He would have said more, blaming Tonkin for the circumstances that had so nearly cost his life, but then the lawman made a remark that surprised him. "We've been expectin' you," he said. "Let's have our talk in private."

Without further explaining this puzzling remark, Tonkin turned and led the way obliquely toward the far walk. Bill, more curious than angry now, followed along with the two deputies.

17

II

"LAWMAN'S PROTECTION"

Tonkin led the way to his office at one end of the frame courthouse in an open square at the town's center. It was a sparsely furnished room fronting the low-built, thick-walled adobe jail. As soon as the sheriff had lit a lamp on his battered mahogany desk, he waved to a chair.

"Have a seat, stranger," he invited. "Strip off your shirt and we'll have a look at that back. Meanwhile, you can tell us what happened."

Some instinct and the few facts he had learned of Tonkin warned Bill Legell to keep his identity a secret. Ordinarily, when after a man in unfamiliar territory, he would ask a sheriff's help or at least let him know who he was. But in this case, bearing in mind the things Ed Bond and his sister and the oldster Grubstake had said about Tonkin, he told his story briefly and with no explanation as to his reasons for riding into the country.

Tonkin had a face that was deceiving. Minutes ago on the street, his leathery visage had had given him the look of being simply a harassed and angry old man, his brown eyes never quite losing a kind of soft-

18

ness that seemed the sign of patience. But now, in the privacy of his office and in the company of his two silent, hard-faced deputies and this stranger, the grizzled face took on the set of granite, and the brown eyes began to glint with a killing light as he listened to the story.

When Bill had finished, the lawman muttered an explosive oath: "I should have thought of them blocking that trail and had you come in another way!" he growled. "We'll have to warn the others away from the pass."

He turned and spoke crisply to the pair standing behind Legell at the doorway. "Rabbit, you head up there tonight. Stay clear of the cañon but by sunup be coverin' the pass. Send Holly's men across to the rim and down that old trail past the Longhorn line camp. We can't take any chances. Barker, you can take that roan to the livery barn and turn in. Be ready to ride at sunup."

There was a short silence as Rabbit and Barker went out of the door. The interval gave Bill Legell time to get over his surprise, to let his lean face assume an inscrutability that hid his utter ignorance of what the sheriff was talking about.

"How many more is Holly sendin' in?" Tonkin asked with sharp abruptness.

Bill lifted his wide shoulders in a shrug. "How should I know? I told him I could handle it alone, but he had a different idea." He watched Tonkin's eyes widen a bit at the arrogance of his words. "How about gettin' to work on my back?"

The sheriff moved across to help him with an alacrity that showed a new respect. He helped Bill take off his shirt, then went to a locker behind his desk, and took out a bottle of iodine and a roll of bandage. Bill winced as the iodine burned into the flesh wound along his back.

"So that little she-cat gave you this, eh?" Tonkin muttered once.

Bill waited until the bandage was on, until he had donned his shirt once more, before he spoke again. "Now you'd better start at the beginnin', and let me have it all, Tonkin," he said. "I want to know who's holdin' cards on this play, and where I wind up if I draw a hand."

Tonkin eased himself onto the corner of his desk, took a sack of tobacco from his pocket, rolled a smoke, and then handed the makings across to Bill.

"There's nothin' much to tell," he said easily. "I've got a warrant out for Ed Bond . . . the same Ed that you met upcañon this afternoon. Three weeks ago a gent named

Sims was cut down in the alley back here. Him and Ed Bond had had some words over a poker game. It looked all along like Bond had done it, but we didn't get proof until a week ago. One of our deputies, Barker, found Bond's pocket knife lyin' behind a rain barrel out there near where it happened. At first, we only wanted to ask Bond some questions. When we rode out to his place to ask him to prove where he was the night Sims was killed, he spooked."

"Wouldn't talk?"

"Wouldn't even show himself. It seems he was warned we were comin' . . . why we were comin'. Him and a couple of his crew poked rifles out the bunkhouse window and told us to make tracks. We made 'em. Since then we've tried three different times to arrest him. Once they shot my horse out from under me. So I sent a letter up to Holly at Willow askin' for a few good men I could deputize to go out and take Bond. That's why you're here."

Bill Legell squinted one eye against the curl of smoke that lifted from the lighted end of his cigarette. That slightly contorted expression of his face and the fact that he hadn't shaved for three days in his hurry to get down here must have stamped his visage with a hardness that fit the part he was

21

playing. For when he drawled — "What else?" — the sheriff's expression of puzzlement was obviously put on.

"There's nothin' else," Tonkin said. "I want Bond arrested, that's all. We found out later that this Sims was a U.S. deputy marshal. We can't let things. . . ."

"What else?" Bill cut in with a knowing smile.

Tonkin frowned. "I don't get you."

Bill stood up, flipped his still burning cigarette to the floor, and stepped on it to put it out. He hitched his gun belts a little higher about his waist and shrugged. "Have it your own way," he said. "Only tomorrow mornin' I'm ridin' north again. Holly didn't tell me this was a penny-ante game." He started toward the door.

"Don't be in a hurry," Tonkin said.

Bill turned, leaned back against the wall to one side of the door. "Either you get it off your chest or let me get over to the hotel for some sleep."

Tonkin's brown eyes narrowed shrewdly. "You're one of maybe half a dozen Holly's sendin' down here. I can't let you all in on it."

"I told Holly I would swing this alone. I'm tellin' you the same. Holly said you had savvy. Now I'm not so sure." Bill let an insulting shade of arrogance edge his tone.

The lawman's tanned visage deepened a shade in color. "You're makin' big talk, stranger. Is it all wind?"

Bill's smile tightened. "The quickest way of tippin' your hand is to bring in a pack of gun dogs. With only me" — he tapped his chest with a finger of his right hand — "no one will ever be sure exactly what happened."

A shrewd game lay behind his words, for the sheriff's expression relaxed. He even managed a smile. But then some inner thought seemed to come to him. "You weren't such a high and mighty sight when you rode in here," he remarked.

Hardly had he uttered the words before Bill eased his high-built frame away from the wall. Suddenly his two hands came alive in an upward blur. One moment the lawman was looking at a man relaxed, motionless; the next he was staring into the bores of Bill's two Colts. The swiftness of the move, the realization that Bill's two thumbs were hooked on cocked hammers, drained the blood from Tonkin's face.

"You'll allow a man one mistake, won't you, Tonkin?" Bill asked softly.

The sheriff let out his breath in a gusty audible sigh. "You'll do," his voice intoned. "Only swing them damn' cutters the other way."

Bill's gesture in arcing down his two weapons and settling them into leather again was as nicely timed as his draw. When his hands hung at his sides once more, Tonkin's glance was filled with unmasked admiration.

"You'll do," the lawman repeated. He thrust out a foot, hooked it over the rung of a chair, and drew it toward him. "Have a seat and listen to something big, friend," he said cordially.

Tonkin took his time about building another smoke. When he lifted his glance from the cigarette and once more regarded Bill Legell, there was none of the awe that had touched it a moment ago. He was once more sheriff of Malpais, the lawman who had brought the stranger into the country as a hired gunman. He ended the long silence by coming directly to the point. "Arrest Ed Bond and deliver him to me and I'll pay you five thousand in gold. Prod him into a shoot-out and pack him in dead and you get ten thousand."

Bill nodded. "All under the protection of the law?" he queried.

For answer, Tonkin reached down between his boots and pulled open a drawer of the desk. His hand fished into the drawer and came out holding a deputy's badge.

"Pin this on." He paused, for the first time realizing he didn't know what to call his new deputy. "What's your handle?"

"Call me Legell," Bill answered, a thin smile on his lean face. "It'll do as good as the next." He took the badge, pinned it on the left pocket of his shirt. "And what comes after that . . . after Bond's out of the way?"

"You slope out of the country. The rest will take care of itself."

Bill's brows came up in a query. "Something that big, eh? Who really cut down this deputy marshal?"

"Ed Bond," Tonkin answered. But the cunning deep in his guileless brown eyes betrayed the fact that he wasn't telling the truth.

Bill had a thought then that prompted him to rise out of his chair, run his left hand gingerly along his back, and say: "I'll get out and see Bond the first thing in the mornin'. Right now, I can stand some sleep."

His instinct was to glance around for his Stetson. Then abruptly he remembered that his hat had been missing when he rode into town. He saw that Tonkin had read his thought. "Looks like I lost it up the cañon," he remarked regretfully. "It might fit that old gent they call Grubstake."

"Watch out for that jasper," Tonkin advised seriously. "Grubstake has been with the Circle B ever since old man Bond started the brand twenty-five years ago. He likes those kids, Ed and the girl, and he'd fight for 'em. Watch him."

"For ten thousand I'd take on ten like this Grubstake," Bill said, crossing to the door. He paused there. "I'll go out tomorrow . . . alone."

"You'd better take Barker along."

Bill laughed derisively. "Barker's kind should never give up cow-nursin'," he retorted. "What would I do with him in the way?"

Tonkin had evidently gone to some pains in choosing his deputies, for Bill's pointedly arrogant words now brought a trace of that former awe into the sheriff's eyes. "Don't be too sure about Barker," he said, and for his answer had Bill Legell's low chuckle as he went out the door.

Bill went along the street to the livery barn, found his roan stabled there, and unlaced his bedroll from his saddle, which had been thrown across the rail at the side of the stall. On the way to the hotel he stopped in at the only store he could find open so late in the evening and paid eleven dollars for a new dark-gray Stetson.

His room at the one-story hotel was at the

end of the hall. He drew the blind of the room's single window, after looking out through the raised sash and noting with satisfaction that it fronted on the alley. The shade drawn, he lit the lamp on the washstand and took his time about shaving. When he had finished, he put on a clean shirt, blew out the lamp, and lay on the bed without taking off his clothes.

He had been lying there for fifteen minutes, fighting against the sleep that wanted to crowd in on him, when he heard a board creak along the hallway beyond his door. He drew his feet up, took off his boots, and then soundlessly crossed the room to the door, palming the weapon from the holster at his right thigh as he moved.

Standing well to one side of the door, he reached out with his left hand and suddenly twisted the knob and threw the panel open. Barker stood directly across the dimly lit hallway, his spare tall frame leaning against the opposite partition, a cigarette drooping from the corner of his thin lips. Bill's move was so abrupt that the deputy had no time to straighten from his shock. But his pale face lost what little color was in it as he stared into the snout of Bill's gun.

"Drag it!" Bill said tersely.

Barker, his face inscrutable, spoke around his cigarette. "You didn't hire this hall."

It was plain that he had been sent by Tonkin to keep a watch on the new deputy. Understanding that immediately, Bill followed his first impulse. His weapon leveled at the killer, he stepped out and across the hall, and lifted Barker's twin Colts from holsters.

"Go on home," he ordered, backing out of reach again.

"Go to hell."

On the heel of Barker's words, Bill moved in. He threw his weapon to his left hand and feinted a blow with his empty right. Barker ducked, raising an arm to shield his head. At that exact instant, while the man's eyes were lowered, Bill brought his six-gun swinging down in a blow that crushed Barker's Stetson crown and landed solidly against the side of his scalp. Barker's knees suddenly gave way, and he fell forward into Bill's arms.

It occurred to Bill that the best place to put the unconscious deputy was in the jail that was almost next door. It was a ticklish job to lug the man out of the hotel and not make too much noise about it, but the town lay under a blanket of sleep so heavy it would have taken more than a few stealthy footsteps to rouse it.

Five minutes later Barker was lying on a cot in one of the jail cells, his keys on the sheriff's desk. If Bill was any judge of the effects of a bull-dogging, the gunman would be unconscious until well into the next day.

Bill was thankful that the livery barn floor was of hard-packed dirt and that his horse was in one of the rear stalls. He saddled quietly, led the roan out the back, and through the corral and through its gate.

The commissioner had said that Ed Bond ran an outfit that lay north of Malpais, toward the mountains. Bill headed that way, swinging west until he found a trail that struck directly north toward the hills.

He rode hard for better than an hour, alternately running and trotting the roan since he didn't know how much distance he had to cover. At the end of an hour he came to a fork in the trail. One path angled off into the west. Bill took the other.

The trail lifted him well up into the timber in the next five miles. He was crossing the far side of a grassy pasture, climbing, when suddenly a wink of powder flame lighted the darkness from the cobalt shadows of the trees directly ahead, and a bullet fanned the air past his shoulder. A moment later the explosion of a rifle racketed down, and on the heel of that sound Bill reined in on the roan and raised his hands high above his head.

"Who is it?" a gruff voice called down.

Bill recognized it as Grubstake's. "Take another look!" he yelled. "You know me."

There was a short silence, then the incoherent mutter of Grubstake's voice. Bill clearly heard the levering of the oldster's Winchester but wasn't prepared for what happened next. He was sitting with hands raised, the reins looped about his saddle horn, when abruptly another shot exploded from the trees.

This time the bullet flicked a shred of cloth from the sleeve of his shirt. He had a moment of panic but didn't move. But he did call loudly. "The commissioner didn't say the Bond crew was a bunch of bushwhackers!"

His stomach muscles crawled as he awaited his answer. It would probably be a bullet, he was thinking, and, while he sat there, he cursed inwardly at the trust he had put in this man Grubstake who had the look of an honest, hard-working old-timer.

Then, after a pause crowded with ominous silence, Grubstake spoke. "What commissioner?"

"The U.S. commissioner at Hodges. I'm his deputy marshal."

"What the hell do you want up here?"

"A talk with Ed Bond."

Grubstake's hollow laugh echoed out of the shadows ahead. "Uhn-huh, mister. Not while I'm able to throw my eyes along a sight. You're after Ed and you can save yourself a lot of trouble by ridin' back the way you came."

"You can have my guns."

Grubstake was evidently considering this, for he took a long time answering. "Ed don't want to talk," he said finally. "Besides, you came in over High Pass. That means you're Tonkin's man. You're lettin' off wind with your talk about the commissioner."

"Did you find my hat up the cañon?" Bill asked, thinking he'd found a way of convincing the oldster.

"What's that got to do with it?"

"You'll find my badge pinned into the band of that Stetson."

This time the silence became so prolonged that Bill half wondered if Grubstake had gone back up the trail and was riding for the cañon to prove the truth of his statement.

Then, finally, Grubstake called tensely: "Shed your irons. One forked move will buy you a wooden outfit, brother."

Bill lowered his hands slowly and deliberately unbuckled his belts and swung them far out to let them fall into the grass alongside the trail. Only then did Grubstake ride

31

out from the impenetrable shadows of the trees. Alongside Bill, he sloped out of the saddle with surprising ease, picked up the guns, and mounted once more.

"Keep straight on up the road," he said gruffly. "It's two miles, and I'll have this smoke-pole lined at your backbone the whole way."

Bill had ridden a good half mile before either of them spoke. He turned in his saddle and looked back at the oldster. "They've worked a nice frame-up on Bond," he remarked.

Grubstake grunted in what might have been disgust. "You better watch where you're goin'," he retorted, and from then on neither made any further effort to break the monotony of the ride with conversation.

III

"ANOTHER STORY"

The Circle B was the kind of a lay-out Bill Legell would have liked to call his own. The house, built of logs, stood high on the broad shoulder of a hill belted with piñon and an occasional tall cedar. It overlooked a broad, grassy valley, one of many, Bill was later to discover, that lay inside Circle B fence. A small lake filled the valley's bottom directly out from the house. Deep along one side, almost out of sight of the main building, laid the barns, the bunkhouse, cook shanty, and corrals.

A light showed from one window of the log house. Bill lifted his roan to a trot and headed for it. Once up onto the bench he could see a clean, grassy yard enclosed by a white picket fence. He dismounted alongside the hitch rail that flanked a white stone walk at the gate.

"Nice place," he remarked.

"Too nice," Grubstake growled, coming out of his saddle without letting the rifle drop out of line with his prisoner. "That's what comes of workin' for a girl."

"I thought Ed Bond ran things up here."

"He does. She runs him." Although the sarcasm was sharp-edged, Bill had the feeling that Grubstake was pretty proud of the looks of the lay-out and of the fact that he worked for Helen Bond. "Go on up the walk," Grubstake directed.

Bill took the graveled path toward the wide, slant-roofed porch, and the oldster followed. He was approaching the log beam of the single step up onto the porch when Helen Bond's voice spoke out of the shadows along the building's wall.

"Who are you dragging in, Grubstake? I thought we were rid of him."

"Says he's a U.S. deputy marshal. He wanted to see Ed."

Bill could discern the girl now, could make out the quick reach of her hand as it went up to her throat in an impulsive gesture of alarm. She was taller than he had guessed she would be, and the erectness of her lithe body aroused an immediate admiration within him.

"Grubstake!" she cried in alarm. "Do you know what you've done?"

"All I know is he sat down there and let me part his hair with two bullets without battin' an eye. Short of luggin' him off dead, I don't think he'd have budged. So I brought him along." Grubstake gave a weary sigh. "This is comin' sooner or later, and we'd best have it out now."

Helen Bond stepped out from the shadows at the back of the porch, standing directly in front of Bill Legell and looking down at him.

"One thing you must understand," she said, her voice low-pitched and full of emotion. "We aren't letting you or anyone else take Ed away. He was framed, and, because we know that, we'll fight."

"I've seen Tonkin," Bill answered. "He's offered me five thousand dollars to bring your brother in to him alive, ten thousand if I bring him in dead."

The girl's glance sharpened. Even in the darkness Bill could catch the unwavering intentness of her look. All at once she breathed softly: "You're either a fool or you're the man we've been looking for." She stepped backward to the door behind her, threw it open. "Come in. Grubstake, hold that gun on him."

The room Bill Legell stepped into was low-ceilinged, large, and he at once detected the evidence of a feminine hand in furnishing it. Clean, starched curtains hung at the four deep-set windows. Two large bear rugs were spread out before the broad stone fireplace. The sofa that flanked them was deep-cushioned and comfortable-looking. Helen Bond had mellowed the roughness of log beams with the rich coloring of faded old Navajo blankets. Gaming prints hung at each side of the fireplace, and the gun-rack on the front wall was an ornament rather than an ugly fixture.

Bill turned to face the girl just as she held out a hand to Grubstake.

"Get Ed in here," she directed.

The oldster reluctantly handed her his rifle and disappeared through an inner door that, Bill realized, must lead to the bedrooms.

Helen Bond nodded toward a rawhide-backed chair alongside the huge slab center table. Bill took the chair, not knowing what to say. Finally he decided that he'd wait until the others were back before he attempted to explain the many things that would need explaining.

Helen Bond sensed his reluctance to talk and crossed to the far side of the table to lay the Winchester out of his reach but well within hers. An unshaded lamp at the table's center gave Bill his first good look at her.

He saw that she had a delicacy of feature and coloring that made her beautiful. While Ed Bond's face had been long, rather sharply chiseled, this girl's was a true oval, gently rounded, and with the angles of cheek bones and chin less severe than her brother's. Another thing Bill noticed, as he had that afternoon, was that her deep chestnut hair caught the light and shone like copper.

Having seen the girl, her beauty, and understanding from the looks of this house just what she and her brother had built here and might lose, Bill Legell had a momentary feeling of mixed regret and helplessness. Then he realized that he had already promised himself to do all he could to save Ed Bond. The man wasn't a killer, wasn't guilty of the charge that had brought Bill down here.

When Grubstake's boots finally pounded in the corridor beyond the closed door, a lighter tread blending in with them, Bill could see that the girl felt a measure of the same relief that came to him. The wait had been long and embarrassing.

Ed Bond was first through the doorway. His hair, lighter than his sister's, was uncombed, his keen blue eyes slightly narrow-lidded and heavy with sleep. But his first words were crisp and betrayed his look. They showed, too, that Grubstake must have done some talking during his absence.

"Let's have it, straight from the shoulder, stranger," he said without preamble.

Bill used a good bit of patience in telling his story. He began with his last interview with the commissioner and ended with the telling of how he had locked Barker in the jail and started out blindly for the Circle B. When he told of riding into Malpais that night, of the mixed reactions of the crowd as they heard the note read aloud, Ed Bond's face lit up.

"We have a few friends left," he muttered.

"One, at least," Bill said. "A man by the name of Miles stood up to your sheriff and had a thing or two to say."

"Lew Miles was drunk," Grubstake growled. "Otherwise, he'd have kept his mouth shut. Go on with the rest."

When Bill Legell had finished, he fished into shirt pocket and took out tobacco and offered the making's first to Ed, and then to Grubstake. Both answered with a shake of the head — to Bill an ominous sign. So he had to be content to build himself a cigarette and sit there smoking while the silence dragged out, waiting for their verdict.

At length, Ed Bond snapped out: "All right, supposin' all this is true. What'll you do with me?"

"Use my own judgment in carrying out orders," Bill told him.

"Meanin' what?"

"That this is a different law, not Tonkin's. Where were you the night Fred Sims was killed?"

"Here. Sis was away on a visit to relatives. Grubstake and me had the place to ourselves. The crew was in town spendin' their pay. We turned in early and were in the saddle before sunup next mornin'."

"How about the clasp knife Tonkin found near the place Sims was cut down?"

Ed Bond's thin lips twisted in a wry gesture. "Rabbit Bude did that. I'd fired him that same mornin' and missed the knife later

38

in the day. Outside of bein' lazy and not worth his pay, Rabbit always picked up anything he took a fancy to, like a pair of spurs, a bottle of whisky, or a fine horsehair bridle. Once it was a Derringer with a busted hammer."

"We could talk from now until sunup," Helen Bond put in. "What we want to know is where you stand, Legell."

Bill spoke to Ed Bond rather than to the girl. "As far as I'm concerned, the law doesn't want you, Bond. I'll make that report to the commissioner."

"Then you're heading back for Hodges?" Helen Bond said.

Bill shook his head slowly. "Not until I've found Fred Sim's killer. Fred was a friend of mine."

"And who the hell knows who cut him down?" Grubstake's voice boomed.

Bill lifted his shoulders in a shrug. "No one . . . yet. I think I'll go on a few days as one of Tonkin's law dogs. There's a thing or two about this man I don't understand."

"He's poison," Grubstake growled.

"It might help if you told me what you know about Tonkin," Bill said. "Why is it that he'll personally pay a reward for Ed, here, to be brought in to him, preferably dead?"

On the heel of that question he caught the looks that flashed between these three. They were looks of some unspoken understanding, and served to put him outside their confidence as surely as though they had bluntly told him that what he was asking was none of his business.

A slow irritation mounted within him. It made him rise to his feet, say tersely: "Empty my guns and hand 'em over, and I'll be on my way."

The fatality of his words widened the girl's eyes. As she looked at him, understanding that he was willingly leaving without trying to force them to tell what they knew, a flash of embarrassment swept across her face. She shot one pleading look at her brother.

"Ed, we have to trust someone," she said impulsively.

"Don't be fools," Grubstake warned.

But Ed Bond raised a hand, gesturing the oldster to silence. Then he looked squarely at Bill Legell. "It's taken a little time to work off the spookin' you gave us this afternoon," he drawled. "Sit down, Legell, and we'll tell you what we know."

Grubstake was evidently a person to be reckoned with, for before Ed Bond started talking he made an excuse to send the oldster out of the room.

"There's some coffee out in the kitchen," he said. "Grubstake, you go out and light a fire under it."

After Grubstake had gone, slamming the hall door with a solid bang as evidence of his displeasure, Ed sat down in the chair opposite Bill. "Dad died two years ago," he began quietly. "We never were quite sure how he died. It was on a day he and a geologist from the coast were looking over a fault along the foot of the rim north of here. He'd brought in that geologist on the hunch that he had found a gold and silver-bearing outcropping along the ledge of a dry wash."

"He prospected in this country once," Helen explained. "He was sure he'd found something."

"The geologist . . . his name was Cribbins, as I remember it . . . packed Dad home that night roped across his own saddle." Perspiration stood out on Ed Bond's forehead as he continued. "Dad was dead. Cribbins claimed that the ledge trail had let down under him, dropped him into the wash shortly after they'd started home with some ore samples. We went up there, and it looked like that was what happened. But the strange thing is that the ledge, as it fell, buried the outcropping that had given the samples. And another thing that's never tied

41

in right was that Bruce Tonkin was here at the lay-out lookin' for Dad that day. We told him where to go, and he came back later and said he hadn't been able to find him."

A short silence followed. "You think Tonkin and this Cribbins might have murdered your father?" Bill asked finally.

Ed Bond shrugged. "We aren't sure. But we do know that Cribbins had been seen talking to Tonkin in town the day before he came out here."

"What about the samples?" Bill queried.

"Cribbins stayed in town long enough to work them through at the assay office," the girl answered. "They showed nothing but a little lead. It was mostly fool's gold, iron pyrite."

"So you gave up the idea of following your father's hunch?"

"Wouldn't you?" Ed asked. "It's the spot where he was killed. I wouldn't like to work up there."

"Tonkin might have been in with Cribbins," said Bill. "But if he was, he'd have done something since then to finish what he started."

"We think he has," Ed said.

Just then Grubstake came into the room, a steaming pot of coffee in one hand, four china cups dangling from the fingers of the other.

"So you told it all, eh?" the oldster queried, eying Ed sourly.

Ed nodded. "Dad had a mortgage on this place," he resumed. "I haven't been able to lift it, even though it's for only five thousand. But since I was framed with this Sims killing, the bank's called the note. I'm not considered a good risk any longer."

"That's natural," Bill agreed. "But once you're clear, your note will be renewed."

"*If* I'm cleared. Another thing is that Tonkin is Boyd Smith's brother-in-law. Smith is president of the bank. His money has elected Tonkin the last two terms."

"Forked?" Bill asked.

"No, just close," Grubstake put in dryly. "Maybe if you was dyin' of thirst, he'd give you one swallow of water . . . if he wasn't thirsty himself."

Bill lifted a spoonful of sugar into the steaming cup of coffee Grubstake set before him. As he stirred the hot liquid, the others were silent, obviously waiting for his reaction. It was plain, too, that they had told him all they knew of the elements that had involved Ed Bond in this breach of the law.

"The whole thing will take some thinkin'

out," he said finally. "I'll go back and be on hand tomorrow to start things with Tonkin. I may even ride out here and make a fake try at corrallin' you, Ed."

"Come alone, or damned if I won't have to shoot one of Tonkin's skunks!" Grubstake shot out. "We aren't goin' to let Ed set foot off this place until this thing's settled."

"Maybe you ought to take to the hills and hide out until it's over," Bill suggested.

Ed shook his head, his face taking on a slow flush that showed the quick temper in him. "This is all guesswork. Maybe you can help, maybe you can't. The minute I leave here, Tonkin will be serving foreclosure papers. He tried it once last week, and we drove him off. That's why he's bringing in his gunnies. Once he throws a crew in here, I'll grow gray hair before he moves 'em out." He shook his head again, this time with more conviction. "I won't run."

There was still more talk, most of it Bill's questioning to clear up a few minor points. He left the Circle B ten minutes short of midnight. He wore his own guns out of the house, loaded, and by that time even Grubstake had lost his surliness and suspicion and was civil enough as he wished him a good night.

It was ten miles back to Malpais. On a

44

good part of the ride Bill Legell found it hard to put thought of Helen Bond from his mind. Even as he took to his blankets in his hotel room an hour and a half later, the clear image of the girl was still with him.

IV

"UNDER ARREST"

Bruce Tonkin's wife answered the persistent knocking at the door at three that morning. She let Rabbit Bude in the door, woke her husband, and went back to bed.

Rabbit waited in the living room until the bedroom door was closed and the sheriff in his nightshirt had finished a long yawn and turned down the smoking wick of the lamp. Then he took his hand from behind him and threw a soiled gray Stetson onto the table.

Tonkin frowned, obviously irritable at being wakened at this hour. "What the hell is it?"

"Look," Rabbit said. He was a man of few words, but now his shifty eyes held an amused glint.

"I'm lookin', ain't I?" Tonkin picked up the hat, thumbed its brim a moment, and tossed it back to the table. "Quit stallin'."

"Take a look inside the band."

Tonkin took the hat in his two hands once more, turned it bottom side up, and thumbed down the sweatband. Halfway through with his job his forefinger encountered a hard object that reflected the lamplight as it was turned into sight.

"Deputy U.S. marshal, huh?" Tonkin grunted. "Well, I've seen one before."

"It was layin' up there in the cañon where this stranger tangled with the Bond crowd this afternoon."

Tonkin reached out and clutched Rabbit's arm in a grip that made the other wince. "Say that again. I thought I told you to keep clear of that cañon on your way to the pass."

Rabbit reached down and removed the lawman's fingers from his arm, rubbing the spot gingerly. "That's gratitude," he complained. "Bring in something like this and you give me hell for not ridin' eight miles farther on a circle. Them Bonds aren't nothin' to be afraid of. Hell, I worked. . . ."

"Get on with it. You didn't follow orders, but we'll let that go. How do you know this is Legell's hat?"

"There was sign. Four horses, as well as I could read it in the dark by the light of a match. Alongside the hat there was somethin' that was brown and looked like

46

blood. This stranger had blood all over his shirt, I remembered, and. . . ."

Tonkin didn't wait for more. He disappeared through his bedroom door, leaving Rabbit with his sentence unfinished. He was back in less than two minutes, fully dressed, buckling on his gun belt.

On the way to the front door, he said — "Come along, I'll need you." — and from there along the street toward the hotel, until they were in front of the courthouse, he had nothing more to say. But in front of the courthouse he stopped so abruptly that Rabbit, two steps behind, walked into him.

"We'll go to the office and get that sawed-off shotgun," Tonkin said. "I saw Legell make a draw tonight. He's fast enough to cut down all three of us before we could get the drop on him."

"Three?" Rabbit echoed.

"Barker's watchin' his room in the hotel."

Tonkin swung along the wall that led to the jail at the far end of the courthouse. He took out his keys, inserted one in the lock, and twisted it to the left. It didn't throw the lock. He tried the knob, and the door swung open under the pressure of his hand. Some inner wariness made him stand back as the panel swung out from him. He reached down and lifted his gun from holster.

"You first," he said to his deputy. Rabbit hesitated, not understanding, and the sheriff reached back and took a hold on his arm and shoved him inside. When nothing but silence greeted the tread of Rabbit's boots, Tonkin called: "Light the lamp."

Rabbit was getting suspicious. "Uhn-uh," he said positively. "I'll cover you while you light it."

Tonkin, already fairly certain that no danger threatened him from inside, stepped gingerly across the room, struck a match, and touched it to the lamp's wick. As the light steadied to a bright glare, he looked toward the cell door. He went over there, found it locked. But still curious, he unlocked it and went inside, the lamp in his hand.

His yell brought Rabbit into the cell-block, six-gun cocked. Together they worked over the still unconscious Barker. Rabbit ran out to the watering trough in front of the courthouse and returned with a can full of cold water. He tossed it full in Barker's face. The wounded deputy opened his eyes.

It was five minutes before he could talk. He didn't remember anything after the instant he had ducked to avoid Legell's fist in the hotel hallway.

"We'll go corral him right now . . . if he's there," Tonkin said, as he finished cursing Barker for his carelessness. "Rabbit, you cover the alley. Take a shotgun. Barker, you and me'll go on to the room. If he bats an eye, let him have it. You know what this means?"

Rabbit shook his head. Barker looked up from where he sat on the cot, his forehead creased in pain at the throbbing in his head.

"It means that I've told this gent enough so that he can guess the rest if he ever gets to see Ed Bond. It means I'm through here, and you two along with me. If he's in his room, we're safe. If he isn't there, we'd better be headin' for the border." Tonkin turned, led the way out, leaving both cell and office doors open behind him.

Tonkin and Barker crossed the hotel lobby without waking the clerk sleeping behind the counter up front. They had waited a few minutes to give Rabbit enough time to get back into the alley. It was Tonkin who tried the door to the room Barker indicated. The door was locked. With a meaningful nod of his head, Tonkin stepped back and raised a booted foot and kicked the door in. Barker, remembering the humiliation of having his guns taken away, didn't hesitate in stepping

49

through as the door crashed open, his cocked shotgun halfway to his shoulder.

Bill Legell sat up in his bed, clearly outlined by the light that washed in from the hallway. It took him only a second to realize what was happening, to raise his hands.

"Back again?" he said to Barker.

Tonkin reached around Barker and pushed down the upswinging barrels of the shotgun. Then, reaching into his pocket, he drew out Bill's badge and tossed it across onto the blankets.

"So Holly sent you down ahead of the others, did he?" he queried mockingly.

Bill picked up his badge and knew that nothing he could say would change the fact that the sheriff was now sure of his identity.

Tonkin, too, seemed to understand that talk wouldn't count now. "We'll give you half a minute to get into your pants and shirt, friend," he said flatly.

As he swung his feet over the edge of the bed and began pulling on his clothes, Bill Legell dismissed any idea of reaching for the guns that hung from the bedpost.

Ten minutes later he was standing inside the cell where he had placed Barker's unconscious body a few hours before. Tonkin, outside in the corridor, was standing with hands on hips, eying him soberly.

"It'll take some thinkin' to work this town up into a lynchin'," he said, "but me and Barker and Rabbit can do it. And, brother, you won't have a chance. You won't get to talk to a lawyer . . . you sure won't get to stand trial. By this time tomorrow night you'll be stretchin' a new rope from the low branch of that cottonwood in the court-house square."

"You make big tracks for such a little squirt," Bill said, trying to disguise his feeling of helplessness behind a show of arrogance.

Tonkin ignored him. "The only thing I'm not sure of is what happened tonight after you slugged Barker," he muttered. "Think I'll go down to the stables and have a look at your horse."

"He's drippin' wet," Bill told him, glad that he had thought to rub down the animal with a blanket at the end of his ride.

"You could have got out to the Circle B and back again," Tonkin mused. "If you've seen Ed Bond, it may make things a little tougher to swing."

"I saw all three of 'em," Bill told him blandly. "They invited me in, and we had a cup of coffee."

Tonkin laughed raucously. "I was forgettin' the combin' over they gave you yesterday afternoon." His confidence was visibly returning. "Guess I'm spooked over nothin'. And why did you belt Barker alongside the head with your cutter?"

"So I could ride out to see Ed Bond." Bill's smile was inscrutable.

Tonkin laughed once more, turned, and went to the cell-block door.

"I'll bet you're wishin' you'd thought to do it," was his parting shot.

V

"LYNCH TALK"

Helen Bond slept less than two hours that night, closing her eyes only as the first gray light of the false dawn relieved the darkness at her bedroom window. The feeling of utter helplessness that had kept her awake most of the night had its way with her even after she answered the clanging call of the cook's gong from the bunkhouse at sunup. She wasn't putting much faith in this stranger, Legell, simply because she knew Bruce Tonkin so well.

She was as silent as Ed and Grubstake as they ate their breakfast. Afterward, gripped by a nervousness that she couldn't conceal, she walked to the corrals and told one of the crew to catch up her team of bays and hitch the buckboard.

"You can't go outside our fence without runnin' a chance," Grubstake complained bitterly. "Stay here, Miss Helen."

"And sit and wait?" she flared hotly. "For what?"

Neither Ed nor Grubstake made any further attempt to check her willfulness. She drove out the trail, intending to take the west fork for a long, hard drive along the foot of the rim. But at the forks, a sudden decision made her keep straight on toward town.

Lew Miles's place lay two miles north of Malpais, a half mile off the trail. She swung in at Miles's gate without slackening the speed of the team, and, when she drew rein in the hard-packed yard under the locust trees, Miles was already on his way down from the house.

"Someday you'll kill yourself drivin' like that," he said reprovingly as he took her arm and helped her from the seat.

He was a milder man than Bill Legell had seen last night. His kindly brown eyes were bloodshot, and his hands shook a little, the only remaining evidence of one of his rare bouts with the whisky bottle. Everyone in Malpais knew Lew Miles's shortcoming and accepted it with the stoicism even his wife showed. Except when drunk and in jail — where he wound up every time — Lew Miles was a righteous and law-abiding citizen.

"I suppose you heard about it," were his first words as he and Helen walked up toward the house.

"Yes. You've been drinking again."

"Not that," Miles said impatiently. "Early this mornin' the stage was stopped three miles out the east road. Old Clem Wallis was cut to doll rags without even gettin' the chance to drop his ribbons and go for his gun. There was less than five hundred dollars in the boot, an' all of it was gone when the sheriff got there. Him and his two deputies took out on the sign and in less'n two hours was back with the gent that done it. They're makin' lynch talk in town right now. Clem Wallis was a right fine man."

As the man spoke, Helen Bond felt a tightening in her throat. A grim conviction grew within her. "The prisoner," she said quickly. "Have you seen him?"

Miles shook his head. "No one has. Tonkin's got the jail under guard. His name is Legell. He may have friends, and Tonkin ain't takin' chances."

It was all Helen could do to make the thoughts that raced wildly through her mind take on some pattern. At first she was frantic. Finally she gave up trying to guess what had happened to put Legell in Tonkin's jail. All that mattered now was that he would die along with Ed and Grubstake, and, perhaps, herself.

"Miles, you must listen to me," she said suddenly. "You're the one friend we're sure of, the one man who can do this."

She talked on, and only twice did Lew Miles interrupt her. Once to ask incredulously — "You mean I'm to throw the whisky away?" — and again to say — "Hell, no, they never search me."

By ten o'clock that morning nearly everyone within a radius of twenty miles of Malpais knew that two very important things had happened. First Clem Wallis, for seventeen years driver of the Willow-Malpais stage, had been brutally murdered by a killer named Legell who was now under guard in Bruce Tonkin's jail. Second, and perhaps more remarkable, was the rumor that Barker, Tonkin's new deputy, had struck it rich on some gold-mining stock he'd picked up for a song. The noteworthy thing about it was that Barker was buying free drinks for anyone who'd take the trouble to drop in at Abel Deems's saloon, the Silver Dollar.

Deems himself questioned the truthfulness of Barker's story of his gold-mining stock. But Barker had put two hundred dollars on Deems's counter at eight o'clock that morning, enough to buy thirteen cases of whisky. Deems, not seeing that kind of money every day, kept his doubts to himself and pocketed the money. Barker and Tonkin were the only two who knew that the two hundred was Tonkin's money and that the gold-mining stock was nothing but Tonkin's brain child.

By mid-afternoon the town was crowded, the thirteen cases nearly gone, and better than half of Malpais' citizens well on the way to being drunk. Barker bought ten more cases and set up a bar in the hotel lobby. At five, when Tonkin openly expressed some alarm over the safety of his prisoner and sent Barker and Rabbit Bude down to guard the jail, the elements for a lynching were already shaping.

By five o'clock, half the town knew that Lew Miles was on another tear. But Lew Miles was the only one who knew that, for the first time in his life, he'd gotten drunk on only one glass of whisky. He'd overstepped

Helen Bond's strict order by that much, that one glass, before he carried the almost full quart bottle he'd bought with her money back into the alley to cache it inside an empty ash can.

At six, Miles joined the small crowd gathering around the courthouse. He had timed his arrival nicely. The crowd was boisterous, not ugly yet. The drunks were still having a good time, the more sober not yet worked up to such a pitch that they would make a try for the jail, which Bruce Tonkin pretended to be guarding, having stationed his two deputies front and back, each with a loaded shotgun.

Lew had wondered about the next part. Finally he decided to get it over with as quickly as possible. He hadn't carried a gun for years, but today he wore a holster at his thigh, weighted down by the Frontier Model Colt .45 he'd bought twenty-two years ago. As he lurched into the crowd fronting the jail door, purposely weaving on unsteady legs, he let out a shrill whoop and drew his gun and emptied it barely over the heads of Barker and Rabbit, his bullets kicking adobe dust down onto the crowns of their Stetsons.

A few thought it was funny and laughed. Others thought it wasn't funny — Rabbit and Barker among them — and growled warnings to Miles. He was standing there, reloading the old .45, when a man stepped in behind him, laid a rough hold on his arm, and reached around with his other hand to yank the weapon from his grasp.

It was Bruce Tonkin. "We'll have no more of that," he growled, pushing Miles in through the crowd toward his office door. "You would pick a day like this to go on one of your sprees. We'll put you in here to cool off a little."

Miles protested, swinging his arms about wildly, making the pretense of trying to hit the sheriff. But Tonkin, long trained in Miles's ways, took a firm hold on his prisoner's left ear, twisted it, and grinned. "Be good."

"Let go!" Miles screamed. "Let go, damn it. You always catch me by that sore ear."

This brought the best laugh from the crowd. Almost everyone there knew about Lew Miles's sore ear, about the time he'd been caught with a broken leg at a hill line camp in the dead of winter and had that ear nearly frozen off before he could crawl out to gather wood for a fire. The ear had been tender ever since. It was the only vulnerable part of his anatomy.

Opening the inner steel door of the jail,

Tonkin pushed Miles in. "You ought to have more sense than to tote a cutter, Lew," he said roughly. "You might hurt yourself."

He put Miles in the cell opposite that of the jail's only other prisoner, and shot the bolt in the lock.

"I'll have your supper sent up right away," he said. "Eat it and go to sleep."

Tonkin had done this at least twenty times in his five years as sheriff. The hot supper he brought over from the Chinaman's was a courtesy he rarely showed other prisoners. But Lew Miles wasn't exactly like any of his other prisoners.

As soon as the outer door was closed and bolted once more, Miles got up of his cot and came to the steel-barred door of the cell. "Legell," he called.

Bill Legell, thinking his hearing had deceived him, paid no attention.

"Legell, I got something for you," Miles called again.

This time Bill got up off his cot and came to the door of his cell. He took a close look across the half-lighted corridor, saw who it was.

"So it's you," he said. "You're sure on a stiff one this time."

Sober, Lew Miles was always offended at having his weakness called to his attention.

"I ain't drunk," he protested. "I'm doin' this for Helen Bond." He rubbed his sore ear gingerly. "You get ornery and I won't give you this."

"Give me what?"

Miles's round, loose face took on a cunning smile. He bent over, pulled up the leg of his baggy trousers until the cuff was above the knee. Against the white flesh of his fat thigh lay the blue steel barrel of a six-gun. "This," he said, as he reached in under his pants leg to undo the knot of the rawhide thong that bound the weapon to his thigh. "Damned if this didn't about put my leg asleep. I tied it on too tight."

He finally pulled the weapon loose, reached it through the bars, and slid it across the stone floor until it hit with a clatter against the base of Bill's cell door.

"Helen sent that," he explained, as Bill reached through to pick up the weapon. "Here's a handful of shells." He proved beyond doubt his soberness for the next two minutes, tossing a dozen .45 shells accurately across toward the opposite cell so that Bill had little difficulty in retrieving them all.

"You're to wait until dark and make your try," Miles said. "Helen wanted me to tell you that her and Ed and Grubstake will be watchin' the door to the sheriff's office. If you get that far, they'll have guns to cover you from the courthouse roof."

"They can't run that chance."

Miles chuckled. "You don't know that girl. She's got more spunk than a pack mule." Then, seeing that Bill still frowned, he added: "It oughtn't to be so hard. With all this whisky workin' into the crowd, they can get away."

It was dusk at seven-thirty. Not on the street, however, for tonight more store lights were burning than on any Saturday night within the memory of Malpais' oldest citizen. But at least the courthouse square was in semi-shadow, a fact that was encouraging to Bruce Tonkin as he left the end of the street's plank walk and started across the courtyard.

Today, three of Holly's men had come in through the pass and were now mixing in with the crowd, thickening in front of the jail. Tonkin had only to give his signal — which was to take off his hat and scratch his head — and those three would start things.

Tonkin intended to be near his office door, although not too near it, and to put up a fight to keep the crowd back. Holly's three men were to take his guns away and clear

61

the way for the mob. Tomorrow the town would remember that Malpais' sheriff had tried to do his duty and stop a lynching.

As he approached the loose outer fringes of the crowd and looked over the heads in front of him, he was surprised to see that Barker no longer stood by his office door. Rabbit was out back, guarding the rear. The door, too, was standing open, a fact that made the sheriff hurry as he pushed his way through and up the steps into his office.

The heavy steel door to the jail was standing open, and a light was shining into the office from the cell-block.

"Barker?" Tonkin called.

A five-second silence greeted his words and sent his hand crawling up toward the butt of the weapon at his thigh. But finally Barker's voice called from beyond the door: "In here, boss."

Tonkin breathed a sigh of relief. He crossed the room and stepped through the door. But there he stopped, too stunned to move farther. Bill Legell stood in the narrow corridor between the four cells, two six-guns in his hands, one pointed through his open cell door at Barker, who lay on the cot bound with torn strips from the blankets. The other was centered in line with the sheriff's belt buckle.

Barker was in his underwear. Bill Legell wore the deputy's trousers, shirt, and hat, the latter a trifle small for him. "Come in, Sheriff," he drawled. "We've been waiting for you."

When Tonkin hesitated, Bill jerked his weapon a bare inch to emphasize his command. "You're to go in there and gag Barker. Stuff a piece of that blanket in his mouth and wrap another around and tie it. First, maybe you'd better step over and let me take the weight off your holsters."

So much had happened in the past thirty seconds that the lawman had little time to think of a possible way out of this. He was relieved of his guns, and he gagged Barker so tightly under the threat of Legell's gun that the upper half of the killer's face turned a dark red. He was acutely aware of Lew Miles's snoring in the cell across the corridor the whole time.

"Miles did it, eh?" he queried with sudden insight.

"Miles? Who's Miles?" Bill Legell asked blandly. Then: "Uh . . . the gent across there?" He laughed, shook his head. "Guess again. I had this gun strapped to the inside of my leg when you locked me in here this mornin'."

It sounded convincing, as Bill had hoped

it would, and Tonkin immediately forgot Lew Miles.

"Now what?" the sheriff asked, undisturbed, for he was thinking that the crowd out front would soon sense that something was wrong.

For answer, Bill Legell calmly shucked the shells from the cylinders of Tonkin's two .45s. He handed the guns back to him.

"We're goin' to walk out of here, side by side, and pay a little call on your brother-in-law," he said coolly.

He was watching the sheriff closely, saw the quick way the pale blue eyes took on a hard light before their look became carefully blank. Then Tonkin smiled.

"I'll lay you a hundred to one you don't make it across the courtyard alive," he said.

Bill shrugged. "If I don't, you don't."

Bill's words lightened Tonkin's coloring a shade. Perhaps he remembered the swift draw he had witnessed in his office the night before.

"We'll be on our way," Bill said. "You'll keep on my left side, even with me. Walk right along but don't hurry."

The men in the front ranks of the crowd, less than twenty feet from the steps into Tonkin's office, were the least sober of all. They were the only ones who had a close look at Bill Legell through the semidarkness before he stepped down and was swallowed by the crowd. Tonkin and Barker had gone in and out of the jail many times in these few hours. Now Tonkin's appearance caused little comment. If anyone noted that his deputy had grown a good four inches in the last ten minutes, it wasn't mentioned.

Once Tonkin's right hand came up to touch the brim of his Stetson. He was about to lift it off his head and give his signal to the three men waiting in the crowd.

"Put that hand down," Bill said quickly, not because he understood the gesture, but because Tonkin's hand, upraised, might have whipped in a blow alongside his head.

Tonkin sobered as he realized that he had failed, that his guess had been wrong. Someone at the front of the crowd called — "How about givin' it a try now, boys!" — and took the attention of the crowd, which pressed forward a little, although still lacking the impetus to carry out the suggestion.

They were clear of the courthouse square and had taken to the plank walk when the first shot at the jail cut loose.

"Faster," Bill ordered, as they went along the walk.

Bruce Tonkin thought of many ways to make his break on the short walk to Boyd

Smith's house. He dismissed them all, finding his encouragement in the mounting roar of the crowd back at the jail. Soon Barker would be discovered. Soon they'd start hunting for him as men remembered the too tall deputy who had left the jail with him minutes ago.

Tonkin smiled to himself as he turned in at the gate to Boyd Smith's huge white frame house. He could stall this off long enough to give Barker a chance to come after him.

His knock at the door was answered immediately. Boyd Smith himself opened the door. He was a short, paunchy man with a shiny bald head who stared up at them through spectacles poised midway down his fat nose.

"Oh, you, eh," he grunted. "Come in."

Bill Legell let the door close behind him before he palmed up a .45. "We've got some business with you, Smith. "Where can we talk . . . alone?"

Boyd Smith's face went pale as parchment. He swallowed thickly. "The library," he gulped, and led the way out of the high-ceilinged hallway and into a room to the left of it, a carpeted room with two windows heavily draped, containing an upright piano, a polished walnut desk, two comfortable leather chairs alongside a horsehair sofa, and shelves well filled with books, mostly in sets. A lamp burned on the table in the room's center.

Bill closed the door, leaned back against it. "This won't take long, Smith," he said. "I'm a United States deputy marshal. I'm here to arrest whichever one of you is guilty of having paid a man by the name of Cribbins to murder Ed Bond's father."

VI

"RATS RUN TO COVER"

The accusation came so suddenly, so flatly, that Boyd Smith's hand whipped up and guilt was mirrored plainly on his face. "Not me," he breathed, his voice no more than a whisper. "I had nothing to do with that."

"Then your part was to foreclose the Bond mortgage, to get the ranch. How soon were you going to start taking out that gold?"

"Gold?" Smith was incredulous. He shot an angry look at Tonkin. "You told me it was lead, not. . . ." He didn't catch himself until the words were out.

Bruce Tonkin smiled thinly, his hands busy with a cigarette. He was sitting on

Smith's desk, and now he ignored the six-gun in Bill Legell's hand. "Go ahead, Boyd," he said acidly. "Tell him the whole business. He won't be alive an hour from now . . . ten minutes from now." His words all too clearly emphasized a muted, throaty wave of sound coming from far down along the street. The mob was on the loose.

Bill was well aware that the crowd must be moving from the courthouse and down the street by this time, probably with Barker leading it. "Talk, Smith," he said tersely. "It may save you a few years at Yuma."

Boyd Smith, hands shaking and his bald head glistening with perspiration, looked angrily at the sheriff. "Tonkin's done this," he said bitterly. "It was him that paid Cribbins to give a false report on assaying that ore of Bond's. I don't know how old Bond was killed . . . but I can guess. Cribbins wasn't the man to do it."

Tonkin laughed, leaning over to pull open a drawer of the desk and take out a match with which he lit his cigarette. "Cribbins didn't do it," he admitted brazenly. "I took care of that. Bond's skull was crushed before he even started to fall."

"Go on," Bill said. "Tell the rest. You killed Sims?"

Tonkin nodded. A few shouts came from

68

almost directly in front of the house. Tonkin reached down, as though to push shut the drawer, his gesture deceptively casual. "Sure I got Sims. After that row over the cards, him and Bond got real friendly. I had a hunch Ed had told Sims a little too much. It was easy. Sims didn't even know when the bullet cut him down."

Suddenly his hand whipped up out of the drawer, holding, tight-fisted, a double-barrel Derringer. At the same time he pushed himself sideways off the desk.

Bill Legell's six-gun was hanging at his side. He had suspected Tonkin's first move toward the drawer, but not the second. In the split second it took him to raise and line his .45, Tonkin's weapon blasted smoke and flame. Along Bill's right arm ran a flood of pain. His grasp loosened against all his effort to tighten it, and the next instant the heavy .45 dropped to the floor.

He moved by instinct, lunging toward the desk, not minding that the lawman dodged out of the way. His fist swept the chimney and shade off the lamp, wiped out the flame so that the room was plunged into darkness at the exact instant Tonkin picked up the fallen six-gun. Bill's lunge carried him on past the desk, and he crouched behind it barely in time.

Smith, until now too frightened to find his voice, spoke from far across the room, in back of Bill. "Bruce, you'll pay for that."

"I've got your iron, Legell." Tonkin's voice sounded from the direction of the door.

Bill's shirt sleeve was soggy wet now and sticking to his numbed arm. He could feel the blood running down onto his right hand, dripping off the ends of his fingers. But with his left he drew his other weapon, cocked it.

Abruptly, from the hallway, came a pounding on the front door. Then the tread of many boots sounded along the porch.

"In here, Barker!" Tonkin called.

The lock on the door rattled, someone kicked at the solid paneling, and Bill knew that only seconds remained before the mob would break in. He moved slightly, to make himself more comfortable. His elbow touched a bit of metal, hard and cool. He felt of it, recognizing it as a metal scrap basket. An idea prompted him to lay his weapon on the carpet and pick up the basket.

"Tonkin!" he called. As he spoke, he came to his feet and hurled the basket through the darkness in the direction of the room's door where the sheriff crouched. Leaning down as the missile left his hand, Bill snatched up his weapon again.

The basket's hollow crack against the door set up a racket of sound. It must have fallen directly down upon Tonkin, taking him by surprise. Far above the *bang* of it as it hit the floor, Bill clearly heard the lawman's startled grunt. Then he saw the thing he had hoped he'd see. Along the dark outline of the sill of the front window closest to the door, Bill saw a moving shape. He lined his gun before it and pulled the trigger. In the red flash of the powder flame he glimpsed Bruce Tonkin crouched before the window's level. The lawman's gun, he could see, was out of line.

With that target clear in his mind, Bill threw two more shots, stepping quickly to one side. An instant later a lance of flame answered his fire. In the hallway outside, the pound of boots against the hardwood floors resounded. Someone threw the door open to let in a long shaft of light.

Tonkin lunged erect then, and they stood face to face. The left side of the lawman's shirt was splotched with red. He was hurt but not badly, for his move to level his weapon was as sudden as Bill's, the grin on his face showing no touch of pain.

Their weapons blasted out at almost the same instant. Bill's was a shade faster. His bullet, ripping the length of the sheriff's forearm, was what saved his life. Yet Bill felt a hard blow slam into his hip, a stunning blow that immediately numbed his left leg as Tonkin's shot cut loose.

As he fell, he thumbed his weapon empty, seeing the sheriff's body jerk backward and into the window. The last shot drove Tonkin off balance. He fell backward, hands all at once forgetting his gun and clawing at his bullet-chewed shirt front. The window gave way in a crash of falling glass, and Tonkin crushed back through it.

Two shapes darkened the doorway, one tall and erect, the other shorter and slightly stooped. Bill could see nothing but the outlines of these two against the light in the hallway. Pushing himself up onto one elbow, he threw his empty gun at them.

The heavy .45 hit the tallest squarely between the shoulders. He grunted audibly, half turned to show Bill the vaguely familiar profile of his lean face. Then Grubstake's booming voice sounded warning. "Back, you murderin' fools!" he boomed.

Bill realized suddenly that it was Grubstake and Ed Bond who stood there in the doorway, for the oldster suddenly stepped farther out into the hall's light and swung up a shotgun to menace the surge of men who tried to crowd through the front door.

Crawling a little farther toward the door, Bill could see Barker standing there. The man had a six-gun in his hand that he now dropped under the threat of Grubstake's lined shotgun. He was barefoot and wore a dirty, patched pair of Levi's, and a shirt too small for him. He had evidently ransacked the locker at the jail and found some of Tonkin's discarded clothes. Now Barker pushed backward against the press of people behind him, trying to get out of range of Grubstake's shotgun.

"You there, Legell?" Ed Bond called.

"I'm all right, Ed."

"Where's Smith?" There was an unmistakable urgency in Bond's tone.

"Smith," Legell said, "get out there and quiet that mob. I'll have a gun lined at your back, so make it good."

Ed Bond heard him speak and turned to look into the room.

The light from the hall doorway showed Smith's form as he rose up from the chair behind which he had been crouching. He went toward the door slowly, reluctantly. "Get a move on, Smith!" Ed Bond called when the banker stepped into the light. "Talk, and talk fast."

There was no need now to urge the banker. The men in the outer doorway had pushed

Barker aside, and half a dozen had stepped into the hall. Those on the porch were shouting, anxious to know what was stopping those in front. Someone out there emptied a gun in a deadening staccato to prod Boyd Smith into action. Facing those inside the door, the banker threw up his hands, commanding a partial, grudging silence.

"Quiet!" he shouted in an authoritative voice. He was one of the town's most respected citizens, and his word checked those inside the door who had been ready to rush Ed Bond and Grubstake. While they hesitated, Smith went on: "We have a United States deputy marshal in here. He's taken full charge now that Bruce Tonkin's dead."

"Deader'n a bear rug!" someone on the porch shouted. "But to hell with the marshal. He killed Clem Wallis, and his badge won't save him gettin' his neck stretched."

Bill Legell had crawled to the doorway. Ed Bond, hearing Bill's moving behind him, turned and saw him for the first time on hands and knees within a few feet of the doorway.

"Help me up, Ed," Bill said, and Bond willingly lifted him to his feet.

Bill staggered into the doorway, leaned weakly against the frame, blood matting his shirt along his right arm, and his Levi's were stained redly along his left thigh.

Smith was hesitating uncertainly at that unanswerable challenge from the porch. Those inside the doorway saw Legell now. One or two stepped menacingly forward. But Legell's glance had settled on Barker. "Barker, tell them who shot Wallis. It was either you or Rabbit or Tonkin. Which one?"

"Rabbit. . . ." Barker hesitated, his eyes in sudden fear.

A man alongside Barker laid a rough hand on his shoulder. He turned to call to those behind: "Get back to the jail and get that other deputy! He's the man that got Wallis."

The sound of hurrying footsteps sounded out along the porch, down the steps. But as the men in the hallway turned to go, Bill Legell called: "Hold on a minute!" When they hesitated, he said levelly: "Barker, are you sure it was Rabbit?"

That heavy hand on his shoulder and the granite-like quality of Bill Legell's glance did something to Barker. His nerve broke. He made a sudden lunge that jerked his shoulder clear, and then he was stooping for the six-gun he had dropped a moment ago. He snatched it up, whirled so that his back was against the wall. "Back!" he snarled. "Back, or I'll drill the lot of you."

Bill Legell's weaponless left hand hung at his side. He felt Ed Bond's presence alongside. Barker, a gleam of frantic fear in his eyes, looked away from Legell toward those at the door for a fleeting instant. And in that brief space of time Bill reached across, and his left hand lifted Ed Bond's second heavy .45 from the holster at his thigh.

Barker must have caught a hint of that move along the margin of his vision. He swung his six-gun around as Bill's arced up. The two guns exploded in one deafening roar. Barker's body jerked convulsively as Bill felt the air-whip of the man's bullet hot against his cheek. Then Barker bent at the waist, lost his balance, and toppled forward.

The man nearest knelt beside him, turning him over, and putting a hand to the killer's chest. "He's still good for hanging," he told the others, and before Grubstake or Ed or Bill could stop them, they had lifted Barker to his feet and dragged him out the door.

"Stop them if you can, Grubstake!" Bill called, and the oldster went out the door, calling to the men who had Barker.

"Smith, get a light in here," Ed Bond said. "Legell's bleedin' like a stuck pig."

Smith managed to light the lamp in the library and to help Ed Bond lift Bill Legell onto the couch. As soon as Bill was lying full-length, the banker said hurriedly: "I'll run down for Doc Ackers." He started toward the hall doorway.

"Just a minute, Smith!" Bill called.

The banker paused and turned to face the couch. A thin smile was turning up the corners of Legell's wide mouth.

"Ed, see if you can find a pair of handcuffs in Tonkin's pockets," he directed.

As Ed Bond left the room, after a puzzled glance at him, Bill looked at the banker. "I'm not up on my laws," he drawled, "but there must be one that'll put a man in Yuma for a few years for conspiring to robbery. It wasn't just plain robbery, either. We just might even make you an accessory to these murders."

Smith's face drained of all color. A sudden, furtive look crept into his glance. He backed away toward the door. Just then Bill Legell raised the hand hidden behind him at the back of the couch. Ed Bond's six-gun came up, and the bore of the weapon fell into line with the banker.

Later, when Grubstake had found Helen Bond after his futile attempt to stop the double hanging — the crowd had caught Rabbit in back of the jail — he brought her back to Smith's house. Ed Bond had already summoned Doc Ackers, who was working on Bill's arm when Helen and Grubstake came into the room. Grubstake took one look at Smith who sat handcuffed to the arm of a straight-backed chair. Grubstake swore softly. "I was wonderin' about him, Bill," he said. "Was he in on it, too?"

Legell didn't have time to answer Grubstake, probably couldn't have summoned the strength had he had the chance. For at that moment Helen saw the blood on the cut away sleeve of his shirt and went quickly to the couch.

"Bill, you're hurt!" she exclaimed. "You've done this for us."

Her voice was unsteady, full of an emotion that made Bill Legell look up into her face. Some measure of the same emotion that was holding her must have showed in his glance, for she suddenly flushed and looked away.

"Is it serious, doctor?" she asked Doc Ackers. "Will he . . . ?" She was afraid to go on.

The medico took Helen by the arm and led her out of Legell's hearing. "That depends."

"On what?" the girl asked.

"On what kind of care he gets. He's lost a lot of blood."

Helen turned to Ed Bond. "You and Grubstake go on home. I'm staying. Send some of my things here in the morning."

Grubstake and Ed went out onto the street and walked toward the center of town where the crowd was still thick in the court-house square.

"I've got a hunch, Ed," Grubstake said meditatively.

"What's the hunch?"

"That'll he'll pull through. Helen's a damn' fine nurse."

They walked along another half minute in silence.

"Something else," Grubstake said abruptly. "Did you catch the look on Helen's face when she saw him? Ed, I'll lay you a hundred to one Legell turns in his badge and starts houndin' us for a job."

"He'd be a handy man to have around," was Ed Bond's answer.

Lawman of Latigo Wells

"Lawman of Latigo Wells" was the third Peter Dawson Western story to be published. It was completed in late March, 1936 and was sold to F. Orlin Tremaine, editor of Street & Smith's *Cowboy Stories*, on June 16, 1936. The author was paid $80 for it upon acceptance. It appeared in the September, 1936 issue of the magazine. Jon's brother, Fred Glidden who wrote under the name Luke Short, had one of his stories in the same issue, in fact directly preceding Jon's story.

The news traveled by word of mouth, and in less than two minutes the one crooked street of Latigo Wells was deserted. In that lowering silence, a buckboard swung into the street and proceeded toward the center of town. A girl drove the team, her slight figure sitting erect, her chestnut hair unruly beneath the broad-brimmed Stetson. Beside her sat a gray-haired man, his well-pressed black coat and trousers seeming a little out of place with the weathered tan of his lean face.

The girl's gaze shuttled from boardwalk to boardwalk, and her eyes were troubled. "Something's going to happen, Dad," she said to the man beside her.

He nodded grimly. "You drive, June," he told her briefly, his voice gentle, if decisive.

"A shoot-out?" she persisted.

He glanced at her. "That last, I hope."

"Is it . . . ?"

"He'll come out of it," her father said shortly, confidently. "He's the kind that does. Now drive for the livery stable. This is none of our business."

In a moment the buckboard was out of sight, and the town was quieter than ever.

From the white-spired courthouse came three strokes of the clock bell. Its jangling tones had not yet died in the still air when two men stepped into the street, as though this were a signal. They faced each other seventy yards apart, then advanced, closing the space between them.

The two were entirely different, one tall and flat-hipped, with loosely hanging arms. A deputy's star glinted brightly from the shirt front of the tall man. As he drew abreast of the hardware store, an onlooker who stood in the doorway said: "Watch out for the iron in his shoulder holster, Jim."

The deputy nodded once, without taking his glance from the man who came toward him. The deputy was a shade taller than was common in this country of tall men, and his flat-muscled body was lean and hardened, face and hands bronzed to a color deeper than tan. It would have been hard to judge his age, for his blue eyes were those of a man who has lived beyond his years; yet he was young-looking, and moved with a sureness that gave a hint of limitless energy.

"Cut the tin star to doll rags, Morg."

The words came from under the awning in front of the Golden Sunset Saloon, addressed to the man who faced the deputy.

Morg heard, and his ugly scowl deepened as he shuffled onward through the dust. Thirty yards separated the two when Jim stopped, his legs spread a little, thumbs hooked limply in his belt, close to his revolvers. At this, Morg hesitated uncertainly.

"Keep comin'," he snarled. "Yellow?"

"Save your wind, Morg," Jim replied, his face breaking into a slow smile. "I can beef you from here."

A blinding rage contorted Morg's sun-blackened face, and his dull gray eyes narrowed. "By heaven, I'll gut-shoot you, Rand."

"You're just workin' your jaws," Jim Rand drawled tauntingly, then added: "Before you make your play, I'm givin' you one last chance to foot it out of here. We're through with polecats."

With an oath, Morg raised his down-hanging right arm. It was too far for Jim to be warned by the look in the other's eyes, yet he sensed the move and followed it. Lazily it seemed, yet swift as lightning, his hand blurred to his revolver. The hundred pairs of eyes that watched could not follow the move, yet saw the six-gun suddenly nestled at his hip, blasting out. Morg stumbled sideways at the exact instant his .45 took up the crashing echo, and the bullet that was intended for Jim Rand's heart splintered a hitch rail.

Frantically Morg tried to swing the big revolver around, but the blended thunder of Rand's shots drove him backward in convulsive jerks. The doomed man's bulk went suddenly limp, as a blue hole appeared beneath one eye; the contorted expression held. As he pitched his length in the dust, his face was a ghastly mask.

Jim Rand moved with abrupt, quick steps

to the shade of the walk, and stood there, both guns out now, waiting. Across the street from the Golden Sunset a half dozen men poured out of a building, raced across the street and into the saloon.

Seconds later there came the echo of shots from the alley behind, followed by the drum of hoofs. Then out of an alley, farther down the street, rammed a cavalcade of horses, turning and racing out of town. Men with rifles knelt in the dust and sent shots after the fast-disappearing riders. One of these threw his hands in the air, fell out of his saddle to the ground, to roll loosely over and over, and then lie still.

Later, a loosely knit group of sober-faced young men stood around Morg's sprawled figure. The ring opened as a little man wearing a sheriff's badge pushed his way through.

"Clear out," he grumbled, jerking his head officiously. "Here, a couple of you rannies help me with this buzzard meat."

Three men stepped forward and picked up Morg's remains.

"Damned good thing this town's got one good lawman," someone spoke up.

"Who the hell said that?" snarled the sheriff, wheeling to search out the speaker.

"Aw, don't get proddy, Abe," said an oldster who was helping to move Morg. "Let the boys have their fun."

"There's two good lawmen in this town, and whoever says there ain't is a side-windin' liar," the sheriff said levelly, his brows contracted in a frown better to emphasize his words.

The men carrying the body moved off down the street. The sheriff finally fell in with them, after having out-stared the rest.

"Come right down to it, it is a good thing Jim Rand's our deputy," said the oldster, as Abe walked alongside.

"You're damned right it is," Abe admitted belligerently. "I pick my deputies, Jeff."

"You what?" howled Jeff. "Why, you didn't pick Rand. He come into town askin' for the job, when Morg's wild bunch was swingin' Latigo by the tail. You was even givin' two to one odds he wouldn't last a week after you'd hired him."

"Takes that kind of odds to pry you rannies loose from your money," Abe retorted, seeing a way out. "Where'd Jim go?"

"He don't never seem to be around when they want to wring his hand," Jeff said. "He ain't the gun-notchin' kind."

"If he was, he'd have to buy new handles for his cutters."

The sheriff and his cortège had no more

85

than disappeared into the livery stable when three riders entered the far end of the street and brought their horses on at a slow walk. They were dissimilar in appearance: one tall and loosely framed, another of middle height and stocky, and the third a man of small stature, whose sharp features were heightened by the pallor of his skin. This man was the only one of the three who wore twin revolvers; they were cedar-handled and jutted fin-like, tied low on his thighs. His gray eyes had the hardness of steel, at once cunning and wary.

"You'd better be right about this, Stretch," he was saying, his tone level and clipped.

"I'm right, Ben," answered Stretch, the tall one. "I tell you I had a good look at him this morning. There's only one Jim Barrett."

"And he was wearin' a deputy's badge?"

"Yeah. Ask Pug here."

"He was," spoke up Pug, shifting his thick-set figure in the saddle. "It seemed damned queer to me. Last time I saw Jim Barrett he had a price on his head."

They rode on toward the center of town. Ben said: "We're gettin' in now. Pug, you let the red-eye alone, or I'll bend the barrel of my cutter over your skull."

"That's right, Pug," Stretch joined in. "Every time. . . ."

"You, Stretch," Ben cut in. "You keep your mouth buttoned. If I'm in on this, I don't aim to have it go haywire because of your jawin' where you shouldn't. Let me do the talkin'. Savvy?"

There was something in Ben's level glance that backed his words. Neither of the others answered.

Fifty yards farther on, they turned in as if by mutual consent to the hitch rail in front of the Golden Sunset. Ignoring the quizzical glances of the men standing on the walk, they shouldered their way into the saloon.

They hung about the saloon until after dark, saying little, but listening to the excited conversation of the men about them, who were discussing the fight in which Morg had met his death. Only once did Ben speak, and that was to address the dirty-aproned man behind the lunch counter at the back, who brought them their supper of beefsteak, fries, pie, and coffee.

"This Rand must be hell on wheels," Ben said. "Been here long?"

" 'Bout three months," answered the waiter, after looking Ben over carefully. He shrugged expressively, wiping his hands on his apron. "He come into town last May from over the hills. Tore down the sign at the livery stable the council posted . . . advertisin' for a deputy. First night in town he made Hib McGee take water. There ain't a hardcase left in these parts worth mentionin'. Rand's cleaned 'em all out."

Ben made no answer, but finished his meal in silence. After he had downed his coffee, he nodded to Stretch and Pug, and the three of them left. Out on the street, the darkness was cut by feebly thrown splotches of light from the store windows.

"There's an alley down by the sheriff's office," Ben told the two of them. "Saw it when I came in. We'll wait there. Stretch, you do the talkin', only handle him right, or we'll get a damned good dose of lead poisonin'."

The three lost themselves in the inky blackness of the alley. For an hour they waited, watching the men who filed past the opening. Pug once started rolling a cigarette, but Ben knocked it from his hand. "Want the whole town down on us?" he snarled, and got no reply.

Then, thirty yards down the street, Jim Rand's flat-hipped figure was outlined in the doorway of the Cozy Café. He paused a moment to roll and light a cigarette, then came toward them.

"The way he outlines himself, you'd swear

he didn't have a back trail," Stretch murmured. They watched him come toward them, walk across the mouth of the alley.

"Barrett."

That name out of the past, spoken so softly from the alley's darkness, made Jim whirl and lunge into the cobalt shadows. In one easy sweep his revolver was out and lined at the three figures that were a shade darker than the frame building in the background. Then came an abrupt remembrance of the voice, and with it a stark foreboding of lurking danger.

"Swing that damned cutter out of line," came the voice again. "It's Stretch Edwards."

"Kinda out of your territory, aren't you, Stretch?" Jim asked, tense and waiting.

"Just lookin' the lay-out over," Stretch answered evenly, with a confidence that made Jim instantly suspicious. "We thought you'd be glad to see your old partners."

"We?"

"Yeah. Pug's here, along with a friend of ours. Come on back here a ways. We want to make medicine."

"I reckon here's as good a place as any to do your talkin'," Jim told him.

"So the deputy decides," Stretch sneered. "All right, lawman. How much is your back trail worth?"

Here it was, the thing Jim had been dreading. Yet his answer came in a drawl that gave no hint of his feelings. "Too much to let a couple of fake hardcases bother me."

"What's the deputy game, Jim?" Pug put in. "We hear you got this tank town by the tail."

"I'm dealin' off the top of the deck, Pug," Jim said levelly. "And I don't aim to have it any other way."

"Jim Barrett reformin'?" Stretch laughed hollowly. "We ain't green enough to take that in."

"It might come in handy for you to know my correct handle's Rand . . . Jim Rand." There was something in those soft-spoken words that cut through Stretch's laughter and suddenly quieted it. "It might be smart, too, for you rannies to ride out of town and forget you ever saw me."

"Uhn-uh," Stretch said. "We figured you might advise that. We're stickin' . . . at least till we finish a little job we got planned. Tonight we're bustin' the Wells bank wide open, and you're helpin' us."

"Try that, and I'll be collectin' the rewards posted for you," Jim said, straining his eyes to catch any hint of a move.

"You're forgettin' somethin', Rand," Ben cut in, speaking for the first time. There was an unfeeling quality to those intoned words, warning Jim that here was the most important member of the trio.

"Forgettin' what?"

"That you're wanted back in Broken Wheel for bank robbery."

The turmoil of Jim's mind made him, for the first time in his life, undecided. Ben's open threat was no idle one. A year ago, he would have shot it out with these three, with no thought of the consequences. But now, having built an honest name and good reputation, he hesitated in risking them. His standing in Latigo Wells had been hard-bought, and he was unwilling to see it taken from him.

"If you listen, you'll save us the trouble of lettin' the sheriff know who's workin' for him," Ben went on. "All we want is for you to leave town tonight until we've finished the job."

"Why toll me in on this?" Jim asked, sparring for time. "Why didn't you do the job and hightail it?"

"Our cayuses are gaunted from a diet of post oats," Ben explained. "Can't start a long run. All we need is your word you won't get up a posse to trail us. We need an hour's start."

"I can't keep the sheriff off your trail."

"We'll take care of the sheriff," Ben said grimly.

The sound of Pug's heavy breathing was all that broke the stillness in the silence of the next few moments. The three stood unmoving, waiting for that word of Jim Barrett's.

"Clear out when this is over," Jim told them levelly. "If I ever see one of you again, you'd better come thumbin' your irons."

He turned and had taken three steps away from them when Ben spoke again. "Ride out of town within the next hour. We'll be keepin' an eye out for you."

In the street, Jim turned toward the upper end of town, hoping that a walk would take the raw edge from his nerves. His seething thoughts were a jumble, and it was with an effort that he finally looked at the thing with any clarity of thought.

These past months had not softened him; he had worked hard toward something lasting and well-ordered. There had been great danger in his work here in Latigo Wells, yet it offered him the opportunity to put forever behind him a past that he hated and did not want.

Jim's thoughts were jerked back to the present as a hand touched his sleeve. He turned abruptly to face the person who had intruded on his thoughts.

"Jim Rand. You'd walked right on past without noticing me."

It was June Wheeler. The sight of her always confused him, seemed to throw him off his guard and aroused in him an emotion he could no longer put down as being a casual interest.

"Howdy, June," he greeted her. The uncertain yellow lamp glow from a nearby store window softened the outlines of her slender, rounded figure. The burnished gold of her hair made a misty frame for a fine-featured face that was the color of old ivory in this light. As the vision of her crowded in on his overly alert senses, he knew that she was the most beautiful girl he had ever seen.

She flashed him a quizzical glance. "Anything wrong?"

"Nothin'," he answered lamely, as ever at a loss for words when she was near him. "How come you're in town tonight?"

"Dad's staying over for a meeting," she explained. "I'm looking for someone to ride out home with me. He'll be out too late for me to wait."

All at once it came to him that June Wheeler was furnishing him the excuse he needed for leaving town as Ben had directed. Now that she was here, the presence of Stretch and the others seemed unreal, as did the thing they planned to do. June Wheeler was far more important, for unconsciously during the past weeks Jim's hopes had centered around this girl.

"A little saddle stretchin' would do me good," he said. "Let's ride."

As they gained the open country, the low-hanging moon thrust up out of the horizon at their backs and lighted the broad sweep of rolling land ahead. Off toward the misty hills the coyotes took up their mournful chorus, and for a while they listened without words.

"I meant to tell you about the meeting Dad's attending tonight," she said at last. "Did you hear about it?"

"No."

"He's done what they've wanted him to do for years . . . gone into the bank."

"Bank?" Jim echoed, a sudden horror numbing him. "Al Wheeler's a rancher."

"I know. But they wanted to make him a director," she told him. "He's influential, and they claim they need him. Today he decided. And you're the one who's responsible."

"Me?" Jim breathed the question, uncomprehending.

"Yes, you. Dad always claimed he'd never invest any money in the bank until the town was cleaned up. Said the bank would never thrive until this became a law-abiding community. You've finally made it that. I'm proud of you, Jim."

Her intended praise caused a slow, but insistent, realization of what this meant to mount up within him. After months of fighting to gain back his self-respect, he was now faced with the betrayal he had made — a betrayal that would ruin Al Wheeler, June's father. A feeling of self-reproach hit him, at once intense and awful, and of a sudden he knew the reason for it. He loved June Wheeler, knew it now above all other things.

"Your father shouldn't have done that." He spoke evenly, trying to hide his inner emotion. "The town isn't a safe place yet."

She laughed lightly. "It's as safe as any place ever is, Jim."

"You say he's got money in the bank?"

"Just about all he has," she said, and her softly spoken words cut at him like a whiplash. "He's not really very well off. But what he has is invested in the bank now."

Jim became wordless. They dipped through a shallow coulée, rounded a large outcropping at the far lip of it, and for a time were busy with the horses as they shied at a coyote slinking off into the night.

"You're quiet, Jim," she said finally, giving him a sideward glance.

"Thinkin'," he replied non-commitally, looping his reins over one arm and reaching for tobacco and papers.

After a moment she said: "I saw you, Jim."

He gave a violent start, and the tobacco sifted off the paper he held in his hand. "You what?"

"I saw you fight Morg," she explained. "You shouldn't have run the risk."

He sighed with relief. "That's part of the job," he said. "A deputy's carcass isn't worth much."

"I've wondered about that, Jim," she said. "You don't seem to care much what happens to you."

He shrugged, forcing a laugh. "Guess we get that way after a while." He felt her quizzical gaze upon him, yet did not look over to meet it.

"Jim, you talk as though you were an outlaw. As though your life didn't mean much to you."

Her remark took him unaware, jerked him away from his thoughts to a realization of how casually she had touched upon the truth. Then came a question. Did she really suspect that he had ridden the dark trails? All at once he knew that he must give her some hint of what his life had been.

"You don't know who I am, June. Neither you nor anyone else here knows my back trail. It isn't pleasant."

For several seconds she rode without comment. Should he tell her more? Then he realized the absurdity of thinking it would be important to her.

Her even tones cut in on his torrent of thought. "What you have been doesn't matter to me, Jim."

Her voice was low and the words full of intended meaning. There was no denying them. As their impact took quick root in his mind, he experienced a surge of emotion that was overpowering.

Before he could hold back his words, he blurted out: "You can't mean that, June."

"I've never meant anything more in my life."

He would have swept her into his arms at that moment, but he sat chained by the horrible understanding that this was not to be.

"You don't care?" she asked finally, taken aback by his silence.

"Care?" he said. "Sure. It's nice to hear you say it."

She winced, visibly shaken by his seemingly indifferent tone. His face, as she looked at it in the half light, was expressionless, a mask.

Out of the gloom ahead loomed up the shadowy cottonwoods that arched over the Wheeler ranch house. It took all his self-control to keep back the words he would have uttered. He did not have the right to admit how much her words had meant to him, neither could he deny them. So he remained silent for those last few minutes of their ride, knowing that he was hurting her.

The last few rods over which their horses carried them seemed an interminable distance, taking an endless time. The only sound was the creak of saddle leather and the sound of the hoofs of the horses that had slowed to a walk, seeming to prolong intentionally the torture for both of them.

He opened the gate for her, and then turned and went back the way they had come, not looking back. And when he had left her, he knew that the thing that had made his life worth living was suddenly gone.

Jim's rangy chestnut was foam-flecked and glistening with sweat as he slid to a stop in front of the Golden Sunset. He swung from the saddle and walked over to look inside, over the swinging doors. What he had expected to see met his eyes. In the smoke-fogged room there were the usual late drinkers, but far back, at a table, sat Sheriff Ames. His head was lying on the table at which he sat, pillowed by one arm. Ben and the others had done their work well.

That one glance at Ames told Jim Rand that little time remained. He headed up the street, leaving his horse haltered at the rail in front of the saloon.

Jim took to the middle of the deserted street as he made directly for the bank. The inborn caution of his hunted years was thrown aside as he approached the building. It did not occur to him that he might be beforehand or too late to meet Ben and his friends; there was only that consuming desire to right the wrong he had committed. He left the street and was swallowed by the moon shadow at the side of the building. He headed for the rear entrance. The scrape of his boots in the gravel sounded hollowly between the walls.

Suddenly he was rewarded by the glimpse of the outline of a man's head, thrust for a brief instant around the rear corner of the building. His nerves were calm now, and the old fighting instinct of his dark-trail days came back with a rush.

He paused an instant, flattened against the wall just inside the corner, and thumbed out the butt of the right-hand revolver that rode at his thigh. Then, with no thought or care of the consequences, he sprang out, whipped around, and saw the man standing there. It was Pug's figure that loomed up out of the darkness, poised and waiting, his revolver already sweeping up to cut down the intruder.

Jim's response was instinctive, and the two guns blasted out together. Pug's bullet, thrown wildly at a moving target, whipped the air past Jim's left forearm. Jim heard the *whap* of his slug as it found its mark. The outlaw's hands clutched claw-like at his chest, and, as Jim bounded past, he saw the other sink, turning, to the ground, already dead.

He hit the door with all his weight, felt it give, and he went down, rolling across the floor inside. As he fell, a sudden crescendo of gun blasts greeted him, and the sting of a bullet bit into his cheek. He rolled over twice, was on his feet again, and saw the head and shoulders of a man dimly outlined against a side window.

Instinctively he thumbed the hammer of his revolver at the target, felt the solid buck of the gun in his hand. The purple fire lance of his revolver had hardly shown before he stepped away from the two answering shots that smashed out at him. He saw the man he had made his target sink suddenly out of sight, and in the momentary silence there was a pulpy cough followed by the dull thud of a body falling.

For seconds the silence hung suspended. Two of the three were down. That outline of a man he had blasted into eternity had been Stretch. There remained only Ben, and, as a momentary remembrance of the little gunman speaking out of the darkness came to him, he knew that he was up against the most deadly of them.

With his left hand he took out a match from his shirt pocket, changed his revolver to his left hand, and palmed the match in his right. With one downward and outward sweep of his arm, he hurled the match far out, to the floor. Before it had struck, his revolver flicked back into his waiting right palm. The match flamed, casting a two-second brilliance over the interior of the room.

Out of the corner of his vision, far to his right, he caught the shadow of Ben's outline. He turned his head and saw that Ben's eyes were peering, slitted, directly at him. Both swung their six-guns around, and they thundered out simultaneously.

Jim's right arm and side went suddenly numb with the blow that hit him. His revolver thudded to the floor, and in one leap he was away from the spot, swinging for his other six-gun with his left hand. As it left leather, he saw the flame stab of Ben's second shot. Then two, three times Jim fired, and the thunder of the .45 beat at his brain. His sudden indrawing of breath sent a knife-thrust of pain through his chest, and he knew that he was badly hit. Even in the darkness he could feel the blanket of blackness that threatened to blind him.

He tensed, summoning all his strength to retain his senses. Then came those faltering, heel-clicking steps that told him Ben was moving. He tried to raise his revolver to send a shot at the sound, but his arm would not respond.

Finally, in the rectangle of pale moonlight framed by the door, he saw the little gunman. Ben weaved, walked aimlessly two unsteady steps, and then pitched his length on the ground outside, his revolver still clutched in his hand.

The blackness settled down, and Jim knew no more.

Dimly at first, but then with greater clarity, came his return to consciousness.

All about him he felt the coolness of fresh sheets, and the fragrance of flowers was in the air. Jim turned his head to see the vision of June Wheeler's loveliness beside the bed. Her deep blue eyes were brightened by the tears that glistened in them, and the look on her face was one of supreme happiness.

"You're back, Jim," she said, her voice low and husky from emotion.

"You here?" he asked. "I thought that . . . ?"

"I wanted to be, Jim. You've been sick, awfully sick. But you're getting well. It's been three long days."

Gradually, piece by piece, the happenings at the bank came back to him. Yet the thought of them left him strangely calm, and there remained nothing but a mild curiosity.

"They found the three of them, Jim. The little man lived until the next morning, then he died. The other two were dead."

Hardly caring what the answer would be, he asked: "Did the little man talk?"

"No."

It suddenly struck him that he need never explain his past to her now; it could be completely buried. But he knew that it would be the wrong way. The barriers his words had built up between them must be broken down, and he felt a longing to let her know

103

why he did not have the right to return her love.

"June, there's something I want to explain," he began. "Two of those men. . . ."

"Does it matter?" she asked lifelessly, and in her words he saw that hope had died within her. Bitterly he thought back over the moments of their ride together, when he had said the thing that had killed that hope.

"It does. It can be my apology for treating you the way I did," he told her, pausing to look at her averted face. "I knew two of those men. Years ago, I sided with 'em, rode the Owlhoot. They came back here to blackmail me into letting them rob the bank. I was with them when they robbed a bank down at Broken Wheel. I'm still wanted for that robbery."

"But you're deputy here," she said, uncomprehending. "You stand for the law."

"I've spent four years outriding a past I never wanted, June. I thought it was behind me. But it wasn't. Knowing what I am, you can't still feel the same way."

In the silence of the next few moments the ticking of the clock in the next room seemed to measure out the time that took her further away from him. He closed his eyes, not wishing to torture himself with the loveliness that would be forever denied him. He heard her move, thought she was leaving the room. Then he felt her presence, and abruptly there came the soft touch of her lips.

"There's my answer, Jim," she said when he let her go.

"But, I. . . ."

"You're mine, Jim. Tell me you care."

"I do. More than for anything in my life." His words trailed off as a weakness assailed him.

"The rewards for those men are in the bank under your name," she told him. "Six thousand."

"That's all goin' to the bank at Broken Wheel, June," he said slowly, after a moment, "and the dark trail is buried for good."

She must have seen the appeal in his eyes, for she was in his arms again.

The Boom-Camp Terror

Jon Glidden completed this story in January, 1937. He did not have a title for it. His agent submitted it to Rogers Terrill, who edited *Dime Western* for Popular Publications, and it was bought on February 20, 1937 for $135. When it was published in *Dime Western* (6/37), the editor gave the story the title that it retains for this first appearance in book form.

I

"RENDEZVOUS WITH DEATH"

They picked old Mel Whitlow out of his diggings one cold, gray dusk late in March. Sheriff Hugh Fogarty and Sid Temple, his deputy, hauled the body down out of the gulch in a buckboard. They drove in through the street mire, flanked by Pay Dirt's tarpaper and slab shacks, and carried Mel into the lean-to at the rear of Fred Snavely's general store, laying him out on a couple of sawhorses. Hugh Fogarty threw a tarpaulin over what they brought, and turned around.

"Get a box built, Fred," he told Snavely. "I don't want that girl to see him when she comes tomorrow. The back of his head's all caved in, and one of his arms washed ten yards down the creek in the rain today. All the pieces is there."

"Who did it, Hugh?" Snavely asked, his voice a little sharp-edged and a futile rage showing in his watery blue eyes.

Fogarty was a massive man past his prime and with a paunch sloping out from the star that rested on his brown flannel shirt front. He had to look down at Fred Snavely as he answered: "This time we know. It was Hawk Skuller."

"Skuller?" Snavely echoed. "Hugh, there ain't no one here has ever seen Hawk Skuller. His country is a hundred miles north. I'll be damned if I don't think someone's tryin' to pass the buck onto him."

Hugh Fogarty shot a look over to his deputy, nodding significantly and saying: "Show him, Sid."

Temple reached in under his sheepskin to a shirt pocket and brought out his fist and opened it. In his palm lay a gray feather. He told Snavely: "We found this stickin' between Mel's teeth."

Fred Snavely's pinched and wrinkled face went an ashen color as he looked at that feather. "Goddlemighty," he breathed. "It's Hawk's sign. He's comin' out in the open now." He paused and swallowed with difficulty before he went on. "Hugh, I'm sellin' my outfit and headin' back down into the valley. I wouldn't give a plugged *peso* for this whole damned country right now."

"Sell if you want to, Fred, but keep your mouth buttoned about this. Me and Sid have trouble enough without you startin' a stampede."

With this word of warning, Fogarty and his deputy walked out into the dripping grayness of the dusk, and Snavely, watching their receding backs as they went down the street, felt a little reassured. These two lawmen — Hugh Fogarty and Sid Temple, half a head shorter but wiry, quick, and deadly with his guns — should be able to take care of law enforcement in this town.

But they haven't, Snavely mused, his alarm rising once more. *Mel's coffin is the eighth I'll have hammered together in the last six weeks. To hell with this. I'm pulling out.*

Fred Snavely did keep his mouth buttoned — until after he'd collected the two thousand dollars the restaurant-owner next door paid him for his store that night. When he had his money in gold safely strapped to the belt around his waist, Snavely told three of his friends about that feather.

By morning the news had spread, and the diggings above the town were deserted; the four hundred hardy souls who had come up into these hills to make their fortunes milled aimlessly about Pay Dirt's muddy street, oblivious of the misty rain that soaked through their clothing and chilled them to the bone. Hawk Skuller and his wild bunch were on the prod, and from now on a man's life wouldn't be worth any more than the gold he carried in his poke.

Louise Whitlow, Mel's daughter, coming up from the ranch, arrived in town early that afternoon with Tom Lemson driving her buckboard, shouting, and using the whip to get his team through the crowd. The girl rode, silent and tight-lipped, beside her father's old foreman, and, when they pulled in at the hitch rail in front of the jail, she didn't make a move until Hugh Fogarty came out and reached up to help her down. Then, as if walking in a dream, she stepped down and went into Fogarty's office, unwavering but with a helpless, stunned look in her hazel eyes. Men stared at her because of the look of freshness that was so strange to this camp, but when they caught the grief in her set expression, they looked away, knowing who she must be.

It was shortly after the girl's arrival that Fogarty saw the stranger riding up the street. Hugh had taken the girl over to the Bonanza Hotel, the only two-story structure in the town. He didn't notice the stranger particularly at first; what took his eyes was the chestnut stallion the man rode. The stallion was deep-chested and big and straight-legged. Fogarty's eyes didn't leave the animal until the stranger rode in at the hitch rail across the street in front of Ace Hartley's saloon tent. By the time the man had tied the reins and thrown his slicker over his saddle, Fogarty was across the street and leaning against the hitch rail.

"That's hossflesh, stranger," the lawman said admiringly. "How much do you want for him?"

Fogarty really looked at the man for the first time then — and immediately forgot the stallion. The stranger's eyes were of the color and coldness of black porphyry. From that lean, square-jawed, and sun-blackened face, those eyes studied Fogarty. Fogarty was tall, but as this newcomer stepped up onto the boardwalk, the lawman had to raise his glance a little to meet the other's. He saw those black eyes abruptly lose that flinty look and an amused glint take its place.

"There's not enough gold in these diggin's to buy that horse, lawman," the stranger drawled. As he spoke, he pulled a glove off his left hand — he didn't wear one on his right — and stuffed it into a pocket of his leather vest. Then, as though he had given the sheriff the answer he wanted, he went on: "I hear there's an epidemic of buck fever takin' the town."

Two things displeased Fogarty about this man: he owned the finest horse the lawman had ever seen and wouldn't sell him, and he was evidently taking the talk about Hawk Skuller as a joke. It riled Fogarty, so he told him: "Hang around a bit, and maybe you'll catch a dose yourself, stranger."

There was mocking laughter behind those black eyes now, although the lean face wasn't smiling. Again came the even drawl: "I rode up here to take a look around and maybe stake me out a claim. From the looks of things, there's plenty already worked I can buy for the price of a box of shells. Someone's runnin' a sandy, Sheriff."

"What in hell you meanin' by that?"

"Meanin' that Hawk Skuller's nothin' but

a gent that was framed and took to the hills to save his hide. He doesn't work this way, Sheriff. I know. I came from his part of the country."

"I reckon he's changed since you knew him," Fogarty answered. "In the last eight weeks eight men have died of lead poisonin'. And enough gold has gone with 'em to plate their headstones. We found a hawk's feather on the last."

The stranger was smiling now, broadly and spontaneously, and Fogarty's irritation mounted. The stranger told him: "Feathers are easy to get. Comin' up the trail today, I knocked down a hawk just for practice. I could've had a hatful of feathers. Would that make me Hawk Skuller?"

"I don't know. Would it?"

"Sure. I'm Hawk Skuller. Now you tell me you're Wyatt Earp."

The stranger stepped around the lawman and pushed in through the crowd in front of Ace Hartley's saloon. Fogarty's eyes followed him, taking in his outfit — the dark red flannel shirt under the buckskin vest, the two horn-handled Colt .44s riding low on thighs. When he had disappeared inside, the lawman shrugged and turned once more to inspect the stallion. And when he finally crossed the street to his office, the covetous gleam had crept back into his gray eyes.

The saloon was crowded. Liquor was a welcome bracer against the fear that gripped the town. Picking his way through to the bar, the stranger heard Hawk Skuller's name mentioned time and again, and at the bar he stepped in alongside a man who measured only up to his shoulder, to hear him telling his neighbor: ". . . me and these others that caught Hawk and brought him in. He's tough as rawhide, fast as a rattler with his hardware, and you couldn't count the men he's dry-gulched on your ten fingers. Sure it's him that's doin' it. He'll use a knife, a shovel, a pick . . . hell, anything he can lay hands on, to kill a man."

"Make mine bourbon," the stranger said to the bartender.

Something in his voice brought the elbows of the little man off the bar top and his hands easing down toward his guns. His head hunched down between narrow shoulders, and, as his eyes swung around and up to center on the stranger's face, a sneer twisted his thin lips. With it, his two hands dove downward.

Easily, almost without effort, it seemed, the stranger rocked back from the bar and waited — waited until the other's guns lifted clear of holsters. Then he moved, and his right hand was a blur for that split second it took him to plant his Colt at his hip. It blasted through the din of the place, punctuating the instant a round blue hole centered the forehead of the smaller man.

A second later, the two blasts of the little man's guns took up the first, but by that time the fingers that clenched the triggers were stiffening in death, and the bullets whipped up the sawdust of the floor. The man's spare figure went suddenly loose, and the dull thud of his head hitting the sawdust slapped out across the sudden stillness.

When those closest looked up from the dead man, the stranger was standing around the corner of the bar, the gun in each hand moving in a tight, sure arc to cover the crowd. He had caught the flash of the deputy's badge on the dead man's vest, and now he was waiting to see how the crowd would take it.

An angry murmur rose from the throng as word went back telling what had happened. But all at once the man who had stood next to the deputy at the bar held up his hand, shouting: "Quiet! Quiet! Gents, I saw the whole thing! Sid Temple drew first, and this stranger cut him down in self-defense."

Over by the doorway the crowd moved a

little; a lane opened through it, and the next instant Hugh Fogarty strode through and stepped over to kneel beside the dead man, disregarding the menacing guns in the stranger's hands. He turned the body over, took one look, and eased it back again. Then he straightened up and looked over at the stranger.

"I heard what Jess Harp just said about this. I reckon Sid Temple lost his temper once too often. But what I want to know is why he'd pull his hardware when he seen you?"

The stranger shrugged his broad shoulders, dropping his two weapons back into their well-oiled holsters, saying: "I'm no good at games, Sheriff."

"Ever seen Temple before?" the lawman asked.

The stranger looked down at the dead man. "I might have. Where's he from?"

"Sand Gap."

"Up near Hawk Skuller's hide-out? Sure, I've been there a few times. Maybe this jasper's wanted up there and thought I'd recognized him. He was real earnest about the way he went for his irons."

"Sid Temple was my deputy, stranger. He wasn't wanted anywhere, and that wasn't his reason."

"Why don't you write the sheriff up in Sand Gap and ask about him?"

Hugh Fogarty's face reddened. He said gruffly: "I know how to run my job. You won't admit you knew Temple, then?"

"I might. Then again, I might not. If I remember later on, I'll come over and let you know."

A ripple of subdued laughter ran through the crowd. Hugh Fogarty disregarded it, staring slit-eyed at the stranger. Finally he said: "We've got trouble enough around here without this sort of a thing, stranger. Keep your irons leathered while you're in Pay Dirt." He jerked his head briefly down to indicate Temple's lifeless body, growling: "A couple of you pick up Sid and carry him over across the street."

When they had gone, the stranger leaned against the bar and said to the barkeep: "I ordered bourbon."

II

"THE STRANGER MAKES HIS BID"

Mel Whitlow was buried at four o'clock that afternoon. His daughter stood it pretty well, until they began shoveling in the sticky red mud onto the pine coffin. When she saw that, she couldn't hold back the tears, and Tom Lemson put an arm around her shoulders and turned her away and led her back to the buckboard. Those who knew Tom remembered that he'd been Mel's oldest and best friend, and they said the girl was lucky to have someone like that to help her at a time like this.

The sign for the auction went up shortly afterwards, and by eight o'clock that night there were as many people in Ace Hartley's saloon tent as could crowd in, mostly men. Louise Whitlow came in with Tom Lemson and Hugh Fogarty ten minutes later, and, as the trio made its way up to the bar, a hush settled down under the smoke-fogged canvas shelter. They gave the girl and Tom Lemson chairs at the end of the bar, and the sheriff walked halfway down behind it and picked up an empty whisky bottle and banged it on the wood for silence. In the dead quiet, his gesture seemed a little ridiculous, as though Hugh didn't get enough of authority in the ordinary run of his official duties.

He cleared his throat and began: "We're here this evenin' to auction off the best claim in the gulch. It's Mel Whitlow's. There's no need in tellin' you again how Mel was the first up here and how he staked out the best claim of the lot. What I do want to tell you is that I'm here to see Mel's daughter get some money out of this sale. She won't thank me for mentionin' it, but Mel owed the bank down at Ridge City seven thousand dollars. It's money he borrowed two years ago on his outfit in the valley. He had that in gold when he was killed. He'd panned it this winter. His girl will leave here with that much money, or I'll buy the claim in myself. Now who's got a bid?"

A heavy silence hung on after his words, to be broken at length by the low murmur of those farther from the bar. A restlessness pervaded this gathering; most of them had come out of curiosity. What happened here tonight was going to govern the events of the next few days, and Hugh Fogarty and the rest knew it.

Hugh rapped for order again, shouting: "There's men here like Homer Kirchen and Abe Tolman and Wes Rand, who've been itchin' to buy up claims! Let's have a bid. Do I hear seven thousand?"

Again a silence — this time one that lingered.

"I know what's got into you," Fogarty told them, his voice not loud but carrying perfectly. "It's this talk about Hawk Skuller. I can remember the time when some of you brought your wives and kids into Ridge City and rode away to fight the Indians. And now you let a hardcase killer like Skuller scare you away from millions in gold. Let's have a bid."

That brought an angry murmur of protest. Fogarty was playing on these people's emotions, trying to whip them into rebellion over their meekness, so it seemed. Finally, toward the back of the tent, the crowd moved, and a short, black-suited man with a pinched face and gray hair stepped through to the bar. He looked up at the sheriff.

"Hugh," he said, "I've taken four thousand in gold out of my claim in less than a month. Right now I'll sell that claim for another four thousand and call myself damned lucky. The rest feel the way I do. It's invitin' a knife in the back or a bellyful of lead to hang on here any longer." He paused, turning to face Louise who sat leaning forward with her eyes fixed on him, the oval of her face pale beneath her chestnut hair. He said to her: "Beggin' your pardon, miss, but it can't be helped. Me and the rest hate to see you lose what Mel left you, but we can't fight the things we been fightin' any longer. And any man who says we're cowards is a damned liar."

A shout of approval followed these words. For a full minute Fogarty beat the bar top with the whisky bottle before the throng quieted. When he could make himself heard again, he shouted: "I told you what I was goin' to do! I'll put in my own bid of seven thousand on that claim! Do I hear any others?"

"Eight thousand," someone answered.

People turned and started to search out the speaker. The voice had come from the far end of the bar, and gradually the crowd melted back to leave a lone figure standing there. It was the stranger.

"You bid eight?" Fogarty asked, his narrow-lidded stare focused on the man. He caught the other's brief nod, and said: "Then I'll bid nine."

"Make it ten," the stranger drawled.

Fogarty's frown deepened. "How do I know you'll pay it?"

"If I don't, you can buy it in at the original bid," came the answer.

"That claim's worth money in six figures," Fogarty said. "I'll take it to eleven thousand."

"You're only *talkin'* in five figures, Sheriff. If you're wantin' to be fair, give the girl eleven thousand and half ownership of the claim, and I'll drop out of this."

"With Hawk Skuller runnin' loose up in the hills?" flared the sheriff. "I'll be lucky if I get back what I'm puttin' in it. My bid's eleven thousand. That's every damned cent the claim's worth, the way things stand."

"Looks like you lose it, then," the stranger answered. "I'll pay twelve. And the girl gets half interest. She'll get full payment in gold in less than no time. And if any of the rest want to sell out, I'll buy more on the same basis." He faced about and let his glance run over the circle of faces. No one answered him, so he went on: "It's like I told you this afternoon, Sheriff. Someone's gone loco in startin' all this talk about Hawk Skuller. Hawk's a white man. Ask anyone from up near Sand Gap. Looks like someone else wants these people to sell out cheap and leave this gold for him to dig out himself. I'm beginnin' work on Miss Whitlow's claim tomorrow mornin'."

For long moments after the stranger's words died out, the silence held. Then came the low mutter of conversation. It swelled until the place hummed with the excited voices discussing this unexpected development. Abruptly another man pushed through and up to the bar. He was a bearded oldster in muddy clothes, a bearskin hat, and heavy boots. Fogarty rapped for silence.

"What this stranger here says is gospel truth, gents," the old man said. "And I'm goin' all the way with him. I'm from Sand Gap. Folks up there'll tell you Hawk Skuller never harmed any critter, human or otherwise, since he hunted down the man who bushwhacked his father. That man was Judge Beeton, and he deserved killin'. But the judge had friends, and those friends ran Hawk back into the hills. Hell, he's fed half those nesters up in the hills every winter since. Don't tell me Hawk Skuller's runnin' hawg wild and killin' at the drop of the hat. It ain't Skuller, gents."

III

"SECRETS OF THE SHADOWS"

Hugh Fogarty couldn't make himself heard above the din that followed. Finally, after the whisky bottle had shattered under his heavy pounding, he shouted that the meeting was adjourned. As many as could crowded to the bar, while Fogarty and Louise Whitlow and Tom Lemson pushed out of the place and crossed the street to the hotel.

They found the stranger waiting in the unpainted small lobby. He carried a saddlebag under one arm and, when they came up, held it out to the girl.

"You'd better ride the stage down in the mornin' and put this in the bank," he told her.

There was something astounding in the look he gave her. A certain warmth was there, too, but Louise Whitlow was the only one who caught it.

"You don't know what this means to me," she told him. "Our ranch saved, the share in the claim, money in the bank . . . everything."

"I'm gettin' the best of the deal, Miss Whitlow."

She shook her head. "No, you're not. I'm very grateful. I hope I make you a good partner."

"We'll get along all right," he assured her. "Leave Tom Lemson here to help out for a while. After this trouble's over, maybe you'll want to take a little time off from cow nursin' and come up to visit us."

There was a certain directness about him that gave her confidence. It made her feel as though she had known him for longer than a few brief minutes, and she unconsciously decided that he was to be trusted. He had asked her to leave Tom Lemson — the one man her father had trusted above all others

— to look after her part of the claim. It warmed her heart, and for the first time that day she smiled genuinely.

"Thank you . . . ," she began, but then hesitated, not knowing his name.

"Call me Hunt . . . Bob Hunt," he told her.

She laid out her hand, and he took it, a flash of pleasure creeping in to deepen the tan of his face. Then she turned and left them, going up the stairs to her room.

Hugh Fogarty had watched all this. When she had gone, he said: "You're wrong about sendin' her down to Ridge City with all that money, Hunt. The stage isn't safe. It's been held up twice in the last two weeks. Last time a man was shot because he didn't hand over enough dust."

"What could she do with it?"

"Wait a few days," Fogarty advised. "By that time there'll be fifty wagons a day pullin' out down the cañon. The road may be safe then."

"People aren't goin' to leave," the stranger told him. "Not now. They're over that Hawk Skuller scare."

The lawman stood there for a long moment, meeting the level stare of those black eyes. Finally he shook his head and said: "I hope you're right." Then he turned toward the door, adding: "I'll see you boys in the mornin'. There's a little work to do up at the office."

Tom Lemson and the stranger watched him go out the door.

"He's bull-headed. Always was," Lemson said. He lacked inches of measuring up to the height of the stranger, and had to look up at him as he went on: "You did a fine thing for that girl. Mel cashin' in like that left her pretty well busted up. That'll help. When do I start to work?"

"Tonight," came the stranger's abrupt answer.

Tom Lemson was plainly puzzled. He pushed his Stetson onto the back of his head, running his fingers through his gray hair, asking: "How do you figure to work a claim in the dark?"

"The claim can come later. It's this other I'm thinkin' about now . . . this Hawk Skuller talk of Fogarty's."

"Hugh may be right. Someone's raisin' plenty hell."

The stranger shook his head. "There's more behind this than any of you know."

Lemson's brows contracted in a frown as he asked soberly: "You know somethin', Hunt? How would a little straight talk do?"

"How long have you known Hugh

Fogarty?" the stranger queried, ignoring the question.

"Hugh helped drive the first herd of yearlin's in here from Texas eighteen years ago. He rode for Hiccup Sanders for six or seven years after that, until they finally elected him sheriff down at Ridge City. He's been wearin' a badge ever since. When they struck gold up here, he came on up because this is in his county."

"How would he get eleven thousand dollars? How could he bid that much for the claim tonight?"

Tom shrugged. "I wouldn't know. He's been workin' a claim of his own since the rush started. But I wouldn't be sure he had that kind of money."

"Let it go," the stranger said casually. Then he went on: "There's a job you can do for me tonight. You'll be sittin' out in the cold and rain, so you'd better go across and buy yourself a pint of rotgut. I want you to go out and climb into that woodshed in back of the jail where you can see the back door to the lay-out. Keep your eyes open and see who goes in and comes out. Don't stir out of there unless you hear shootin' up front. If anyone goes in, try to remember what he looks like."

Lemson's rheumy eyes inspected the

stranger for a full five seconds before he answered: "Sounds like you're talkin' through your hat, Hunt, but what you say goes. I'll do it."

"I've got a friend in that jail, and I don't want the wrong crowd to bust him out," the stranger explained. "I'll be out front. So, if there's any gun play, we'll have 'em front and back."

Tom Lemson smiled knowingly, saying: "If I didn't hate Hugh Fogarty's guts about as bad as you do, I wouldn't swallow that story, Hunt. Is that all you want to tell me?"

"It's all I can tell you," the stranger answered. "Let's go over and get that whisky."

He led the way across the street, and Tom Lemson had to be content with what little he could make out of the stranger's words. Perhaps it was his knowledge of Louise Whitlow's confidence in this man that strengthened his own.

Fifteen minutes after Lemson had gone over to take up his watch in the woodshed behind the jail, the stranger was astride the chestnut stallion, heading out of town and taking the gulch road, riding with the straight ease of a man born in the saddle.

Three miles farther on, the floor of the gulch widened and sloped to become a part of a rocky hillside. At the foot of this slope a thick belt of cedar made a cobalt shadow against the lighter shade of rock and sand. The stranger rode to the trees, whistled softly, and reined in.

An identical note drifted back to answer his signal. The next moment the regularly spaced rattle of horses' hoofs sounded out across the still night air. Four shadows drifted out from the trees and closed in on him.

IV

"THE HAWK STRIKES AGAIN"

Toward morning, through the whispering of a steady drizzle of rain, came the muffled blasts of two explosions. Pay Dirt's street was nearly deserted, since most of its inhabitants were getting their first sound sleep in many nights, but a few were awake and heard the double concussion. It revived that feeling of restlessness and awakened once more those haunting fears that had been with them for days now. Faces appeared at windows and doorways as men looked up and down the street.

Twenty minutes after the beat of those explosions, a half-crazed mule slogged down through the mud of the gulch trail and into the deeper mire of the street. A rider, forking the mule, beat the animal unsuccessfully with a heavy club. He slid off the mule's bare back in front of Ace Hartley's and waded in through the mud. The half dozen watchers who came to the doorway saw that his face was a smear of blood and dirt, and one of them ran out to help him as he fell to his knees in climbing up onto the walk. It was Charlie Bedford, who had a claim out near Whitlow's.

"They got Matt Tryson," he gasped. "Blew his head off with a shotgun and brained me with a plow handle. Every damned ounce of dust we had is gone. When I come to, I found this in Mel's hand." He opened clenched fingers and a curved gray hawk's feather floated down onto the wet boards. Then the man collapsed, and they had to pick him up and carry him into Hartley's.

The word spread, and the gray dawn that finally dispelled the darkness showed Pay Dirt's boardwalks once more spilling their load of humanity out into the mire of the street. This time there was semblance of order to the panic. Better than a dozen heavy wagons were being loaded with goods — furniture and tools and barrels and clothing — their owners grim and tight-lipped as they went about their work. Hawk Skuller had struck again, and they were pulling out. And to hell with the yellow metal that had brought them up here.

The stranger found Tom Lemson waiting at the bar in Ace Hartley's shortly after nine that morning. Tom's eyes were red-rimmed over his suntanned, unshaven cheeks, and the grim set to his jaw made him look older than his fifty years. He told the stranger: "I'm headin' out with the girl today."

The stranger's glance shuttled over the room briefly, taking in the several small groups where men talked in hushed voices. The poker and faro tables were now deserted for the first time since Ace Hartley had set up his tent. Having seen all this, he looked at Tom Lemson.

"So you've changed your mind about stickin'?"

Tom nodded slowly, saying: "After what happened last night, a six-horse team couldn't keep me from ridin' down to the bank today with Louise Whitlow. Maybe I'll feel different when I get down there. Maybe I'll come back and see what's on your mind."

If he had expected the other to show surprise, he was disappointed. The stranger, leaning against the bar, had picked up a pair of dice he'd found lying there and was turning them over and over in his long fingers.

Tom went on: "There's plenty goin' on 'round here I don't savvy. Last night, for instance. Four men went in through the back door of that jail between midnight and three this mornin'."

The stranger abruptly straightened, the dice in his hand forgotten as he asked: "Any you could recognize?"

Tom shook his head. "It was as black as the inside of my hat back there."

For a long moment the stranger stood thinking, and, when he once more looked over at Tom, all of the softness had gone from his eyes. His lean face was flinty, jaw set, as he told Tom: "Get over across the street. The stage is ready to leave. Don't let the girl out of your sight until you're in Ridge City."

"That's what I aimed to do," Tom told him, a little surprised to see the effect of the news he had brought. "Is there anything you'd like to tell me about all this, Hunt? About Fogarty, I mean."

"Not a thing . . . yet."

He turned abruptly and left, and Tom made no attempt to stop him, knowing by the look on his face how futile it would be to question him further. Two minutes later he crossed the street to the stagecoach, and the stranger was not in sight.

The stage was loaded, and the driver was climbing up to his seat to take the ribbons as Tom opened the door and stepped in. There were only two other passengers besides Louise. He took the place next to her on the seat, explaining briefly: "Hunt wanted me to ride down with you."

He answered her questions as best he could. Then the vehicle moved forward with a jerk, the driver's bull snake cracking out above the heads of the lead team. They were leaving ahead of time, with fifty thousand in gold in the boot, the driver anxious to get to Ridge City before the bank closed.

Tom had seen the three grim-faced guards riding up with the driver, their shotguns across their knees, and now Louise told him that Hugh Fogarty had supplied those guards against any attempt at robbery on the way down the cañon. The seat opposite was piled high with bundles and small trunks, containing the most prized possessions of those who were leaving later that day by wagon. They were sending their valuables down under guard, rather than run the risk of meeting Hawk Skuller's men on the way out and losing everything they owned.

The three teams strained at the traces to pull the lumbering coach through the mud of the street. Then, as Pay Dirt's last slab shack dropped behind, they hit the firmer going of the cañon road and picked up speed.

For brief moments the sunlight broke through the clouds, driving away the haze that hung below in the cañon. The road to Ridge City followed this broad cañon for better than ten miles, hanging for a time high up on one slope but gradually descending until they were riding smoothly along the bottom.

They rode silently. The two other passengers — a nattily outfitted gambler and a fat storekeeper — both rode with eyes searching the cañon to the side and the road in back of the stage. Above, the driver and the guards muttered only an occasional word or two.

It was twenty minutes later that the squeal of brakes and the rattle of double-tree chains reached the ears of the passengers. The lumbering stage rocked to a sliding stop, and Tom Lemson got up out of his seat. Through the window he saw one of the guards climbing from the roof. The man stepped down off the hub of the wheel and whirled suddenly, throwing his shotgun within a foot of Tom's face.

"Reach for your ears!" the man snarled.

The next instant Lemson was knocked back into the seat as the gambler lunged forward and swung open the door. He pulled a Derringer from his pocket and was leveling it at the guard when the shotgun roared.

The gambler's frame jerked violently, then he pitched head first out of the coach to the ground. He lay there, unmoving, a crimson patch of blood spreading out around him in the sandy soil.

"He made a cleanin' at Hartley's last night," the guard said, reaching down and taking a bulging wallet from the gambler's inside coat pocket. "If the rest of you want to cash in real sudden, try the same thing this jasper did. Now climb down and keep rubbin' your ears."

Tom Lemson went down first, reaching back to help the girl, seeing that her eyes were filled with a growing horror.

"Joe, get busy on the stuff in the boot," the guard barked, without shifting his eyes from his passengers. "Baldy, rip open them bundles inside. Pull loose the cushions. We'll burn it."

Up front, the driver was hurriedly unhitching the horses. He had led the first team a little ahead and was coming back toward the coach, when the faint thunder of pounding hoofs sounded out from some-where above.

The guard whirled at the sound, shouting to the others: "Someone comin' down the trail! Scatter, gents! Blow 'em to hell!"

He backed away from the passengers, his shotgun leveled menacingly, watching them with an unblinking, wary stare. As the last one of his companions climbed down off the roof and disappeared, he suddenly darted around the end of the coach.

Tom Lemson's hand swung down to his six-gun. He ran out and had a flashing glimpse of the driver as he dodged behind a low outcropping, after the others. The .45 in Tom's hand roared twice, but his bullets were wide of the mark.

In the silence that followed, they all listened. The sound of hoofs had been faint before. Now it had died away altogether.

A moment later, from above, came the brittle crack of a rifle shot. One of the guards screamed, threw up his hands, and lunged out from behind the rock outcropping. He reeled drunkenly a few steps and sprawled onto the ground. Then a ragged volley of shots rang out above the sharp oaths of Joe and Baldy and the driver. They had found themselves trapped by bullets coming from up on the cañon rim.

Tom Lemson edged from behind the shelter of the stage and threw two shots that caught the guard, Joe, just as the traitorous stagecoach man was making a mad dash for the shelter of the aspen grove on the other side of the road. Joe folded to the ground, making one weak effort to raise his shotgun before he fell and lay still.

It was over then. A complete silence held for long seconds, until Louise Whitlow's startled cry rang out: "Look, Tom! Look up there."

Tom Lemson's gaze went up to where she was pointing. He saw high above on the cañon rim a big chestnut horse and his rider outlined against the gray sky. He recognized that figure. The next instant he made out other riders farther down the slope. There were four of them, picking their way warily down toward the road. Once in the road they came on at a slow trot, spreading out to circle the outcropping as they drew nearer. Six-guns were in their hands.

Finally one of the four dismounted and walked in behind the outcropping. In a moment they heard him call: "They're buzzard meat!"

Only then did the others come over to the stage and get down out of their saddles. For a long moment no one spoke. These men seemed out of the same mold — lean and sun-blackened and all wearing double belts. Their bronchos were big and rangy and sleek-coated, and from each saddle hung a rifle boot with a Winchester in it.

"Hawk wanted us to take you on into town," one of them said. "Bill, you and Andy go hitch up that lead team."

Unable to believe his hearing, Tom Lemson looked up to the cañon rim again, searching for the sight of that chestnut horse once more. He was beginning to see the answer to his doubts, and with the thought that came to him he asked: "The man on the chestnut . . . was that Hawk Skuller?"

The rider nodded, saying: "Hawk said you were special friends of his."

Tom looked over at Louise Whitlow and caught the expression of incredulity in her hazel eyes. She spoke in a hushed voice, saying: "Then . . . then Hawk Skuller's men *didn't* do this?" She was looking down at the lifeless body of the gambler.

"No, ma'am," the rider told her. "There's a pack of coyotes been runnin' up here, hidin' behind Hawk's name. He brought us up to find out who was. . . ."

A hoarse shout from up ahead broke in on his words; then came the explosion of a six-gun to drown out for an instant the quick pounding of hoof thunder.

They looked up there to see a horse and rider streaking down the road finally to cut out across the cañon beyond the trees. Tom Lemson recognized that rider: it was the stage driver.

"Let him go!" shouted the rider who stood beside Tom. Two of the others were running over to get their horses. "He can't do anything but save his rangy hide. What happened?"

"He was playin' 'possum, I reckon," explained one of the others. "We weren't looking . . . over there toward the rocks. He must have crawled out and grabbed my bronc' when we stepped in here behind his team."

"How about the others?"

The speaker up ahead shook his head. "We'd better bury 'em before we go on."

That took them twenty minutes. They piled loose rocks and sand over the bodies of the three gunmen and the dead gambler. By the time the job was finished, Tom Lemson's mind was made up. He asked one of Hawk's men: "Where did Hawk go? Back to Pay Dirt?"

The man nodded, answering: "He said he had a little unfinished business up there."

"I'm ridin' back to help him, if you'll loan me your jughead."

"Suit yourself," the man answered. "But Hawk don't often need help."

Regardless of that, Tom Lemson went back to Pay Dirt. Knowing now who it was that had killed Mel Whitlow, it was the only thing he could do.

V

"FUGITIVE TOWN TAMER"

Hawk Skuller was a mile below town when he saw the rider coming up on the opposite ridge. He watched the black horse for a full half minute before the animal and rider dropped out of sight below the rim. Then he put the incident from his mind, thinking only of the thing that lay before him.

He didn't hurry; there was plenty of time for what he was going to do. He topped the grade in the trail and looked up ahead into Pay Dirt's street. Going along it, he passed several of the loaded wagons. He permitted himself a smile, thinking how soon their owners would be unloading those same wagons.

He swung in at the hitch rail in front of the jail, threw the reins over the tie pole, and stepped up onto the walk. His instinctive gesture as he approached the door was to thumb out the butts of his six-guns. He felt no sensation beyond a growing desire to get this over with quickly.

Hugh Fogarty sat at his desk with his back to the door and turned slowly in his swivel chair as he heard the door close. When he saw who it was, a faint surprise showed in his gray eyes.

"Did you decide to sell the stallion?" he asked. "Or have you come to tell me where it was you knew Sid Temple?"

Those casual words and the cunning light lurking behind the sheriff's gray eyes sent a flood of warning through Hawk Skuller. He waited a moment longer, his glance shuttling over the small room as he stepped to one side of the door. Then, certain that he had been mistaken at what he read into the sheriff's words, he said: "It didn't work, lawman. Your men are lyin' dead down the cañon road. I thought you ought to know."

Fogarty nodded, his coarse features placid. "I know," he said. "Barney Beeson got away and rode in and told me. Barney's over there." The lawman jerked his head in the direction of the cell-room door.

Hawk Skuller thought it was a trick at first

— until he heard the dull ring of metal against wood at his other side. With that sound, he took his eyes off the sheriff for one minute, in time to see the twin barrels of a shotgun swinging down at him through the square mesh grating of the cell-room door. He laughed, and that move barely took him out of the path of the buckshot blast that cut loose a split second later.

Still moving, his two hands blurred to his guns and swung them up in a blasting crescendo that sent a shower of splinters from the center of that door. Then, too late, the limits of his vision showed him Hugh Fogarty rising out of his chair with a .45 in his big fist. The sheriff's weapon stabbed a purple ribbon of flame, and Hawk felt a crushing blow alongside his head. Then white fingers of light stabbed out to blind him, and he thumbed his guns empty, without seeing.

An iron will sustained a slender thread of consciousness in Hawk Skuller during the next few minutes. He could not see, could not think, but there was a dim awareness of the shouts and the cries and the trample of boot soles on the rough board floor. And above all these sounds came Hugh Fogarty's booming voice.

When they lifted him roughly to his feet,

141

his weak protest was only an inching upward of his right hand. He felt his arms being pressed behind him and tied, and he tasted the salt of blood in his mouth. And then he was being carried outside where the sudden chill of the air cleared his head a little.

His vision returned gradually. The first thing he saw was a maze of gyrating faces that slowly settled into place so that he could look at the roaring crowd and recognize it. Hugh Fogarty's voice sounded above the din, and Hawk listened.

". . . guts to come back and kill Barney Beeson right in my office. You got Barney's story before he died. He was from Sand Gap, and he named this man as Hawk Skuller. Hangin's too good for him, but I'm damned if I let you tear him to pieces like a pack of wolves. Keep back and give me room to knock this sawhorse down."

That shouting, frenzied mob out ahead spilled in a huge semicircle across the muddy street. Hawk Skuller glanced beyond, saw the open maw of the livery stable door, and knew where he was even before his eyes ran upward. That glance above his head confirmed his recognition of the place — it was the gaunt, unfinished framework of a new store. But at the same instant he saw the length of half-inch rope that curled upward and over one of the two-by-fours above him. He hunched one shoulder to feel the thick knot of hemp at his neck. He tried to move, but his arms and feet were laced so tightly that they were robbed of all feeling. A hand was steadying him from behind; he was standing on two planks laid across sawhorses.

Hugh Fogarty, hiding behind the badge of the law and behind the name of an outlaw, had killed and robbed and deceived these very people who now cried out for justice. Fogarty was giving them a victim, the real Hawk Skuller, with a rope around his neck and a plank under him. Hugh Fogarty would knock that sawhorse out from under the plank and strangle the life out of this outlaw. Hugh Fogarty was bringing justice to Pay Dirt.

"Tighten up on that rope!" came his booming voice. As Hawk felt the rope go taut, the shouts out front gradually dropped to a low murmur, and then there was complete silence.

Hawk Skuller looked to one side, saw Fogarty swinging up an axe. The next instant the unwieldy platform beneath trembled under the lawman's first blow. The axe rose again.

143

"Hold it, Hugh!" a voice barked out.

That voice came from behind Hawk. He turned in time to see Tom Lemson edging out from behind a pile of new lumber in back of the square lay-out of the store's newly laid flooring. Tom had a six-gun in each hand.

Lemson stepped up onto the unfinished floor and came into sight of the crowd below. Before that mob knew what had happened, he was standing so that all could hear: "I rode out on that stage today and saw what happened. It was Hugh Fogarty's guards and driver that held it up."

An angry howl drowned out any further words. Tom Lemson had to shout to make himself heard. "Wait! Hold on, down there! The first move you make will lose you a sheriff! I'll let Fogarty have it with both these irons! You'll hear what I have to say!"

There was a ring to his voice that was commanding. A few of those below knew Tom Lemson and did their best to quiet the crowd. Something was happening here that these people couldn't understand, but they finally listened, willing to put off a little longer what was coming.

"The man you're hanging *is* Hawk Skuller," Tom Lemson told them. "But not the Hawk Skuller we know. Hawk heard

144

about the killin's up here and rode in to find out who was using his name. Hugh Fogarty's your killer."

Hugh Fogarty took a menacing step forward, but stopped as Tom nosed up his two weapons. Then the lawman shouted: "It's a damned lie! He's tryin' to turn Hawk Skuller loose, to go on killin' and robbin'."

A roar of approval greeted his words, but Tom Lemson stood there, without moving his guns. The crowd below took this in and instantly quieted, now waiting expectantly for someone to make the move that would send them up after Lemson.

Tom stepped over behind Hawk Skuller, holstered his weapon in his left hand, and reached into his pocket to bring out a knife. He opened it with his teeth, still covering the sheriff.

There was a flash of steel, and in five seconds Hawk Skuller stepped down off the platform, the ropes falling around his feet and his hands working blood back into his muscles. "Some of you know Tom Lemson," he told those below. "You know he wouldn't lie. What he says is true. My own men shot and killed Hugh Fogarty's guards as they were robbing the stage." He paused for brief seconds, letting what he had told them take hold. Then he went on: "Tom Lemson was behind the jail last night and saw the robbery being planned. He saw those guards going in to talk with Hugh Fogarty. He listened and heard what they said."

He turned as he spoke and caught the look of amazed guilt that crossed Hugh Fogarty's ugly face. That last had been a lie, for Tom Lemson had heard nothing, but the lie carried its weight.

Fogarty suddenly darted a look behind him, and in that involuntary gesture condemned himself before the eyes of the crowd. Those below caught the furtiveness of that move and read his guile. Angry shouts mounted in a roar — a roar of: "Hang Fogarty!"

Hugh Fogarty's two hands suddenly came alive, stabbing at his guns. Tom Lemson was caught unaware, looking out at the crowd. He swung his weapons around too late. But in that fraction of a second, Hawk Skuller hurled himself at the lawman. His two hands cracked down onto the rising six-guns in a stunning double blow. Fogarty's howl of pain rang above the tumult, to be cut off as he went down under the driving force of Hawk Skuller's weight smashing into him.

He was a cringing hulk of a man when they lifted him to his feet. The mob below surged up and onto the floor of the building, with cries of: "Hang him!"

Hawk Skuller and Tom Lemson couldn't fight off that mob. Hugh Fogarty was torn from Hawk's grasp. Hawk was pushed aside, along with Tom. He took Tom's arm and dragged him to the edge of the mob, breathing heavily and saying: "Let 'em get it over with."

Fascinated, they watched as the crowd fell back a little. Hugh Fogarty's shaggy head lifted above the others; a noose flicked out and settled about his neck. Then the hollow thud of axe blows beat out. Suddenly Fogarty's head dropped out of sight, and the rope went taut and swung pendulum-like. . . .

Louise Whitlow rode into town an hour later, accompanied by one of Hawk's men. The two of them stared at the grisly thing hanging from the rafters of the new store across from the livery stable. Tears came from the girl's eyes — tears of glad relief.

Someone told her that Tom Lemson was at Ace Hartley's bar, celebrating. She went in there after him.

"Hawk went over to the hotel an hour ago," Tom told her. "Said he'd be back soon."

But they didn't find Hawk Skuller that day, or the next. The girl insisted on waiting for him, but finally Tom Lemson convinced her that they weren't going to find him, and she consented to ride down and out to the ranch. On that ride her eyes were moist with tears, and she looked tired and worn. Tom stood it as long as he could and finally blurted out: "You'd think the ornery owl-hooter could have said goodbye."

During the next two weeks Tom's uneasiness about the girl increased. She wasn't herself; she ate almost nothing, and in her hazel eyes was a look of longing Tom had never seen before.

One evening he went down to the corral and saddled up a horse, thinking he might ride in to Ridge City and get her a bottle of tonic. He was tightening the cinch on his saddle when he saw a rider coming in on the trail.

It was one of Hawk Skuller's men who drew up alongside Tom and told him: "Hawk's up at Pay Dirt. The governor heard what he did up there and wrote a pardon. We're workin' the claim, all five of us, takin' out a hatful of dust every day. Hawk said to tell you he needed his partner up there to look out for her interests."

It was close to a hundred yards up to the

house, and Tom Lemson didn't often walk that far. But this time, even though his saddled horse stood there waiting, he got the idea that the quickest way to get to Louise Whitlow was on his sure legs. He ran.

A Renegade Guards the Gold Stage

This story was completed by Jon Glidden in early August, 1937. His agent submitted it to Rogers Terrill at Popular Publications on August 28, 1937. Terrill bought the story on November 6, 1937, paying the author $126 for it. The author's original title was less than inspired: "A Buckskin-Popper Fades a Back Trail." For its appearance here the new title given it by Rogers Terrill when it appeared in the magazine *Star Western* (1/38) has been retained.

I

"RIDING SHOTGUN"

From the seat beside the driver on the careening stagecoach top, Jim Bourne watched the lights of Twin Strike draw nearer, pinpointing the blackness across the valley. Two thousand feet above the town the fading twilight played across the high, wooded hills, but down here the darkness was complete. The creaking Barlow-Sanderson stage swayed with the unevenness of the trail; the rattle of double-trees and the creak of harness made a monotonous song that had been with them for the past eight hours.

Jim Bourne reached down and placed his shotgun on the hangers under the seat and took out his pipe and filled it. Race Hogan, alongside, shifted his thick-set bulk a little forward and lifted his whip out of its socket and swung it so that the curling end exploded between the ears of the off-wheeler. The three half wild teams strained against the harness and broke from a trot into a run on the slight upgrade. Race Hogan always hit town this way, running his teams no matter how much work he had given them earlier. He liked to put on a good show.

"Quiet this evenin'," Jim Bourne offered in way of conversation.

Race Hogan's only answer was a grunt and an imperceptible tilting of his head. It was only what Jim expected. Race was a sour one, and after two months together on the run between Twin Strike and Millston they were still strangers. Yet they made a good combination. Hogan could get more out of horses than any man in the country, and in the two times a hold-up had been attempted in the cañon Jim Bourne's guns had spoken too deadly a chant to be matched.

Twin Strike took on shape, its frame and adobe building standing out from the lighter shadows of the barren, rocky slope behind. Lights winked out far up the steep hillside, where the shacks and engine-houses of the two dozen mines clung precariously above the myriad fan-spread scars of the muck dumps. The gold-fever was over, for the big outfits had come in and bought out all but half a dozen claims, and Twin Strike had settled down to a busy, well-ordered existence.

"Damn that ore-wagon!" Hogan growled as he reined the teams into the far end of the street. Shouting out a curse as he passed, he deftly swung his nervous horses around the lumbering wagon and went on toward the lights of the stores, leaving a pluming cloud of dust in the stage's wake. The way cleared, buckboards pulled aside, and Race coasted into the stage station with his ponies high-stepping and the brake chocks screaming against the iron-tired wheels.

"Far as she goes!" he sang out as the vehicle rocked to a lurching stop. He leaned over and accepted the foaming stein of beer from the swamper of the Twin Strike House bar, while Jim Bourne swung down off the seat and helped the passengers alight. Tom Kennedy, owner of the line, came to the door of the station and stood so that his stooped old figure was outlined by the lamplight in the office behind.

"Good trip?" he called out to Jim.

"Couldn't be better." Jim was up above again, swinging down the boxes and bundles and suitcases from the rack. Last of all came the heavy, iron-bound chest of the Miner's Bank and Trust Company. Three guards tugged it quickly up the street and into the bank, for tomorrow was pay day, and the chest held upward of fourteen thousand in gold.

Finished with his work, Jim tied down the thigh-thong of his holster and waved a casual good night to Race Hogan as Race pulled away toward the stables. Jim saw Eileen Kennedy push past her father and out the door of the station. As always, her presence filled Jim with indefinable excitement. Because any feeling toward a woman was a foreign thing to him, he had made a point of avoiding her.

It was that way tonight. He pretended not to have seen her and started down the walk, when her low-pitched voice called after him: "Jim!"

He stopped and waited for her, unconsciously admiring the slim erectness of her swinging walk. At times like this she had a boyish look, almost leggy as a colt, with her wide shoulders and her blue cotton shirt open at the throat. But there were other times when her womanliness was a powerful thing that made him regret what his life had been, and that he could never hope to know her better.

"There's a dance tonight, Jim. You going?" she asked, as she fell in beside him and they made their way along the crowded walk toward the hotel.

He smiled and shook his head. "We start down again at five in the mornin'. If I went out tonight, I'd be sleepin' in my seat within a mile of town."

Her oval face lighted with a look Jim often saw when she was with him. What he told her erased a measure of her buoyancy. She sighed and said: "You work too hard, Jim. Father says so. Why don't you get him to let Barney ride guard tomorrow? You deserve a day off."

He shrugged his shoulders and smiled openly and told her: "Barney might get my job."

She flung her head at the lightness of his words. The orange glow of lamplight streaming from the window of Hardy's general store turned her chestnut hair to burnished copper as they walked past, and, when they were in the half light beyond, he caught the fire in her brown eyes as she looked up at him. There was a question there, too, a disturbing hunger in her glance.

"You don't like me, do you, Jim?" she asked with startling suddenness and candor. It was the first time she had mentioned a thing so personal. It caught Jim Bourne unaware, and he felt his face take on a tide of color as he looked away. He was framing an answer — a dangerous answer for him, for it would have been an admission — when he saw the stranger leaning against the awning post in front of the Miner's Luck saloon across the street.

Something startlingly familiar about the expressionless face of the man across there wiped out whatever emotion had been riding through him. So he didn't answer Eileen Kennedy, and his silence seemed to strike her like a blow. But an instant later she was smiling, her head held proudly. "Jim," she went on, "I wish you'd speak to Bobby. He's down in the Nellie Barr mine again tonight. Father doesn't know, or

Bobby'd get a whipping. O'Shaunessy told me he went down with the night shift in the cage. Of course, nothing may happen, but then again. . . ." She shot a glance up at Jim Bourne and caught the tight-lipped expression on his lean face.

Then, before she could define his bleak look, he swung his glance around to her again. The chill went from his gray eyes, and again he was smiling. "What can I do?" he queried.

"You're the only one Bobby will listen to, Jim. Go up to the Nellie Barr and see if you can find him. Then, please, for me, ask him not to go underground again. Any one of a thousand things can happen."

"I'll do that," he promised. They were at the bottom of the steps that climbed to the porch of the Frazer House. Reaching up and touching the brim of his wide Stetson, he said: "Sorry about the dance, Eileen. Some-day we'll take one in."

Her smile was tight, forced. She shook her head ever so gently and said softly: "I wonder, Jim Bourne. I wonder what goes on in that head of yours." Then, before he could answer, she swung off down the walk and into the crowd that milled beneath the awnings.

Jim Bourne's glance followed her until

she was lost in the crowd, then it shifted across the street to intercept the hard stare of the man, leaning against the awning post of the Miner's Luck. An unspoken message passed between these two for the brief moment their gazes locked, and then the man was stepping across the street toward the hotel.

Jim waited, knowing that this meeting must come sooner or later. He watched Dude King's choppy stride as he crossed the street, remembering another day when Dude's stiff-legged, saddle-born walk was a familiar everyday sight. It brought something back to Jim, something he had hoped was gone from his memory, and a strange bitterness took hold of him as he waited.

Dude King sauntered past the hotel, not once looking up at Jim, but as he came abreast, he drawled distinctly: "Come along behind, friend. We can make medicine."

Reluctantly Jim Bourne fell in a dozen paces behind Dude. A thing he had thought gone forever from his life was tonight reborn; and the inevitability of its coming rankled within him, yet he knew he was powerless to fight it down.

Dude didn't stop until the last slab shack of the town had fallen behind. By that time they were well up the cañon, where the walls closed in and rose high and forbidding toward the myriad stars. There Dude turned and waited until Jim stood before him.

"You could have knocked me over with a wheat straw, Jim."

"Me, too." Jim couldn't help but smile.

Dude's gusty sigh was plainly audible. "I was wonderin' how you'd take it, friend. No hard feelin's?"

"No hard feelin's," Jim echoed. Then, after a moment of awkward silence, and in a half-bantering tone: "What's the play, Dude? You're lookin' seedy."

Dude's harsh laugh was mocking. He was of medium build, slight, and now his two thin hands ran up to finger his frayed tan vest and the faded yellow flannel shirt that so loosely draped his narrow shoulders. "The handle don't fit any more, does it, Jim? I've had lean pickin's for a year now. Jake Troy messed up a job down at Ames right after you pulled out. He gut-shot a mail clerk and put the law on us. The last I saw of him he was swingin' off the arm of a telegraph pole. So we hightailed and split up. I ain't no damn' use by myself."

"So Jake got it at last," Jim mused. "No surprise, the way he always trusted to his gun." He waited then. Dude had something on his mind.

"Nice town," Dude said. "Prosperous place. You're ridin' guard on the stage, now?"

"For two months."

"Hmm," Dude said, "what handle you usin'?"

"The real one."

"Far enough south so that you can get away with it, eh?" Dude's sharp tones took on a taunting edge. "Gettin' ready to leave soon?"

"I hadn't thought of it. Why?"

"I've been pokin' my nose around yesterday and today. They say a big shipment of bullion goes down to Millston tomorrow mornin'."

"Someone's been pullin' your leg," Jim told him, hoping the words sounded convincing.

Dude chuckled mirthlessly. "Don't go upriver with me, Jim," he warned silkily. "How about it?"

"How about what?"

"We can make a cleanin'. I've got it all thought out." Dude's voice grew smoother as he explained his plan. "The Apaches busted out of the reservation ten days ago. I've spotted the right kind of a place down the lower cañon, the place where the road takes to that high shelf. You know it?"

"I know it," Jim admitted, his voice crisp with a rising inner uneasiness.

But Dude was so engrossed in his story that he overlooked this danger signal. "Right there you can slug the driver. We can run the whole works off the cliff. Afterwards, we can go down and leave a couple of arrows stuck in the driver's chest. It'll look real enough. You can bloody yourself up a bit and foot it back to town and make a real hero of yourself. We'll split the gold even."

"Dude, I could kill you, here and now," Jim Bourne breathed.

Dude's slight frame came taut in a half crouch; his two clawed hands were within inches of his guns. "We never did decide that, did we?" he drawled. "I still say I'm faster, friend. Want to try it?"

This cold, calculating calmness was a thing Jim Bourne had not felt for months. It took possession of him now, and backed by reason it formed a check on his rising temper. If he killed Dude, it would take a lot of explaining to convince the sheriff, for a dead man is a dead man, and this was a peaceful community. He had started to build up a life here, a quiet life, but in thinking of Eileen Kennedy once again he asked himself what good he was doing in settling down? The vision he had of her brought up a bitterness he could not suppress, and he realized with startling clarity that he could never be one of these people. Someday now, as well as any future time, he would take up the old life where so much depended on his wits and his guns.

Dude had been quick to take up the challenge; the man had guts, a thing Jim Bourne had never doubted. Dude King had an evil streak in him, yet he didn't lack courage. There were worse men. Thinking that, Jim's lean face took on a slow smile. Dude saw it, and he relaxed.

"This would be a damn' fool play now, wouldn't it?" Jim queried smoothly.

For all the years he had spent hiding his emotions, Dude's face showed utter amazement. He cursed softly, not once but many times, and, when the edge had worn off his fury, he looked across at Jim Bourne and said: "You sure do beat hell, brother. I can remember how you used to get these spells. Now, why in tarnation hell should you talk like that, at a time like this?"

Jim shrugged his wide shoulders, and let that be his answer.

Then Dude laughed. "You're a card, Jim. You always was proddy." He was suddenly serious and asked: "How about it?"

Again Jim lifted his shoulders. "Why not? There's nothin' else for me here."

II

"THE STAGE MUST GO THROUGH"

This backwash of his past had left Jim feeling helpless as he walked slowly alone, following the trail that would take him to the shaft house of the Nellie Barr. Suddenly he heard a shrill whistle high above him. He took out his watch. It was eight-thirty, and then he stopped and listened to the screech of the whistle's continued high note, his heart quickening. For five seconds longer he waited there, then started a frantic run on up the trail.

There is no mining community on the face of the earth but what lives under the dread of the off-time whistle. To hear it turns sober men crazy and crazy men sober, for its meaning brings to all a feeling of bottomless dread. To hear the high whistle of the steam siren now made the hackles rise along the back of Jim Bourne's neck. It was the Nellie Barr's whistle, and Eileen had said that Bobby Kennedy was down that shaft — twelve-year-old Bobby whose every waking hour was spent dreaming of the day

162

when he would be superintendent of a mine like the Nellie Barr.

Closer, Jim made out shouts above and looked up to see hurrying figures running back and forth, silhouetted in front of the naked glare of the single lantern that hung beside the door of the Nellie Barr's shaft house. He ran like a man possessed, climbing that last fifty yards and crossing the narrow shelf to the door of the shack in long, reaching strides.

Jerry O'Shaunessy's solid bulk collided with him as he stepped into the doorway. O'Shaunessy's face was flushed and twisted as he mouthed a curse and shoved Jim out of the way. Then, seeing who it was, he shouted above the screaming note of the whistle: "For the love of God, Jim, get down there and help. It's a cave-in on the second level. Grab a shovel and go down the next trip. Goddlemighty, will someone turn off that damned steam!"

O'Shaunessy turned and bellowed an order to a begrimed oldster whose upheld arm bore its weight on a short length of rope beside the donkey engine. The oldster let go the rope, and the sudden silence was more awful than the tortured scream of the alarm.

"Keep your boiler hot!" O'Shaunessy bellowed, his voice ridiculous in the utter stillness. Then he turned to Jim Bourne and said quietly: "Bobby Kennedy's down there, with four others."

People were streaming up the trail from town, arriving out of breath and with eyes fear-filled and faces blanched. O'Shaunessy put a cordon of men about the shaft house to hold back the crowd, then went in and asked the man at the engine: "No signal yet?"

The oldster straightened up, a shovel in his hand, and the red glare from the boiler's open door made his sweat-streaked face glisten. He shook his head. O'Shaunessy went over to the open maw of the shaft and jerked madly at a rope that dropped out of sight below. Two seconds later the bell above O'Shaunessy rocked over from an answering tug on the cord below, and the big Irishman said: "Give her steam, Al. All you got."

Al dropped his shovel and reached for a valve that let steam into the donkey engine of the winch. The geared drum of the winch began turning slowly, then faster, until the outline of the dogs on the big wheel made a blurring, solid surface. "To hell with the pressure," the oldster muttered.

O'Shaunessy went outside and called for volunteers to go down and do shovel work, his voice surprisingly calm and reassuring. Half a dozen sober-faced men came in through the door and stood alongside Jim Bourne, near the closed gate of the shaft. Suddenly the winch stopped its furious winding, and the cage crawled into sight. The gate swung open, and a single, grimy man with a miner's lamp on his billed cap stepped out and said gruffly: "Get your hats and climb in, boys. It's bad down below."

O'Shaunessy opened a wood locker to one side of the door and took out hats. He lighted the lamps and handed them to the men who were going down. Ready, he ushered them into the cage, Jim along with the rest, and said: "We'll send down as many as can work at one time. Give it hell, boys!"

As the cage dropped suddenly out from under Jim Bourne and he reached out to steady himself, he looked across to the door of the shaft house and caught one fleeting glimpse of a face in the reflection of a lantern. Eileen Kennedy stood out there. Her face was chalk-white, yet there was a set to her lips that made them a thinner line than he remembered, and her eyes were strangely bright.

That vision stayed with him all the way down. The pressure came on, and he swallowed thickly, again and again, clearing his ears. The cage abruptly jolted to a stop, throwing a man behind to the floor. The door swung open, and in the eerie light of the arching, timber-vaulted shaft stood a man whose blackened face looked much like the one Jim had seen above a half minute ago.

"All out," this one said, waiting until the cage was unloaded. He swung shut the door, the shadow of his squat figure leaping on down the floor as a lantern silhouetted him. "This way, gents."

Down here the low ceiling with its solid timbers seemed a weight ready to fall and crush these helpless men. Jim Bourne, at home in the saddle, having lived all his life in open air where he could see for miles in any direction, had the feeling that he was doomed. He forgot about Dude King, about the world above, and thought only of Bobby Kennedy and Eileen and the tragedy that had so suddenly settled down over them all.

It wasn't far to where a slanting pile of rubble blocked the adit. Half a dozen times Jim and the others had passed men wheeling track loads of loose rock down the adit and into offshoots. Now they saw the eight weary men who were filling the trucks, men who had spent the last half hour futilely attacking the slanting mass of rock that lay between them and those entrapped beyond.

Jim and the others peeled off their shirts and took the places of that first shift. With a new frenzy they attacked the muck heap, and, when they had to wait for a truck, they cursed the slowness of the men who pushed it.

It went on that way for hours. Jim Bourne refused to give up the shovel to new volunteers, until, at last, exhaustion dropped him in his tracks. Soon afterward, someone yelled: "Stop!"

In the hushed silence that followed, every man straightened from his work. They all heard the muffled tapping on the other side of the muck heap — as though a carpenter in some far town across the prairie was driving home a nail in a green pine board.

"They're alive," someone muttered.

"Get a doctor down here," Jim ordered, and took a shovel from a man alongside him and started at his work again. From there on he worked tirelessly, blindly, inching his way into the endless rock heap.

Doc Blake came down the shaft and stood with them. It was Jim whose swinging pick at the top of the heap went loosely through the last few inches of the cave-in. O'Shaunessy was down here now and spent precious minutes with two of his men wedging in new reinforcing timbers. Then they shoveled away a passage large enough for a man to crawl through, and Jim forced his frame through the opening and held a lantern before him. In the blackness beyond he saw five huddled figures.

They were all unconscious, and all but Bobby Kennedy appeared safe and breathing. It was when Jim lifted Bobby's small body from the floor that he made the discovery. The boy was alive, but one of his legs was broken. Jim laid him back again and bellowed for the others to let Doc Blake through.

The sawbones crawled through the opening, dragging his black bag after him. And there, on the damp cold floor of the adit, they tore the cloth away from Bobby's leg and laid open the wound. Doc Blake took one look and slowly shook his head.

"Smashed," he breathed. "We'll have to take him down to my house before I touch him."

It took them twenty minutes to enlarge the opening enough so that they could lift the boy through on the improvised stretcher. Jim and Dr. Blake went up with him, Jim cursing time and again at the slowness with which the cage hoisted them. Then they were out and in the shaft house, and Eileen Kennedy and her father were standing there, looking down at the boy. The cage winch shrieked once again, as the cage was lowered for the others down below.

Eileen knelt beside the stretcher and took Bobby's head in her lap and looked up at Jim with a mute plea showing in her glance. It was old Tom Kennedy who asked in a quiet voice: "Any hope, Doc?"

Blake gave the stage owner a hard look, a trained look that bolstered the man better than any words. "If you'd all clear out and give me a little room, we could do something. 'Course, he's all right."

They carried the stretcher down the trail and through the town to Blake's unpainted pine house far up the street. Jim stayed with the sawbones while he set the leg. After the operation was finished, Blake straightened up and pulled the sheet up over the bandaged leg.

He looked at Jim and said, low-voiced: "You'd better take him down to Millston with you this mornin', Jim. I've done all I can with what I have. Harry Jaeger, down in Millston, has better equipment. There's danger of gangrene settin' in, and I'd feel a lot safer if he was in Harry's hands."

They hadn't been looking at the boy. But Bobby's soft, high-pitched voice said eagerly: "Am I goin' to ride with you, Jim?"

Bourne looked down at the youngster, remembering how often Bobby had teased for a ride on the stage. He forced a smile and said: "You sure are, bub. This mornin'. You can lay between the seats and look out the window." He took Dr. Blake by the arm and led him aside and asked: "Can we wait that long?"

Blake took out his gold watch and looked at it. He smiled grimly, and showed Jim the time. It was four thirty-five. The night was unbelievably gone.

Quite suddenly Jim felt again the weariness he had realized before. He was worn out. He left the house and went down the street and stopped at Chin Louie's lunchroom for two steaming hot cups of coffee and ham and eggs. He felt better after that, and stepped back onto the street just as Race Hogan wheeled the teams of horses out of the alley alongside the livery barn.

They had planned it the day before. Race was to load the gold bars into the boot in the stable, out of sight, then they were to get out of town quickly. No passengers this trip.

Race stopped the stage and let him climb aboard, announcing curtly: "She's loaded. Ten bars under the seat."

When Jim answered that they were taking

Bobby Kennedy down to Doc Jaeger, Race's only answer was a scowl. They drove up to Blake's house and rigged up a bed of planks between the cushions of the two seats. Eileen was there to watch them lay the youngster on the improvised bed, and, after they were through, she came up and took his hand and said: "I'll be there to see you tomorrow, Bobby." Then, looking up at Jim, she added: "Take good care of him."

Race flicked out the whip, and the teams fell to with a will.

Jim's last look at Eileen showed him a smile wreathing her countenance, and a measure of that same quality in her eyes that he had found so disturbing the night before. Race Hogan happened to glance back and intercept her expression. He turned around and shot Jim a surprised look. Then he smiled wryly and said: "You might do worse."

And Jim, irritable and tired and disliking the man's presumption, answered shortly: "Your job's drivin', not talkin', Race."

When it happened, the thing was as much of a surprise to Jim Bourne as it was to Race Hogan. Jim was dozing, his body instinctively bracing itself against the lurching of the stage, the shotgun in his lap, when he felt

Race nudge him with an elbow. He pulled himself into wakefulness with a protest on his lips.

"Rider up ahead," Race announced briefly. "Keep an eye on him."

Even then Jim didn't catch the full significance of the thing. It wasn't until he'd centered his attention on the rider, waiting beside the road ahead at the point where it topped the rise and ran along the high bench, that he suddenly recognized Dude King's faded yellow shirt.

Jim sat up suddenly, swinging the shotgun around in readiness, and then his mind was frantically running over their meeting of the night before and groping helplessly for a way out of this. It was Dude's plan that Jim should strike Race Hogan down. Then they were to send the stage, teams and all, over the cliff and frame it so that the blame for the robbery would fall on the raiding Apaches. Clearest of all came Doc Blake's warning: *There's danger of gangrene settin' in.* And the look in the man's eyes as he had said it. Blake had been plenty worried, more worried than he let on, if Jim was any judge.

Race was pulling in on the teams, seeing that Dude had rested his six-gun on the saddle horn. Race threw Jim Bourne a worried look, his blunt face twisted with fear. "Better plant a load ahead of his bronc', Jim," he said hollowly.

Jim shook his head. "I'll go down and have a word with him."

"You know this jasper?"

Jim nodded, and a strangely suspicious glint shot into Race Hogan's slitted blue eyes. "What is it?" he croaked. "You two . . . ?"

"Pull in and let me handle this," Jim commanded tensely.

When the stage had rocked to a stop, Jim laid his shotgun on the seat and swung to the ground.

"Why we stoppin', Jim?" came Bobby Kennedy's voice.

"Boulder in the trail up ahead," Jim told him, and gave Race a look that was potent in its meaning. Then he was walking up ahead of the coach, catching the first hint of Dude King's wary uneasiness.

Dude waited until Jim was within ten feet of him, then he turned in the saddle so that his right arm hung out of sight. "A double-cross?" he asked.

"You heard what happened at the mine last night," Jim said, keeping his hands in sight and away from the holstered weapon at his thigh. "The Kennedy boy's leg was busted bad. We're takin' him down to the

sawbones in Millston. He's in there now,"
he added, jerking his head in the direction
of the coach.

Dude's pale blue eyes shifted toward the
coach. He had seen Jim put his shotgun
down on the seat alongside Race Hogan,
and he wasn't taking any chances on being
surprised. "All right, there's a kid in there,"
he drawled softly. "That'll make it look even
better for our play. You can still swing it. Get
on back there and give the jasper a lick
alongside the head with your cutter."

"We're not goin' through with it, Dude.
We'll be bringin' bullets down another time."

"That means another two weeks or a
month," Dude reasoned, shaking his head.
"I can't wait that long. I have to get out of
the country *pronto*."

"That's final," Jim said. "Slope out and let
us through, Dude."

"You think I'll miss this chance?" Dude
barked, his voice rising. "We've framed this,
and I'll see you go through with it or blow
you to hell. Take your choice."

Shouting the words, his right arm moved.
Jim Bourne raised his own right hand in ac-
companiment with the gesture of the
smaller man's. Dude's eyes held a killing
light as he lifted the heavy weapon out of
leather with blurring speed.

Long hours of practice had trained Jim Bourne's muscles for this moment. He never doubted his ability at beating Dude, whereas there was a doubt even now showing in Dude's frantic eyes. It was that confidence that made Jim Bourne's flat muscles swing true. Their two guns flamed in unison, so that the double gun thunder sent far echoes beating up the corridors of the cañon. Jim felt a searing burn down his left side in the fleshy roll above his thigh bone. But his attention was centered on Dude King, and he thumbed back the hammer of his weapon on the heel of its falling.

Dude swayed drunkenly in the saddle. His right arm fell loosely to his side, and the heavy Colt .45 slipped from his grasp to fall to the trail, leaving a little puff of dust to mark the spot. Dude's gray gelding, shying at the sound of the explosions, shifted nervously and threw Dude's weight off balance. Then Jim Bourne saw the blue hole that centered Dude's forehead, and read the lifeless swaying of the man's body. Dude pitched sideways from the saddle, spreading loosely as one shoulder hit the ground, and the movement of his fall rolled him over onto his back.

"Jim? Jim, what's happened?"

It was Bobby Kennedy's cry that first reached Jim's ears. He turned, then, to find Race Hogan sitting calmly atop the stage, the shotgun in the bend of his arm, its twin barrels lined at Jim's chest.

Something went out of Jim Bourne, yet there was a gladness in him as he walked slowly back to the stage. "He's dead," he announced to Hogan.

Race Hogan's gaze was edged with a cunning deliberation. Once more Bobby Kennedy spoke, this time with his face showing at the open window. "You all right, Jim? What was it?"

Jim took the time to look back at the boy, to tell him calmly: "A robber, Bobby. But I chased him away." Then he once more met Hogan's measuring gaze.

For five seconds Hogan surveyed his partner with that unreadable glance. Abruptly his look changed. He swung the shotgun away and laid it on the seat beside him. "Climb up, friend Jim," he said. "We'll send the sheriff up from Millston. I reckon you saved my life."

Unbelieving, still not trusting the man, Jim Bourne climbed to his seat. Race whipped up the teams, without so much as a single glance at his companion, and in another half minute they had topped the rise, and Race was driving home the brake on the downgrade.

They traveled this way until the stage rocked into the level a full mile below, and the teams were running hard across the smooth trail in the lower valley.

Then Race asked: "What's your right name, Bourne?"

"That's funny," Jim answered dryly. "It's Jim Bourne."

Race's lips compressed in a tight smile. "And that gent was a friend of yours, eh?" he asked quietly. Then, after a few more seconds: "It would have been a smart play. What were you goin' to do with me?"

"Run the stage over the rim and leave a couple of arrows sticking in you, to look like the Apaches had done it."

Race's ruddy face blanched, yet his look remained rock-like. "A smart play," he repeated. "A smart play. Why didn't you go through with it?"

Jim shrugged his shoulders but gave no answer.

"The kid?" Race queried. Again he got no answer. After a moment he picked up his whip and laid it across the rumps of the swing ponies. "If he means that much to you, we'd better get him down to Doc Jaeger."

III

"THE SHOTGUN GUARD TAKES CARDS"

They brought Bobby Kennedy home ten days later, Eileen with him. She had gone down the second day, riding the stage, and for those ten days she had nursed the boy and seen the crisis pass. The wounds had healed cleanly, and Dr. Jaeger was profuse in his praise of the job Dr. Blake had done in setting the shattered bones.

It was a bleak ride home with the boy and the girl below inside. Jim had seen little of Eileen, and for a very good reason: one man in this country knew of his past now. Race Hogan had seen and understood that shooting on the ledge trail. Worse than that, he had kept silent about it. He had praised Jim's handling of his gun at the sheriff's inquest the day after the hold-up, telling his story of how they had been stopped by the bandit, how Jim had drawn against the threat of the other's gun, and shot the man dead.

Bobby Kennedy might have told a different story, but he was down in Millston, and his memory of what had happened was hazy. He told Eileen about the fight, but disconnectedly and only sure of one thing that Jim Bourne was "the bravest man and the best shot that ever lived. They say he put a hole through that man's forehead, Sis."

That first night Jim had wanted to saddle his sorrel horse and ride away. One man shared his secret now, and sooner or later Race Hogan would tell what he knew. Jim knew that this country was no place for him, yet somehow he couldn't leave. He thought of Eileen more than he cared to admit and of the tantalizing elusiveness of her gaze the morning they had taken the boy down to Millston.

It was on the ride home with Bobby and Eileen that Race Hogan's attitude suddenly changed. He usually made these trips in silence, his attention centered on the driving, his wish to be alone with whatever were his thoughts. He had been even more silent and glum since the shooting, and Jim had seen in this a subtle warning.

But today, with the sun playing its yellow light across the yellow bank of aspens that fringed the valleys, Race was talkative, less surly than Jim had ever seen him. "There's a little place above Rimrock I got spotted, Jim," he said as they slanted across the grassy meadow of one of the small valleys this cañon made. "It's like this valley . . . plenty of grass and water and a place for a

179

man to throw up a cabin. Someday I'll buy that place and settle down."

"On the pay you're drawin'?" Jim asked banteringly. "How many years will it take you?"

"Not so long. Not as long as you'd think," was Race's cryptic answer.

Later, as they climbed the trail and put Twin Strike in sight, Hogan said: "Tomorrow we'll have better luck than we had last trip."

Jim remembered then that Kennedy had told them they were to take down another load of gold from the smelters the next day. The bank at Twin Strike never let more than a two weeks' supply stack up in the vaults. The mines were taking out a lot of the yellow metal, and Cap Frobisher, president of the bank, didn't feel any too safe with so much of it in his tiny vault.

"We'll never have the kind of luck again, Race," Jim told Hogan. He hadn't intended this, making an unspoken plea for Race Hogan to keep his secret, but the vision of Eileen Kennedy this morning had made him anxious to stay here.

Race's thin smile was disconcerting. Inwardly Jim cursed the unreadable quality in the man that made him seem to be nursing a constant threat. Jim knew little about Race, except that he lived by himself in a small shack on the outskirts of Twin Strike and that he had few friends.

At the office in Twin Strike, with Eileen and Bobby safely delivered to the Kennedy house and the boy once more in his own bed, old Kennedy came out and told the two of them: "I'm lettin' Barney ride shotgun on that trip tomorrow, Race. Jim, you can have the day off."

Jim wasn't looking at Hogan then, so he wasn't able to catch the man's expression. But he heard him say awkwardly: "Not tomorrow, boss. I . . . that is, I'd feel a damned sight safer with Jim here ridin' alongside. Barney's all right, but we'd better use Jim with the load we're takin'."

As Jim wheeled to look at Hogan, sensing the absurdity of this request, Tom Kennedy said in alarm: "Why, Race? You expectin' something to happen?"

Race's look was uneasy, strangely flustered. Tom Kennedy didn't notice it, but Jim did. Hogan forced a laugh and said: "No. But in case anything comes along, I'd rather have Jim with me."

Tom Kennedy's weathered visage took on a more sober look. "Maybe you're right," he muttered. He looked up and said: "You'd better take the ride, Jim. I was sort of hopin' you could come up for dinner tomorrow and spend the day with Bobby and Eileen. But we'll save it for another time."

Later in his room at the hotel, Jim Bourne sat on his bed and filled his pipe, forgetting that he was grimy and his clothes soiled from the dust of the trip. Race Hogan's insistence on having him along tomorrow set up a vague alarm in him that he was at a loss to define.

Barney was a good guard, fast with a gun and a good shot, and there was no logical reason why he couldn't take Jim's place. What had Race been thinking of in insisting that Jim ride guard? He peeled off his shirt and was lathering his face and arms when a light tapping sounded at the door of his room. He reached for a towel and was wiping his face with it when he heard the door hinges squeak open and wheeled to see who had the presumption to enter his room without being asked.

Race Hogan was stepping in, while closely behind him followed two others, strangers to Jim. Race's broad face was set in a tight smile as he swung the panel shut and indicated his companions with a jerk of his head.

"Meet Roardan and Jenkins, Bourne. Friends of mine."

Jim nodded and reached for his shirt and put it on, sensing something here that was connected with the request Hogan had made earlier. He waited silently as Race, catching a hint of Jim's restlessness, laughed nervously, and said: "The three of us came up to make medicine with you, friend."

Jim forced a toneless answer: "Glad to oblige, Race. What's on your mind?"

"It's like this. Tomorrow mornin' we got a little job for you. That is, we were thinkin'. . . ."

"You're talkin' in circles, Race," cut in Roardan, a massively built man who stood nearly as tall as Jim. His voice was powerful and gruff, and for an instant he gazed directly at Hogan with a hint of contempt showing in his glance. Then he gazed directly at Jim and said: "Race has cold feet. What he's tryin' to tell you is that the four of us are snatchin' that gold shipment tomorrow, splittin' it an even four ways, and leavin' the country. You're the fourth."

This was it, then, the thing Race had so lamely tried to clear the way for earlier that night by asking Tom Kennedy to let Jim ride shotgun in the morning. Jim understood instantly how these men could so brazenly come to him with the suggestion, for Race Hogan had learned his secret, learned that

183

the man who rode beside him was an out-law. These past few days Hogan had been planning this, searching for a way of using the knowledge he had of Jim's past.

It was a long training that made Jim Bourne put down his real feelings and say easily: "I tried it once. It didn't work."

Jenkins, patterned after Dude King in body and obviously a man who relied on his guns when it came to trouble, drawled: "We heard about that. It gave us the idea." Having spoken so briefly, he leaned against the wall, hooking his thumbs in his gun belt, and waited, his expression masked in a studied inscrutability. Seeing the way the man so easily controlled whatever emotion was within him, Jim Bourne immediately la-beled Jenkins as the most dangerous man in this trio.

Race Hogan was speaking more firmly this time, now that he had been relieved of the task of explaining. "We thought you'd come in with us, Jim. What you tried the last trip was what I've had in mind for a long time. Hell, we're workin' our guts out for a hundred and a half a month, with nothin' to show for it at the end of a year . . . or two years, for that matter."

"You've got to use your head, Race," Jim said. He knew now, as never before in his life, that he must play out his desperate game in pretending to go along with them. "The only reason a gent ever takes a job like this in the first place is so that he can make a cleanin' later on. That's why I hired out to Kennedy."

A new respect shone in Race Hogan's eyes as he looked at Jim. Roardan smiled crookedly and said: "That's the way I like to hear a man talk. We sorta expected something different."

Jim laughed, reaching into his shirt pocket for tobacco, and began shaping a cigarette. "Did you ever hear of Jake Troy's bunch, Roardan?"

The big man nodded. "Who hasn't?"

"I sided Jake for three years. He was dumb, and trusted his irons more than he did his brains. Last I saw of him, he was swingin' from the cross arm of a pole along the Denver and Río Grande tracks. Maybe we ought to think the thing through a bit further before we make our play. I won't go in on anything that has a chance to fall through."

It sounded convincing. Even Jenkins, logically the most skeptical of those present, relaxed a little where he stood by the door.

Roardan, bluff, hearty, and easily convinced, had been awed by the mention of

Jake Troy's name. "It's simple. We frame it like you did the other time. Run the outfit over the ledge above Williams's place and skip the country. Headin' south, we're across the border in two days."

Jim shook his head slowly as he flicked a lighted match to his cigarette. "It won't work. We've got to have more time." He let his look turn thoughtful for a moment, then said: "I'd do it this way. The gold is bein' shipped in that big box of the bank's. Down in Millston they'll put it in the vault without even checkin' it in until Monday mornin'. If we'd deliver that box loaded with rocks, we'd have an extra day to make the getaway. We could use the extra day. Race and me can make the drive home to make it look right, and then hit the high lonesome tomorrow night."

A light of suspicion flared in Race Hogan's eyes. Before he thought, he blurted out: "But what about the split? Why couldn't these two . . . ?" He stopped, biting off his words, flushing when he realized he'd said too much.

Jim Bourne smiled, seeing that Hogan had reacted the way he had intended. He said coolly: "The split? We'll make it right there on the trail. We'll take our half and hide it under the seat inside. Roardan and

Jenkins can do what they want with theirs. You're gettin' spooky, Race." He gave Race Hogan a cold, examining look that was not lost on the others.

Roardan caught it and scowled. Jenkins focused on Hogan an inscrutable look that was betrayed only by the coldness of his pale gray eyes. It was what Jim had wanted, this planting of the seed of distrust in the minds of all three.

There was an awkward silence until at length Jim Bourne said: "That's all there is, isn't it? You've all got it straight . . . what we're doin'?"

It was plainly a dismissal. Jenkins and Roardan stopped looking at Hogan and nodded and went toward the door. Race Hogan hung back. The other two seemed to accept this situation, and Jim knew that, when they once were alone, they would talk over the thing he had so casually pointed out — that Race Hogan didn't trust them, that they likewise couldn't trust him.

"See you on the road in the mornin'," Roardan said as he opened the door and went out.

Jenkins gave Race Hogan a cold stare. Hogan's glance wavered and fell, and, when Hogan wasn't watching, the spare-bodied gunman jerked his head at Jim. It was as plain as though Jenkins had said aloud: *I'll see* you *later.*

Then they were gone, and, when their steps had faded down the stairs up front, Hogan looked at Jim, his ruddy face two shades paler than usual. "Do you think they'll double-cross me?" he wondered.

Jim held back his answer, pacing up and down in front of Hogan, who was sitting in the room's single chair. A faint scorn showed in his eyes as looked at Race, and he stopped his stride abruptly to wheel and face the man squarely.

"You were a damned fool, Race . . . a plain damned fool. Why didn't you tell me? Why toll two others in on it?"

"I . . . I didn't know how you'd take it," Race muttered, his glance wavering. "I wish to hell I'd never met those two now."

"You didn't trust me," Jim said, pressing his point. "You're crooked, Race. You knew why I was here, workin' this low-down job for more than the pay I'm drawing. It was so I could make a cleanin' and leave the country. We could have swung it alone, but now you toll in these others because you didn't have the guts to come to me."

"But I thought. . . ."

"You didn't think!" Jim snapped. He resumed his pacing, speaking meanwhile:

"Now we don't know what they'll do. Like as not, they'll pull their irons and let us have it right out there on the trail. And they'll split even, with enough to last them the rest of their lives . . . while we feed the buzzards."

Race bridled, straightened up in the chair, and looked at Jim with a cunning glance. "If they can do that, why couldn't we do the same with them?"

Jim stood still. "I don't get you, Race."

"Why couldn't we let 'em have it the way they'd like to cut down on us? Then we can split even and make our getaway."

Jim Bourne allowed his own glance to match Race Hogan's. He was silent a moment, obviously considering the plan Hogan thought his own. Finally he breathed: "It could be done. You'd handle the shotgun and blast hell out of Roardan. I'd use my iron to get Jenkins." He tensed suddenly and softly tiptoed to the door and abruptly swung it open. The hall was empty outside, but he stepped out and had a look down the length before he closed the door and came back to stand before Hogan again. "I'm with you, Race. You'll take Roardan . . . I'll get Jenkins. Will you go through with it?"

Hogan was now more himself, unsmiling, trying to hide his enthusiasm over the idea.

He had one more question: "How do I know you won't cross me?"

Jim smiled bleakly: "I could have cut you down a hundred times in the last ten days, Race. I'm no hog . . . half is enough for me. When we're through with this, we'll head north into the country I know, where we can bury ourselves from the law for the rest of our lives. I don't know Mexico, but I do know that there are a thousand gunslingers down there waitin' to cut down on anyone with money. Up north, it's different. I know what we'll find there."

Hogan was convinced. To hear Jim Bourne include him in his plans was the thing that did it. He impulsively offered his hand, but Jim had turned away and pretended not to notice the gesture.

"I wouldn't sleep at home tonight if I were you, Race. Stay away from town and keep under cover. Jenkins is poison, and I'd hate to see you stoppin' one of his slugs."

IV

"A RENEGADE RIDES HOME"

Jim followed Race Hogan as he left the hotel that night, up the cañon to his shack. Hogan left Jim outside and entered alone. He didn't even light a lamp but was inside for five minutes and reappeared, carrying a rifle and some blankets. Instead of going back toward town, he went farther up the cañon and, after a full mile, took to the trees. Jim circled the place and finally saw the orange glow of a small fire behind a sheltering outcropping of rock. Hogan was back there, cooking his supper in hiding.

Knowing that Hogan was out of the way, Jim made his way back to town, ate his meal at the Chinaman's, and afterward went into the Twin Strike House. Roardan and Jenkins were there, playing two-handed solitaire at a back table.

They looked up at Jim without a sign of recognition and waited until he had finished drinking a bourbon whisky. Then Jenkins caught his eye and nodded his head toward the rear of the building, and the two got up from their table and strolled casually out the batwings up front.

Jim Bourne followed, taking the passageway alongside the saloon and marking the way to the alley at the rear. His hand never strayed far from his gun, and he halted in the shelter of the passageway until he had picked out the two figures, waiting in the shadow of the saloon's rear wall. Then, watching their guns, he advanced with his right hand swinging within inches of his own weapon.

"Where's Hogan?" Roardan asked blandly when he stood before them.

Jim shrugged and said: "He went home." Then, before either could interrupt, he sighed audibly and added: "You sure picked a rattler to side you. Why didn't you come to me for this job?"

"We didn't pick. He picked us," Jenkins said in a surly tone.

"Watch him. He's out to hog the whole thing. I don't trust him."

"We don't, either," Roardan breathed. "I'd love to take a sashay up to his place to-night and plant a bullet through his ear."

Jim smiled and said: "That'd be fine, wouldn't it? Spoil the whole play. Uhn-uh. We need him to do the drivin', so Kennedy won't be suspicious."

Roardan grunted.

Jim waited, wanting the obvious suggestion to come from one of them.

At length Jenkins cleared his throat and said: "We'll wait until tomorrow. You can shove your iron in his ribs and blow him to hell."

Jim shook his head. "He doesn't trust me, otherwise he wouldn't have tolled you two in on the job, and we two could have done it alone. He'll be watchin' me all the way down the cañon. But you might wait until he's pullin' up on the ledge trail and then let him have it square from the front." He paused, seeming to think of something else, and added in a soft voice: "But you might let me have it at the same time. I'll have to remember that."

"You." Roardan laughed — too heartily. "You're in this with us, Bourne."

Jim said: "I'm not worryin' about it, friend. I always manage to take care of my end." There was a mildness to his voice that made Roardan stiffen, that made Jenkins clear his throat restlessly — good evidence Jim's words had hit home. It was easy to see that Jenkins wasn't sure of Jim Bourne, and to make doubly sure that he carried his point Jim added: "I'll roll back off the seat behind the boot just to make sure. And if any of your slugs miss Hogan, I'll get you both before you can slope out of your saddles. Is that clear enough?"

"You're a trustin' jasper," Roardan put in sourly. But his manner was submissive now.

Jenkins's shuffled his feet in the dust at his feet.

"Yeah, I'm like that," Jim agreed. "And remember one thing . . . if you get the idea you don't need me, you can't try a play any place else this side of the ledge. There's a dozen small outfits within hearin' distance any place this side of it, and they'd savvy something was wrong and come to take a look and put a posse after you so quick you'd never make the border. So you'll play along with me. It's your only chance, gents."

"Lay off!" Jenkins snapped viciously. "We're in it with you, and I hate to listen to a lot of damned nonsense about a double-cross. My job's to cut loose on Hogan as he's pullin' in the teams. After he's out of the way, we split what's in the boot between the three of us. Then we're long gone for the border."

Jim permitted himself a confident smile. Roardan started to speak, but then Jenkins touched him on the arm and said curtly — "Let's be goin'." — and the two of them walked down the alley, their figures further melting into the shadows.

Jim went out front again, recalling each step of the plan he had laid, weighing how he might best fit it to the thing he had in mind. Jenkins was the man to watch, he was thinking.

"Here you are, Jim. I've been looking for you."

It was Eileen Kennedy's voice that spoke behind him.

Jim Bourne turned to face her, feeling more strongly than before the hold this girl had on him. The night's happenings had rekindled the flame of hope within him that had died many days ago, when Dude King had appeared in the trail ahead of the stage. But tonight he felt that he once more had a chance — if things worked out the way he planned.

"Bobby wants you to come up and tell him about the stage hold-up," Eileen told him. "None of us has seen you for a long time, Jim. We've all been busy."

They started up toward the Kennedy house that lay fifty yards beyond the last store, and strangely enough the girl reached up and took Jim's arm. This gesture of intimacy sent the blood beating at his temples.

"Why didn't Race want Barney to ride with him tomorrow?" she asked, after they had gone beyond the crowded section.

"Race is gettin' old for the job," Jim told her. "He's spooky. But we'll let him have his way this time."

It was cloudy the next morning, and an unseasonable dampness chilled the air so that Jim and Race sat huddled on the seat atop the stage, for once thankful of the vehicle's ungainly lurching, for the movement helped keep up circulation. Race's eyes uneasily scanned both sides of the trail once they dropped into the cañon out of sight of Twin Strike. Jim noted this and assured him: "They won't try anything this side of the cliff. Too many spreads within hearing. I wouldn't worry, Race. Get a good sleep last night?"

He had noticed Hogan's puffy-lidded eyes and guessed that the man had spent a night in mortal dread and watchfulness. Hogan's only answer was an unintelligible grunt. Though he was suffering from the cold, he refused to button his sheepskin coat because he wanted to make sure that his holstered six-gun was within easy reach. He wasn't using the whip this morning, either, and held the reins awkwardly in his left hand so that his right hand would be free.

They dipped into the valley, and the teams were stretching into their habitual run to take them up where the trail clung to the face of the cliff. Jim said then: "Remember what you're to do. Here's the shotgun. Lay it across your lap and they won't notice until it's too late."

Hogan kept silent, his square-jawed face down and set in an ugly grimace. As the teams slowed against the upgrade, he flashed a sideward look at Jim who was unbuckling his sheepskin and said hoarsely: "What if it don't pan out the way you say?"

"It was your idea, Race."

Hogan clenched his teeth and swore loudly at the horses. At the sound of his voice they buckled into the harness and took the grade at a stiff trot.

Then Jim saw Jenkins and Roardan.

They sat their horses at the almost identical spot Dude King had picked. Jenkins's spare figure looked dwarfed beside Roardan's massive bulk, even though his roan was a good hand higher at the withers than his companion's.

Jim said — "Steady." — as Hogan lifted his foot onto the brake. They were almost close enough for Hogan to get in a sure blast with the shotgun.

As Hogan's left hand let go of the reins and dropped to close on the shotgun's barrels, Jenkins's hand swiveled up from his side, holding a heavy Colt .45. Race Hogan saw that gesture and frantically swung the shotgun up. Jim bent forward, gathered his muscles, and in a sudden lunge rolled backward up off the seat. The next instant, while he was sprawled uncertainly on top of the stage behind the seat, the triple concussion cut loose in a deafening roar.

Hogan and Jenkins had pulled triggers in the same split second. Looking up, Jim saw Race Hogan lurch clumsily to his feet and claw at his chest with his two hands. He heard Hogan's pulpy cough, and then the man's knees buckled, and he dropped limply onto the seat, the reins leaving his hands. He fell against the brake and released it as the ponies, half wild at the sound of the guns, lunged into a frenzied run that sent the stage-coach swaying ahead.

Jim looked out then and saw that Jenkins was still in the saddle, leaning low now as he spurred his roan out of the way of the mad-dened teams plunging toward him. Roardan had pulled his bay horse off the trail, part way up the steep bank, inside it. As he saw Jim's hat appear, he swung up a six-gun and snapped out a shot that sent a bullet whining within inches of Jim's head.

It was as Jim had planned it. The pair had showed themselves according to last night's arrangement, but now that Race Hogan was out of the way, they were gunning for Jim as he had known they would. Trusting to the unevenness of the trail to make him a poor target atop the swaying coach, Jim came to one knee. He pulled his Colt and thumbed the hammer twice as he swung past Roardan. The big man stiffened in his saddle as the two slugs whipped into him, while the bay horse shied.

The fear-crazed teams were at a hard run now, sightless in their terror. In a flashing glance ahead Jim saw that they were swinging perilously close to the outer edge of the trail, that the wheelers were not taking the turn around the face of the high cañon wall. He rolled to the edge of the coach's top, swung himself far out, and triggered his six-shooter at Roardan. The big man returned the fire once, then he was finally down, out of the saddle, lying spread-eagled at the edge of the trail. Jim pushed himself off, shoving his weight as far in toward the trail as his strength would let him.

He landed hard, going to his knees, and his last sight of the stagecoach was blotted out by a smother of dust as the teams pounded over the ledge and dropped out of sight. The next instant, as he was turning to see what had happened to Jenkins, a blast cut out at him, and his right shoulder went numb under a terrific blow. It threw him flat on his face, so that Jenkins's next shot whipped the air over his head.

Jim rolled onto his back, sat up, and reached over with his left to take the big .45 from his useless right hand. He saw Jenkins, sitting the saddle of his nervously prancing

199

roan not thirty feet away. It was the restlessness of the animal that saved Jim Bourne's life, for it gave him time to get an unfamiliar grip on his weapon with his left hand and swing it up.

In the split second the blunt snouts of their guns lined true, Jim saw Jenkins's gray eyes glaze with a sparkling hatred. He let his thumb slip off the hammer and took up the gun's solid buck with a steely wrist, throwing it into line once more. Then Jenkins's weapon blasted, but the bullet plowed up the dust at Jim's feet.

Jenkins coughed thickly so that Jim heard it across the interval that separated them. He caught the telltale flecks of blood that appeared on the gunman's lips and saw him double in the saddle and slide slowly to the dust.

A faintness took hold of Jim for long seconds, and for the first time he felt the pain in his right shoulder. He shook his head to fight off the dizzy spell and crawled to the edge of the trail to look down. Three hundred feet below, in a settling cloud of dust and broken wood splinters smeared with the blood of the horses, lay what was left of the stage.

For the moment he forgot that he must some way get the gold back to town, thinking how narrowly his plan had come to miscarrying. He had hoped that Hogan and Jenkins would kill each other and that he would be able to take care of Roardan by himself. It hadn't worked quite that way, but what did it matter? *A close one,* he told himself. *I'm all right now, and what's over is finished.*

It was then that he heard the rattle of iron-tired wheels and the slogging pound of horses on the trail below. From here he could see nothing, so he waited, slowly shaking his head to fight back the faintness that was taking hold of him. The sound of the oncoming rig grew louder as it swung around the bend. He raised his head to look along the trail and saw Tom Kennedy reining in on a team of bays that pulled a buckboard. Eileen Kennedy, beside her father, was already coming to her feet, a cry on her lips.

She stepped down quickly and ran over to Jim, coming to her knees and pulling his coat away from his bloody shoulder. "Jim," she sobbed, "you're hurt."

He smiled up at her. "Not bad. You look mighty good, Eileen."

There was something in his voice that stopped her inspection of his wounded shoulder. Their glances met, and in hers he saw a tenderness he had never before glimpsed in a woman's eyes. Suddenly she bent her head and kissed him.

Afterward, when he had told them what had happened and after Tom Kennedy had driven down the trail to have a look at the smashed stage and dead teams, Jim gazed levelly at Eileen. "There's something I want to tell you . . . about what I was before I came here," he said slowly. "For years I've been. . . ."

Her hands left the bandage she was wrapping around his shoulder, and she reached out and put a finger to his lips. "I know my own mind, Jim Bourne," she said softly. "I could have married a clerk, or a storekeeper, or a banker, if I'd wanted to. But you're . . . you're the man I want."

And with that Jim Bourne's arm went about her shoulder. As he pulled her to him, he knew that this time he could forget forever the darkling shadows that lay along his back trail.

Bushwhack Heritage

Jonathan Glidden completed the story he titled "Bushwhack Heritage" in early March, 1937. His agent submitted it to Street & Smith's *Western Story Magazine* on March 25, 1937. The magazine was then still being edited by Frank Blackwell, who had been with it from the beginning. Because Blackwell at the time had bought stories further in advance than usual, this story was not accepted until December 18, 1937. The author was paid $81 for it, at the rate of 1½¢ a word.

A slow paralysis settled through Gil Scobee at what he saw in the sand at his feet. It took him to his knees, and he spread his fingers and measured the length of the boot sole print indented there. Nearly two finger spreads — and his hands weren't small. Only

one man on the range wore boots that large
— Bob Scobee, his father.

From behind him the sound of shifting gravel slurred across the stillness. Gil whirled, and his right hand stabbed back to the holstered Colt .45 at his thigh. But when he saw who stood there, he arrested the motion, and his hand came away empty.

He said: "Howdy, Sheriff."

" 'Mornin', Gil." Sheriff George Lane pretended to ignore Scobee's hasty move. "Lookin' around?"

Gil Scobee got up slowly and stepped back in such a way that he kicked the loose sand and rubbed out what he had found. "There was a chance you'd missed something, George."

He was half a head taller than George Lane, yet the difference between them passed unnoticed. For in the sheriff's broad frame and in his rugged features were a foundation that made him measure up to any man. He cast one brief glance downwards now, to where the other had been kneeling, and shook his head.

"You won't find a thing up here," he said soberly. "I reckon whoever did this had wings and left his sign in the air. I spent three hours goin' over this ground yesterday, after they brought the bodies in." He shrugged his shoulders and spread his hands in a gesture of helplessness. "Nothin'."

"There's too much rock up here to tell a man much," Gil observed, attempting a casualness he didn't feel. "You ridin' my way, George?" He sauntered away to where his ground-haltered bay was standing close by, and leaned down to pick up the reins.

"As far as Freeman's place," Lane answered, jerking a thumb to point down the rocky slope. "My bronc's down below."

When they were down on the trail, the lawman climbed into his saddle and took the trail. He had ridden only a few rods when he reined in to point down to a dark brown smear in the sandy soil just off the trail. "That's Freeman's blood, Gil. José Manero was found a bit farther up the slope there. They didn't have a chance."

Gil felt the blood mount to his face as he looked down. All his thought was centered on one question. Had his father spilled that blood?

It was through circumstances alone that his curiosity had taken him above the trail to discover the distressing sign that was now raising the torment of doubt in his mind. For the moment he was thankful that no one else had come upon that bit of evidence; yet the thought did not ease his own concern.

Of course, the presence of Bob Scobee's boot sole print up there didn't mean that he was connected with this double killing. Nevertheless, there were questions he was asking himself, and questions he wanted to ask his friend, George Lane. Questions, however, could be dangerous, and he kept his silence.

Finally the lawman rode on again, muttering: "It's a damned funny thing about Freeman. He was a harmless old drunk . . . never had an enemy." He turned in his saddle and looked back at Gil. "Did you ever hear of anyone hating José Manero bad enough to dry-gulch him? I'm askin' because you knew Manero better than the rest of us."

Neither of the men they had found dead back there on the trail two days ago was the kind who made enemies. Freeman was a small rancher who owned an outfit adjoining the Line S, Bob Scobee's spread. José Manero, a deaf-mute, had been a docile and hard-working young Mexican of Gil's age and had grown up on the Line S. Gil knew him like a brother. No, he'd had no enemies.

"He never said, George." Gil forced a smile at his own feeble joke.

"What a devil of an inquest that was this

mornin','" Lane went on, sighing in worried perplexity. "No motive, no evidence, nothin'. And they expect me to bring in whoever did it."

Gil gave no answer, not trusting himself to speak. They rode on for the better part of half a mile in silence, each man busy with his own thoughts, both depressed over the happenings of the last two days.

"What's eatin' me is this," Lane resumed finally. "Day before yesterday Todd Freeman came to me, wantin' to borrow a thousand dollars. He wanted it to pay off that note to your father . . . the money Bob loaned him two years back. Like an addle-headed old fool, I let him have it."

The news settled like a brain-numbing shock in Gil's mind. He could scarcely believe it, yet he knew what was coming even before the lawman told him.

"Freeman had that money on him when he was murdered."

It was a full half minute before Gil regained composure enough to speak. Even then his words came only because he felt he had to say something to cover his confusion. "Why didn't you tell that at the inquest, George?"

"What good would it have done? I'm the law here. My knowin' is all that matters."

"Then there was a motive. Robbery."

"I reckon."

From then on, George Lane rode ahead in silence. Gil was thankful when the fork in the trail came into sight a few minutes later. Lane took the turning to the right, waving one hand carelessly and calling out: "I'll ride over and let you know if I find anything! This business has me whipped."

Gil watched the lawman's receding back, asking himself how much his friend suspected. Who had killed Todd Freeman and José Manero? And why had they been killed?

A growing bitterness sharpened his feelings when he thought of his father. Bob Scobee was a big man, both in stature and in name. His wealth and power had bought him respect on this range. Gil knew a different side to the man, the side that was so often overlooked now that Scobee had made his mark. To Gil, he was the man who had worked his wife into her grave, for Elizabeth Scobee had done the housekeeping and the cooking for the entire Line S crew during the days when her husband was a poorer man. He had done nothing to lighten her work, and Gil had never forgotten it.

Other things had lessened Gil's respect for his father, including the petty cruelty he often showed in his treatment of horses and men. Long ago he had lost all the feelings a son should have had for a father. George Lane's loan to Todd Freeman was another thing that occupied his thoughts. Two summers ago Lane had lost his outfit and all his money in a severe drought. He and his daughter, Martha, had moved into town shortly before Lane was elected sheriff. Martha had come home from college in Kansas City to live with her father, and Gil was thankful for that, for it had given him the chance of finding out how much he loved her. They were to be married soon now. Surely, if George could have spared a thousand dollars, he would be sending Martha back to finish her last year at college. Todd Freeman was a harmless, worthless, small-time rancher whose liking for alcohol had surmounted his liking for work. Why, then, would George Lane be loaning him money?

Suddenly the muffled thud of a distant explosion cut in on his thoughts, and his glance swung around to the north, in the direction from which the sound had come. Up there, near the face of that low ridge three miles away, was a small mine Bob Scobee had been working for the past year.

Dynamite? Gil asked himself, his curiosity mounting.

He was remembering that only two men had ever worked that mine. Those two were Bob Scobee and José Manero — and José Manero lay dead on an undertaker's slab back in town. *And the old man's over at the Hacksaw today buyin' that twenty ton of hay Joe Knoll had to sell,* he was thinking. His father had sent that message in to George Lane by Gil himself.

Remembering this, he swung off the trail and, spurring the mare into a swinging run, followed the line of Todd Freeman's fence that ran string-straight for the ridge. That heavy, earth-jarring explosion could be nothing but dynamite, coming from the vicinity of the mine, and Gil felt it his duty to investigate.

Minutes later, he topped the crest of a low hill to look across a shallow draw and see the dirty fan-spread of the mine's muck dump at the foot of the ridge. Above it showed the timbered opening to the adit of the mine, fifty yards outside of Freeman's fence. He was about to ride down the slope when a second beating blast ripped across the still air. The mare shied violently as a lazy puff of gray dust billowed outward from the mine entrance, and the next instant a horse and rider cut away from the shelter of a piñon clump in the draw below.

Acting instinctively, Gil wheeled his bay and rode quickly back over the rise and out of sight. Even though instant recognition of that rider came to him, he had the feeling of wanting to hide his presence. For the rider down there was his father.

He dismounted and walked back to a point where he could see below again. He watched his father head his big chestnut gelding at a leisurely walk down the thin line of the trail that would take him back to the Line S. Bob Scobee's huge stature seemed to dwarf that of the animal he rode, and somewhat grudgingly Gil admitted that he made a fine figure of a man — big-boned and wide-shouldered — as he sat the saddle with an erect ease that was good to see.

Afterward Gil tried to define his reasons for not riding home with his father. The best excuse he could offer was that he had wanted to be alone to reason out the things he had learned this morning. Bob Scobee's presence at the mine was perfectly natural, for he had apparently merely changed his mind about riding over to the Hacksaw that day.

Gil stood there watching until horse and rider disappeared a half mile away where the trail swung around a large outcropping. It was then that he heard the beat of hoofs behind and turned to see George Lane riding up the slope toward him. This meant that Lane had heard the blasting, too, and had come to investigate.

"Who's dynamiting?" George asked, reining in ten feet away.

"The old man," Gil told him. "He just rode off toward the lay-out."

"Changed his mind about seein' Joe Knoll?"

Gil shrugged his shoulders, finding the sheriff's presence a little irritating.

Lane rode on past him to the crest of the hill and reined in, looking over toward the mine. Gil noticed that his glance swung off to the right, toward Freeman's fence, and even at this distance he caught the sudden start the lawman gave at what he saw. His curiosity aroused, Gil walked up so that he could look down into the draw himself, and then his glance followed Lane's, taking in immediately what it was that had startled the other.

Freeman's fence was sagging, and one post leaned awkwardly out of line so that the three strands of wire hung nearly to the ground. Across the line of that fence ran a broad trench where the earth had settled. Nature had had no hand in the violent upheaval that had caused the cave-in, for the earth there had settled recently and fresh earth scars showed along the edges.

Lane said hastily: "Let's you and me be ridin' back. There's plenty of lookin' around to do at Freeman's."

"What's happened over there, George?" Gil ignored the other's attempt to divert his attention.

"Nothin' I can see. You go on and. . . ."

"I'm headed down there," Gil cut in, noting suddenly that the line of the cave-in ran in the general direction of the mine opening.

"Stay away, Gil," Lane advised severely. "Don't go messin' into things that aren't your business."

Their gazes locked, but the lawman's was the first to fall. In those brief seconds came an unspoken understanding between these two. Gil read the look of guilt in George Lane's eyes and with it his mind was made up.

He walked back to the mare and went up into the saddle to ride on past the sheriff and down into the draw. At first Lane hung back, but then followed slowly after him. By the time the sheriff had come up, Gil was out of his saddle and standing on the top of the broad trench, looking down into it. He stooped and picked something off the ground, examining it carefully, and finally coming over to hand it up to the sheriff.

"Recognize that, George?"

Lane shook his head. "I don't know much about rocks, Gil."

"Any man would know what that is," Gil rebuked him. "Horn silver. What are you tryin' to hide?"

"Lay off," Lane said testily. "It won't do you any good to ride herd on me this way." In his eyes was something that did not go with his words — that same look of guilt. Gil observed it in grim soberness.

"You know what that blasting meant, George. This was a tunnel from the mine. It ran under Freeman's house and onto his land." He gestured toward the line of the cave-in. "The old man came up here and blew it up. He did it to hide something. How long have you known about it?"

"See here, Gil. Keep out of this. There's no good. . . ."

"Why was Bob Scobee workin' under Freeman's land, George?"

Lane sighed wearily and got down out of his saddle. "Don't say you didn't ask for this," he said gruffly. "Four days ago José Manero rode over to see Freeman and tried to tell him about something queer up at the mine. The poor devil was gesturin' wild like the way he gets when he's excited, and he brought Freeman out here. Then they came in after me and brought me out that night. Bob Scobee had struck a vein of black glance the day before that meant a heap of money in silver to someone. He didn't figure Manero could give it away."

"That's why you loaned Freeman the money?" Gil asked, his tanned face losing color.

Lane nodded silently. "What else could I do? I went to the bank and borrowed it rather than let Bob Scobee steal something that wasn't his."

Gil listened to the accusing words, seeing what damning evidence this was in addition to what he had already learned this morning. Bob Scobee was guilty. But his father was no murderer — some strange coincidence had only made it appear that he was. Freemen and Manero had been robbed for the money Freeman carried, he told himself, and because of these other circumstances Bob Scobee was the logical man for Lane to suspect. "Are you thinkin' of ridin' out to arrest the old man, George?"

"I wasn't sure until this happened. Now I don't have a choice," Lane told him apologetically.

Only then could Gil see Lane's real reason for having hesitated in his duty. He was thinking of Martha and of Gil and of the tragedy it would bring to their lives to have the name of Scobee labeled with murder. Mixed with the shame he felt for his father's actions, Gil felt a certain family pride, a resolve that no Scobee should ever be dragged before the law for such a thing as this. He must have time — time enough to go into this himself and discover who was really responsible for the double killing.

He acted on impulse. His right fist whipped out and smashed at Lane, striking him full in the face and knocking him backward. The lawman rolled out of the way of Gil's rush, then stood up on his feet again, a look of bewilderment in his eyes and his hands up to defend himself. Gil rushed in once more, and Lane side-stepped and delivered a blow that caught the younger man in the pit of the stomach and doubled him up. The force of that driving punch made Gil gasp for breath and raise his hands to cover his head against the blow that Lane now hammered in. The ground whirled before his eyes as he somehow managed to break away and keep out of the lawman's reach until his senses cleared.

Then, coolly, and with a skill his father

had taught him, he fought George Lane. The man was a fighter, but he wore himself out against a younger man who fought with science backed by a hard, lean body. At last, a smashing blow caught the sheriff on the point of the jaw and knocked him flat into the dust.

Gil leaned over him, breathless and a little afraid of what he had done. He lifted the sheriff's .45 from its holster, thrusting it into his own belt and sensing the irony behind the fact that neither of them had for one moment thought of their guns. He sat down and waited the three minutes it took before Lane stirred and finally pushed himself up to a sitting position. He met the lawman's hurt stare and heard him ask: "Where's this gettin' you, son?"

"We're waitin' until we know more about this, George. Bob Scobee would never kill a man. I'll warn him and have him leave the country until I can find the dry-gulcher who's really guilty."

Lane sat there, running his hand along his aching jaw. At length he reached into his shirt pocket and, taking out his tobacco, built a cigarette. When he had lit it, he said without looking at Gil: "I know of a man Bob Scobee killed. I reckon I ought to tell you about it."

Gil kept his silence, only half listening

above the thoughts that were crowding in on him.

"It happened nearly twenty years ago," Lane went on. "You were just takin' your first steps those days. You remember Bob tellin' about the trip across the desert when we first came out here . . . after we'd sold our outfits to the big cattle company back in New Mexico?"

Gil was listening now. He remembered his father's story of that desert trip, and nodded.

"He's told you about how we found the water poisoned at Churchill water hole that first night when we were halfway across that bad stretch of sand. How the horses drank the water, while we were lucky enough to use what we had left in our last barrel . . . all but Tyler Kirk. Kirk took only a couple swallows of the poisoned stuff.

"Well, with our bronc's all dead the next mornin' there wasn't anything to do but walk on to Satan Springs. You were still a yearlin' in your mother's arms, so we left you and her and Jess Hardin to watch over you both. We took three canteens of water, and then me and Bob Scobee and Tyler Kirk started out afoot across the desert. Kirk was sick from the bad water he'd taken, but wouldn't let us go on without him. You'll see the reason for that later.

"That day was awful. Bob Scobee did most of the growlin' . . . complainin' over his sore feet and how thirsty he was. Kirk didn't complain once, but about sundown he caved in with cramps. We had to make camp to give him a rest, and we all went to sleep. I woke up sometime after dark, hearin' a strange noise. I looked over and saw Bob Scobee with our last canteen tipped up to his mouth, drainin' the last drop out of it. After he'd finished, he crawled over and laid it beside Kirk, leavin' the cap loose so's it would look like Kirk had been careless."

Gil was finding it difficult to meet Lane's glance now. "Go on," he said quietly.

"Bob Scobee was big and plenty fast with a gun, and I was scared of him in those days. I pretended to be asleep, thinkin' at the time how handy it might be someday to know just what kind of a polecat he really was. Well, we got Kirk to Satan Springs the next mornin'. He was walkin' on his two feet, too, but weak as a new-born calf. He died later that day, mostly because he hadn't had the water to fight the poison in his stomach. The last thing he made us promise was to get a wagon and head right back with water for you and your mother."

An indefinably significant look accompanied Lane's last words. Gil had a strange foreboding of what was coming, but he waited until Lane spoke again.

"Tyler Kirk was your father, Gil."

The significance of the thing held Gil in awed fascination. He was almost afraid to believe what he had heard. At last, when he fully realized the meaning of all Lane had said, a strange, wild elation took possession of him. He felt as though a great weight had been lifted from his mind. Bob Scobee was not his father — he was the murderer of his father.

In those few brief moments Gil regained a long-lost self-respect. He was not to blame for his lack of a son's affection for the man he had known always as his father. The intense hatred he had been holding in check for all these years suddenly took possession of him, and like wildfire sweeping across a range of dry grass it brought a mounting fury that drove everything else from his mind.

He put a question to George Lane, quietly, but in words that were clipped and hard. "You've let Bob Scobee live all these years . . . knowing what you do?"

"Easy, son," Lane answered. "It's still hard for me to say for sure that Bob had killed Tyler Kirk. When I was younger, I sometimes wanted to have it out with him.

But there was you and your mother to think of. Bob married her two years after we came here. I let it ride."

"What kind of a man was Tyler Kirk?" Gil asked, realizing how little he could blame George Lane for acting as he had.

"You're his image, son. Ty was big and blond and with fire in his eyes just like I saw in yours a minute ago. Your mother loved him."

"Yet she married Bob Scobee?"

"She didn't know what he'd done. I've never opened my mouth to anyone about this."

Gil hastily put aside his regrets, thinking that later he and Lane could talk this out. He would want to know more about his father, more about the times before his mother had come out into this country. What he was thinking now was the way in which the events of the past few days fitted so perfectly together in pointing to Bob Scobee as a murderer. The man had been satanical in his cunning, and his stroke of luck in making the loan to Freeman two years ago had made it certain that he would someday own the land. But he had been too greedy and had gone ahead with his mine, pretending to run it in toward the ridge on his own land, certain that no one would discover what he was finding under Freeman's. José Manero had been the logical one to help him at the mine, but Scobee had trusted the silent Mexican too far.

"If you knew all this, why didn't you arrest Scobee yesterday?" Gil asked.

"What I had wasn't proof that he did the killing, after all," Lane said. "Then, too, I reckon I was thinkin' of you and Martha."

As never before, Gil saw the true nobility of Lane's character. He had fought down his hatred of Bob Scobee in order to bring happiness to the two people he cared most about.

"Let's be ridin', George," Gil said, knowing what it was he had to do now.

The lawman read his thoughts, answering: "You let me handle this my own way. Stay away from Bob Scobee until I've taken him in to jail."

"No. This is my affair now."

Lane shook his head emphatically. "I'm the law, Gil. You keep out of this. Think of Martha."

If he had thought to block Gil's reasoning with this argument, the lawman was mistaken. For the mention of Martha Lane was the one thing needed finally to convince Gil that the way he had chosen was the only honorable one.

Lane caught the light in Gil's eyes and saw his hand stab toward the weapon at his thigh. The lawman tried to lunge away from the blow as it came, but the thirty years' difference in their ages made Gil's move too swift to ward off. The blunt snout of the .45 streaked downward to land solidly above the lawman's right temple. He went suddenly loose, and Gil caught him as he fell, easing him down until he was full-length on the ground.

The fierce torture of the throbbing pain in his head made George Lane lie quietly for a full half minute after he regained consciousness. Then came the memory of the blow that had downed him.

There was only one explanation for what Gil had done. He was riding now to meet Bob Scobee. And with this realization, George Lane was remembering Bob Scobee's skill with a six-gun — a skill that made him the equal of any man on this range.

The thought of Gil's danger helped to give him the strength to struggle to his feet. He staggered over to his ground-haltered gelding, pulled himself into the saddle, and raked the animal's flanks with his spurs. For the first half mile he clung grimly to the saddle horn, his strength gradually returning until he could sit straight and ride.

A growing sense of futility took possession of him then. Common sense told him that he was too late to help Gil, that it would be over before he could make the Line S buildings. But a slender hope drove him on, a desperate hope that sent his gaze roving over the rolling sweep of the range once he was clear of the hills. Finally he saw a faint smudge of dust hanging in the distance, and with sight of it his last hopes were blasted. Gil had too much of a lead over him.

A feeling of utter helplessness gripped him, but he rode on blindly, bending low in the saddle so as to get every ounce of speed out of the gelding. Then, suddenly, he remembered the wide swing the trail made to the south on its way to the Line S buildings. But there was a shorter way through the hills to the west. At the instant this thought came to him, George Lane was reining the gelding off the trail.

He never forgot that ride. He never again experienced the fear that took hold of him when he came to the lip of the dry wash a quarter of a mile behind the Line S buildings to see Gil riding in toward the lay-out.

He spurred the gelding down into the bed of the wash and followed it in toward the buildings until it was too shallow to hide him. Then he came down out of the saddle, feeling instinctively at his holster for his six-gun. The holster was empty. Quickly he reached up to lift the rifle out of the boot below his saddle, knowing, however, that it might prove useless for the work that was to come.

Climbing up over the bank of the arroyo, he had a last flashing glimpse of Gil riding into the yard in front of the long low adobe house. Then the building hid him, and Lane could only guess what was happening. He ran openly now, knowing that Gil hadn't seen him, yet driven on by a fear that he was too late.

The rear of the house was better than sixty yards away as he rounded the corner of the wagon shed. He was breathless, and the last few yards to the front corner of the house sapped him of his remaining strength. Just short of the corner, he hesitated an instant.

Gil's voice traveled out across the momentary stillness. ". . . about Kirk Tyler. He was the first you killed. Those other two don't count with me."

"George Lane lied," came Bob Scobee's booming answer.

Lane stepped out around the corner at

that instant, and what he saw took him to one knee, swinging his rifle up in frantic haste. But he was a split second too late, for Bob Scobee had already lunged at Gil, and Lane was afraid to shoot. His finger eased from the trigger as Bob Scobee's long arms struck out.

Gil side-stepped and whirled with the speed of a striking rattler. Too late, Bob Scobee saw his mistake and dropped his hand to his holster. At that instant Gil's .45 nosed up and cut loose its thunder. Bob Scobee's towering frame stiffened at the bullet's impact, but his hand still groped for his six-gun.

A second staccato blast of Gil's .45 drove the big rancher sprawling to his knees. Then Lane heard the click of a hammer on an empty shell and saw Gil hurl his weapon from him. And it was at that moment that Bob Scobee's tremendous vitality asserted itself. As life ebbed slowly out of him, he reached once more to his holster, lifted out the weapon, and brought it up.

The man's broad chest dropped into George Lane's sights. Lane squeezed the trigger, felt the solid slam of the rifle against his shoulder, and saw the shock of the soft-nosed bullet knock Scobee sideways to the ground, with the rancher's .45 blasting into the dust at Gil's feet. The man lay where he had fallen, sprawled awkwardly, not moving.

Gil stared, a slow look of disbelief coming into his eyes as Lane walked toward them.

"I wanted to be in on this, too," George Lane said.

This One Good Eye

Jonathan Glidden titled this story "This One Good Eye to See With." It was submitted to Frank Blackwell at Street & Smith's *Western Story Magazine*. Blackwell thought certain changes ought to be made in the story. Jonathan Glidden agreed and rewrote it. Marguerite E. Harper, Jon Glidden's agent, submitted the revised version on February 27, 1938, and it was bought on May 12, 1938. The author, upon publication, was paid $121.50 for it, at a rate of 1½¢ a word. The title was changed to "Owlhoot Nemesis" when it appeared in the issue of *Western Story Magazine* dated July 30, 1938. For its appearance here, the author's original title has been partially restored.

I

"THE LETTER"

For the twentieth time that day, Ed White took the dog-eared letter from his pocket and read it with his one good eye, sitting with his back to the fire so that the light was good. Once again he read:

Ed:

Twenty years ago you gave me an address to write to if I ever wanted to get you word. That's a long time, and you may never get this, but it won't hurt to try. Your boy grew up to be a fine man. Last year he was elected sheriff. Since then we've had a gold strike near Hillton and the town has gone wild. Bob is in trouble. Spence Hoff is running a gang and works the stage roads and his average is two killings a week. Bob has been bull-headed enough to try and fight him. You know what that means. If you are still alive and get this, maybe you'll know what to do. I don't.

Cyrus Packett

Ed White didn't know what to do. He sat there with a frown seaming his wrinkled, leather-colored face, until a man hunkered down across the fire drawled: "If you weren't too old, Ed, I'd say your girl had thrown you over."

Ed smiled perfunctorily. He got up off the log and walked out of the circle of firelight to the edge of the cañon rim in front of the cabin. Far below, the muddy waters of the Río Grande reflected the moon's light in a dirty gray ribbon, while to the northward the cañon-shot land was a black ribbed, upslanting country stretching far into the distance.

Ed and these seven others had made a good thing of it the past three years: a bought sheriff, fine grazing land within half a day's ride, and a quick way into old Mexico made it easy to steal, drive, and sell an average of four hundred head of cattle a month. They had so much gold they couldn't spend it. After a hard life, now turning his fifty-seventh year, Ed White had lately been thinking of heading for South America to buy his own outfit and begin an honest life.

Someone called down from the cabin — "How about a hand at stud, Ed?" — and he answered gruffly: "Count me out." He wanted more time to think, for in the three hours since he had received Cyrus Packett's letter he hadn't been able to decide what to do. Hillton was within easy reach, a hard four days' ride north. No longer was it the sleepy cow town he had once known but a booming mining camp. Alone, his chances would be slim against Spence Hoff and his hardcases, but he might take his seven partners along. No, that wouldn't do, either. One taste of easy pickings would turn them against him even though they settled things with Hoff. Some fine day one of them would put a bullet in his back, and it would be worse than ever for Hillton's sheriff.

Maybe I'm getting soft, Ed mused, thinking of his son.

But, sentiment or not, he couldn't forget what he owed the boy. He couldn't forget Bob's mother, young and beautiful, who had given up family and wealth to follow the man she loved, an outlaw. The youngster had been only five when his mother died, looking so much like her that Ed hadn't the heart to bring him up in the wild ways that were his heritage. So he had picked Cyrus Packett, his only friend, as a likely father for the boy, and Cyrus had taken to the idea. But the night Ed took the youngster to Packett's ranch, a quirk of fate had set the scales against the secrecy they hoped would cloud the boy's parentage.

Spence Hoff, saloon owner and gambler, had ridden out to Packett's place on business that night and had seen Ed and recognized him. Later, Hoff had reasoned who the boy was. From then on, he and Ed had been partners in a few deals that concerned stolen cattle, and before Ed left the country he knew that one more man shared his secret. He had trusted Hoff; now he was sorry he hadn't killed him.

Soberly, a little grimly, Ed White considered his chances in going to Hillton alone. Twenty years ago he had been tall and lean and wide-shouldered; now he was stooped a little, his shoulders not as wide because of their old man's sag. Only the eyes were the same — one eye, rather, and it was gray.

Four years back a shard of broken rock flying from a ricocheting bullet had struck Ed's left eye. There had been weeks of pain, and finally a doctor was kidnapped from a border town and kept a prisoner until the wound healed. An ugly scarred lid covered the sightless eye, and the agony he had suffered had engraved deep lines on Ed's face. For the first time in those four years, Ed White was now thankful for his ugliness. No man who had known him twenty years ago could possibly recognize him now.

This assurance was what brought him, a few minutes later, to say to the men ringing the poker table: "I'm headed out of here for a spell, maybe a few weeks. Hal, you're boss until I get back. Watch out for the *rurales*."

It was that easy, his going. Ten minutes later he had saddled and was riding down the steep trail leading off the rim, waving a casual good bye to Seidler, who stood guard.

Ed wasn't tired tonight, and he covered the miles as effortlessly as the roan mare that carried him. Two hours after he had left the hide-out, he suddenly felt the leather of a latigo snap give way, and he cursed softly as he slid stirrupless out of the saddle.

He was halfway across a narrow valley that wound between two high ridges, and a long training in wariness made him lead the roan close in to a high finger outcropping before he started lacing the broken leather together with a rawhide thong. He had been there only a minute when he heard a sound that made him reach up and close his hand over the mare's nostrils. Another rider was crossing this valley tonight, the earthy pound of his pony's hoofs striking softly out of the near distance, coming closer.

Ed waited, unmoving, and shortly saw the rider's outline against the lighter shadow of the slope two miles behind. And with the first sight of that small-bodied shape, Ed White felt a subtle warning of danger flow through him.

This rider was Perez Martínez, the wiry Mexican they had recently recruited from

Laredo, in Mexico, because he knew the *rurales* and had found good markets for their stolen herds. No one had liked Martínez, least of all Ed White. He was young, but his face was stamped in premature wickedness, and he was fast with guns and faster with a knife. A growing premonition made Ed watch him closely, and he was not surprised when he saw Perez suddenly lean low in the saddle and study the ground ahead. He was following Ed's sign.

It was Perez who had brought him Packett's letter today. Remembering that, Ed recalled one thing about the letter he had been too busy to notice at the time he opened it: the flap on the back of the envelope had been dirty and torn, and now he knew that the letter had been opened before he received it. Perez had read it.

Sure of this, watching the man draw nearer, Ed White reached back and lifted his Winchester from the scabbard. When Perez dropped a few feet beyond the outcropping and looked over toward it, surprise written across his thin shadowed features, Ed stepped out with the rifle half raised.

"Lookin' for me, *amigo?*" he drawled.

His speaking wasn't necessary. Martínez moved his body in a convulsive double thrust of hands toward the butts of his guns.

234

And he was that way when Ed's bullet caught him, hands clawed over holsters, bent a little forward. But Martínez never completed that lightning move. He froze, paralyzed, and a wild scream of pain burst from his lips as he pitched head first to the ground from his shying pony.

Ed didn't bother to look. It was hard sighting a rifle with one eye, but where he sent a bullet, it went. And Martínez's chest had been centered by the notch of his rear sight.

During the five minutes it took him to repair that broken latigo, he glanced only twice in Martínez's direction. The man hadn't moved. It was right that he lay there dead, for it took little guesswork on Ed's part to realize now the man had meant to put his knowledge of the letter to use.

Ed took the trouble to catch up Martínez's riderless pony and tie the reins on the saddle horn. Then he went on, and he covered thirty miles that night before he made a fireless camp and rolled into his blankets.

II

"FIRST ROUND"

Four nights later he rode the packed, seething length of Hillton's main street. It

235

was the rainy season here in the hills, and the mud ran knee-deep to a man, foreleg-deep to a horse. New, pine-boarded buildings flanked the thoroughfare, and, even though it was late, lights blazed in the stores, and barkers in front of the saloons bawled lustily above the din. Ore wagons, six, eight, ten-teamed, plowed to and from the flaming chimneys of a smelter at the far end of town, the drivers shouting and cursing as saddle horses or buckboards blocked the way. The walks were crowded, and from every saloon and gambling hall came the din of music and voices pitched in laughter or anger.

Ed White made for the hotel but was only halfway to it when his attention was attracted by a garishly-painted sign above the doors of the town's largest saloon: **Mother Lode Bar — Spencer Hoff, prop.** It was a newer and bigger Mother Lode than the one Ed remembered. From a small beginning, Spencer Hoff had evidently come a long way up a crooked trail.

A rising curiosity made Ed rein aside and pull in at the tie rail in front of the saloon. Inside, he elbowed his way through the crowd toward the bar. Once, a big hulk of a man growled angrily as Ed pushed him to one side, but the growl and the flaring anger on the man's face subsided as he glanced down at Ed. What he saw — one coldly staring gray eye in a face molded of viciousness — was enough to make any man freeze into silence. Ed White was that way. His ugliness could either go soft or hard, and at times like this he used it as a weapon as formidable as the Colt .38 that rode low on his thigh.

He called for rye at the bar, and, when the apron brought him a bottle and a shot glass, he poured himself a drink. One taste of the fizzy liquor and his throat balled up. He picked up the bottle by the neck and brought it smashing down on the cherrywood counter.

"Coyote poison!" he roared at the astonished barkeep. "Fetch me whisky this time."

An outward wave of silence greeted the crash of the broken bottle. Ed felt it, yet he stood his ground. The barkeep swallowed with difficulty, started to say something, and, instead, turned and picked up another bottle off the shelf back of the bar. He was handing it across, uncorked, when a voice behind Ed spoke sharply.

"Put it away, Riley. You, stranger. Who the hell you think you are?"

Ed White faced about slowly, for he had already recognized the voice. When his one-eyed glance settled on Spence Hoff, he was seeing a fleshier man than he remembered and a more prosperous-looking one. Spence's outfit was a long cutaway, a black-and-white checked vest over a white shirt. Above his ample paunch his coat bulged from a shoulder holster, and the heel plate of a pearl-handled gun showed from under the lapel. Yes, Ed even remembered Spence's shoulder holster — also that the man was fast at unlimbering his weapon.

"The name's Graves," Ed drawled evenly. "Once I had my guts poisoned with worse liquor than that, but I can't remember where."

Spence Hoff's pear-shaped face flushed angrily, and his cloudy, greenish eyes narrowed in a look of speculation. But no recognition showed in that look, and Ed White felt an immediate relief.

"Riley, call Charlie and Apple Cheek," Hoff told the barkeep, his glance not straying. Then, to Ed: "That bottle's worth seven dollars and a half, stranger. Pay up, or we take it out of your hide."

When Ed didn't bother to move or answer, there was a stir behind Hoff as men moved out of line. Two men stalked through that opened line a moment later, one tall and gaunt and with weary-looking eyes, and the other half a head shorter, younger and frail-looking. Both wore twin guns in low-hung holsters.

When they stepped in alongside him, Spence Hoff said suddenly: "Throw him out."

Before the two had taken a full step toward him, Ed's right elbow left the bar top and flashed down and up in one deceptively smooth gesture. Charlie and Apple Cheek made a simultaneous move toward their weapons but were caught with hands locked on the butts of their guns. They froze that way, looking into the snout of Ed's Colt.

"I came in here for a drink of good whisky," said Ed, stepping down the bar a little until he had the front wall of the building at his back. "I'll stay here till I get it. You, Riley, slide that bottle down here."

Riley hesitated only a moment. Then, ignoring the glowering look Spence Hoff fixed on him, he slid the bottle down to the stranger. Ed laid his gun on the counter and poured himself a drink. He took a sip, spat into a spittoon, and said: "Better, but not good enough. Another, Riley."

The crowd was enjoying this. Those at the back, out of Spence Hoff's sight, set up a low murmur of stifled laughter. Hoff heard it, and his eyes glittered, but he did not speak. His eyes were filled with threat as he glanced sharply at the two men who had failed him. But they didn't meet that look, for they were watching this calmly arrogant stranger.

Ed caught the third bottle as it slid down the polished bar top toward him. Again he poured a drink, and again he tasted it. This time a pleased smile softened the hard planes of his lean face. "Not bad," he conceded, and emptied the glass. Then he poured another shot and drank it, asking when he finished: "How much, friend?"

Spence Hoff didn't answer. It was Riley who said meekly: "Drinks are a dollar apiece, one-fifty for a double-header."

Ed reached into his pocket and took out two silver dollars and flipped them across at the barkeep. "Keep what's extra, Riley. The entertainment was worth it." He picked up his gun, dropped it in his holster, and sauntered along the wall toward the doors. All that way he had Hoff and Charlie and young Apple Cheek well within his vision.

As he backed out through the swinging doors, a roar of voices suddenly broke loose. Evidently no one had ever twisted Spence Hoff's tail like that before.

Outside, Ed stood alongside the doors and took out his six-gun and waited. In five seconds the batwings burst open and the tall man, Charlie, rushed out, gun in hand. Ed thumbed back the hammer and sent a snap shot at the walk that took the heel off Charlie's boot, drawling: "Back you go, Slim."

And Charlie, wise enough in the way of guns, broke his stride and stepped backward out of sight.

As Ed was ramming the Colt back into leather, a voice drawled out behind him: "You made Charlie like that, stranger. If you've got anything between your ears, you'll slope out of town before he has time to get out the back way. Charlie's a poisonous gent and likes the look of a man's back."

Ed turned and looked at the speaker, who stood alongside him now. He had to look up a little to meet the eyes that were a gray, matching his own, and, when he saw that face, he caught his breath and held it. Then he saw a glint of reflected light from this newcomer's shirt front and let his glance drop. What had taken his attention was a five-pointed star with **Sheriff** lettered across the middle.

This was Bob Packett, and he had the look of being all man. His big frame was his father's, his aquiline face a haunting, more rugged image of his mother's. Ed tried to smile, and in that moment a startling softness wiped the ugliness from his face.

He said easily: "This one eye of mine can see backwards, friend. I reckon I'll stay. A man has to work, and work's what I'm here for."

"So you're after gold like them others," Bob Packett said, a wry smile on his lean face. "It's gettin' so more than a hundred like you drift in here every day after easy money. Meantime, I can't find a man to fill an honest job at honest wages." He shrugged. "Well, suit yourself about stayin'."

"I will," Ed drawled. "But what's this about a job?"

"You wouldn't be interested."

"Tell me where to get one and I'll go after it," Ed insisted.

Bob Packett regarded this stranger speculatively. What he saw must have satisfied him, for finally he queried: "You mean that?"

Ed nodded.

"Then you'll do," the younger man said. "Any gent that can make Charlie take water is good enough to wear a deputy's badge. Stranger, you're a law officer. Come on up to my office and I'll swear you in."

III

"FROM DEPUTY TO MARSHAL"

That first day on duty, Ed White didn't stray far from the jail where Bob Packett had his

242

office. A hunger for the sight of his son brought him back more than once with questions anyone on the street could have answered, and he smoked more that day than was his habit, coming to the office each time he filled his pipe.

Finally Bob noticed it. He didn't say that his new deputy was loafing, but once he remarked: "It wouldn't hurt to make the rounds of the diggin's out behind town, Ed. If anyone so much as cracks a smile when he sees your badge, arrest him and bring him in."

To the outlaw, his own name had a heartwarming sound when spoken by his son. He had given his full name as Edwin Graves — "Ed, for short." — as he put it. But above the inward pleasure at hearing his son address him with such casual friendliness, something else was worrying him. All at once he made up his mind to get it off his chest, and said cryptically: "I heard that about you."

"What?" Bob Packett's eyes showed puzzlement.

"That you were a good lawman but too willin' to fight. That you went around with a board on your shoulder, not a chip."

"A lawman can't be too willin' to fight."

"Somethin' else," Ed went on, ignoring

the statement. "I got it pretty straight that there's a wild bunch in this town that's waitin' for an excuse to dig your grave."

"That'd be Spence Hoff and his crew. What of it? I'll meet his whole damned outfit, any day they say . . . fight 'em with guns, knives, knittin' needles, or buggy whips. The next time Hoff steps out of line, he'll wind up stoppin' a bullet bearin' my brand. I'm through waitin' for proof. It'll never come. He's too slick."

Ed sighed. "Yes, sir," he drawled, with a disarming smile, "you're the gent they said you were. So damned full of vinegar you're goin' to sign your own death certificate if you ain't careful." He paused, and in that interval saw his son's face flush in anger. But before Bob could speak, he went on seriously: "Sheriff, I cut my teeth on a gun barrel. I'm not blowin' off wind when I say I'm fast with a cutter. But in fifty-odd years I've learned a thing or two. One of 'em is that the gent that's lookin' for trouble has about as much chance of livin' out his natural life as a snowball would in a pan of hot lard."

"And I say that a man who's afraid wouldn't last even that long. And I'm not afraid of this job, Spence Hoff, or anyone else." Bob reached down and viciously slapped his holster with open palm. "This is the medicine that'll cure this town's trouble. And the next play Hoff makes . . . whether it's robbin' a stage or steppin' on a stray cat . . . will see the two of us havin' it out, with guns."

"Sure," Ed agreed. "But when you're up against a gent like Hoff, take it a little easy."

The sheriff leaned across his desk, fixing the outlaw with a hard eye. "Get this, Ed. This county elected me to carry out a sworn duty. You know what I'm up against. This is a tough town, with no marshal yet that lived more'n a month. That isn't my end of the business, and I stay clear of the town. But now that every fourth or fifth bullion stage is bein' robbed, the drivers killed, it's up to me to put a stop to it. And I will. I know it's Hoff, and, if I can't stop him any other way, I'll go after him, and we'll have it out." His fist banged on the desk top as he finished.

Ed thrilled a little to see the stubborn courage of his son. Bob was young, perhaps a little foolish, but he would make a real man, one man in a thousand — if he didn't die before he had the chance to learn through experience. But in a town like this, a sheriff wouldn't live long enough to get the experience Ed White saw that his son needed. He made one more attempt to batter down the stubbornness that was his own blood gift to Bob Packett. "Lay low, Sheriff. If Hoff walks off with a little gold, let him. Sooner or later you'll get the proof you need."

Packett chuckled mirthlessly. "I couldn't get a jury he wouldn't buy. No, Ed, my only chance is to cut him down. Once last month Hoff thought I had something on him. He came to me and threatened to tell something he knew about me. Said he knew for a fact that my real father was an outlaw. He claimed that, if I ever arrested him, he'd spread that news through ten counties, get me thrown out of my office."

He was looking at his hands, folded before him on the desk top now, so that he didn't see Ed White's leathery face drain of color. Ed queried after a long minute: "Was he right? Could he get you thrown out of office?"

Packett nodded. "He could, only I don't care. I had a talk with the man who raised me, Cyrus Packett. He knew my father. From what he said, I don't have a damned thing to hang my head about." He got up out of his chair and went to the window, staring out onto the crowded street. "So I'll play out the hand, and, if I lose my badge, it won't make much difference. I won't stop until I get Hoff."

Ed White rose from his chair, trying to put down the panic that rose up within him. There was a welling pride deep in him, too, a thankfulness that he had lived his outlaw life squarely in Cyrus Packett's eyes, that Cy had made his son believe him a good man.

It seemed all at once hopeless that he would ever change Bob Packett's mind from what lay ahead. Sooner or later the sheriff and Spence Hoff would meet. One of them would die, and it took little guessing to see which it would be, for Hoff could hire a dozen men who wouldn't think twice of cutting a man down from behind.

Suddenly Ed was remembering something Bob had said a minute before. No sooner had the thought come to him than he was asking: "Would it make a difference if this town had a good marshal?"

"Some," Bob replied. "But it wouldn't change things much in the end."

"How would it suit you if I turned in my badge this mornin'?"

Packett turned from the window and faced the outlaw, smiling. He shook his head. "Stay away from it, Ed. Marshals don't live long here."

"We could work together, me inside the town, you out in the county."

"You wouldn't last long enough to help."

"Let me take care of that end of it," Ed said.

Bob stood there a long moment, deliberately studying this stranger he'd known for less than twenty-four hours. At length, he shrugged his broad shoulders and said: "If you're goin' to quit, I can't stop you. I could even take you to see the council members and make sure you'd get the job."

"Then let's be about it."

With another shrug, Packett said — "Wait here until I round 'em up." — and went out the door. He was gone fifteen minutes. Back again, he had five men with him.

They were a sober group as they entered the office behind the sheriff. Ed guessed from their respectable looks that they were merchants, peaceable citizens. When they saw who it was — the one-eyed stranger who'd out-bluffed Spence Hoff and his hired killers in the Mother Lode — they were so anxious to hire him for their marshal that they offered him a month's pay in advance, three hundred and fifty dollars.

"That's real money," Ed told them.

"It may be the last pay you'll ever draw, too," put in one of the five warningly.

"Maybe so. But if you'll give me full authority, let me arrest anyone I please, I reckon I'll be around the first of next month after more of this coin."

The man who had spoken a moment ago glanced slyly at Bob Packett, smiled, and said heartily: "Enforce our laws and you can have the town, stranger. It'll be a pleasant change."

After they had gone, Bob Packett said: "You might as well start now. Step into any saloon any time of the day and in half an hour you'll see a fight started. Arrest the man who starts it, and you've taken your first step."

Ed White did exactly that. An hour later he brought in two hardcases, one with a bloody scalp, the other with half his front teeth missing and his lips broken and bleeding.

Bob Packett was sitting at his desk. Ed looked across at him and drawled: "Show me the lock-up. These two wouldn't take my word for it when I told 'em I was the new marshal."

Packett got his keys and went back to the jail, a separate building in the rear, and, as he locked the two thoroughly cowed men into a cell, Ed told them: "You'll leave town by stage in the mornin'. The stage will take you to the county line and dump you out. Walk back into the county and sooner or later I'll fill your carcasses with lead." He looked at Packett, adding: "That is, either me or the sheriff will."

IV

"FROM OUT OF THE PAST"

Ed White was a busy man for the next eleven days, and Hillton's jail was kept crowded. Each morning the stage took one or more of his prisoners to the county line and unceremoniously turned them loose with an eight-mile walk to the nearest ranch. None of them came back, either, for the new marshal had twice drawn his gun from the holster, and there was still talk of the way his two bullets had centered the foreheads of the men he faced. Even those who should have been headed out of town with the others were thinking twice before they robbed a placer miner or shot up the street or picked their quarrels openly. Hillton took on a look of respectability. Even the stages went through without being stopped. Bob Packett looked faintly worried these days; this lull in his official duties was suspicious.

It was on the night of Ed's eleventh day in town that he strolled into the Mother Lode and made his way to the bar for a drink. He asked for rye, and a strange bartender went to get him a bottle. But Riley, standing farther down the counter, called to his partner, and the apron put back the bottle he had taken down first and got another. He set it on the bar before Ed, grinning. "This is on the house, Marshal. The boss' own label."

Ed took his drink without answering, and, when he was through, he laid a dollar on the counter and walked away. Halfway to the doors he found Spence Hoff standing in front of him. This time Hoff met him with a genial and friendly smile, and he took Ed by the arm and said: "There's a man in my office I want you to meet, Marshal."

Ed bridled at the touch of the man's hand, but his instinct was to play a part, so he said casually: "Lead the way."

On the way through the crowd Hoff, alongside, said: "No hard feelin's about what happened the other night, are there? I was feelin' ornery. It must be the hog-swill they feed me at the restaurant for food."

"No hard feelin's."

Spence Hoff's office was at the rear of a long hall that went back from the main saloon. On either side of the hall, doors opened into private dining rooms, cubbyholes where the percentage girls entertained their customers, and one or two poker parlors.

Hoff knocked at the door to his office, and waited a moment before he went on in. The action struck Ed as being odd, so that when he stepped into the office after Hoff his hand hung close to his holstered weapon.

What he saw made him stiffen, first in disbelief, then in acute dread. A man sat behind Spence Hoff's desk, a dark man whose left arm hung in a black sling. It was Perez Martínez, the man he had twelve nights ago left for dead, and Martínez's wicked face was set in a smile that had a meaning behind it Ed could understand.

"This is Miguel Roybal," Hoff said. "He saw you on the street today and recognized you. I'll leave you two alone."

As the door closed behind Ed White, he felt coolness settle along his nerves that was a mingling of a killing urge and a faint curiosity to see what Martínez wanted of him. His years had made him cautious, and, where a younger man would have drawn a gun and put a bullet through the Mexican's throat, Ed now checked the impulse, drawling: "Miguel Roybal, eh? Not such a high-soundin' handle."

"It will do," Martínez said silkily, his English precise but holding a faint trace of accent. "*Señor* Hoff is obliging. He lets me use his office and promised not to disturb us." He lifted his right hand off the desk top and indicated his injured arm. "The moonlight blurred your sights, *amigo*. You shouldn't have been so sure about that shot."

"You've got a minute or two more before I do make sure," Ed told him. "What's on your mind, sidewinder?"

Perez Martínez shrugged expressively, smiling more broadly. "You are my friend, and, when I finish, you will forget your gun. But in case your fingers itch for the trigger, I will tell you this. Tonight I have given *Señor* Hoff a package . . . valuables, I told him. He has put it in his safe to keep for me. If anything should happen, he opens it. And if he opens it, my *amigo* Ed has to leave his *bandido* whelp of a sheriff and ride out of the country. ¿'*Sta bueno, compañero?*"

"Get on with it," Ed said tonelessly.

The Mexican leaned forward across the desk. Now his smile disappeared, and his lips curled down in a sneer. "I have told *Señor* Hoff that I think you can help us in what he wants done. In a week, two weeks, there is talk of emptying the bank vaults and taking the bullion out by wagon. They say there will be twenty, perhaps thirty, men with rifles guarding the wagons. *Señor* Hoff would like to empty the vaults before then. But he fears the marshal. I have told him that for money I will make it safe for him with the marshal. Am I understood, *amigo?*"

Once again Ed White had to check that

253

lustful urge to kill this man, and this time it took more power of will than it had before. Perez Martínez was clever — that much Ed had never doubted — and the cunning the man was using now was no surprise.

Never before had Ed White been faced with such a dilemma. The plan was flawless, for Ed must either come in with Spence Hoff on the robbery of the bank or see his son exposed as the outlaw's whelp, as Martínez had put it. There was no choice here, he told himself despairingly. But he could keep his pride, so now he smiled easily and said: "I wanted it all for myself, Perez. When I found you following me and knew I'd have to split with you, I wanted you out of the way. The play didn't go through, and now I take what I can get. Did you think I was coming up here to save my pig of a lawman son?"

The suspicion in Martínez's eyes was edged out by sheer surprise. "Pig?"

"What happened twenty years ago doesn't count for a damn with me now. I knew there was gold here and that the sheriff was my son, an outlaw's son. I rode up here to cash in on a good thing, the same way Hoff's cashin' in. If I'd been caught and arrested, I could have bribed my way free with what I know. This marshal's job is a front, Perez. When I'd had my look around, I was goin' to make a cleanin' and finish buildin' that South American stake."

Perez Martínez was grinning broadly now, all malice gone out of his expression. He knew how badly Ed wanted that South American stake. He rose up out of his chair. "I see it, *amigo*. I was in the way and that was why you shot me. This *gringo* sheriff mean's nothing to you, eh? I forgive you for shooting me, Ed." Abruptly his expression hardened once more. "Only from now on you play straight. Hoff will want to know about this."

Martínez stepped around the desk. He opened the door and called down the hall: "Tell *Señor* Hoff to come here *pronto*."

In a few seconds Spence Hoff was striding into the room. Eagerly, in a mixture of Spanish and English, Perez explained that Ed was with them. And when Hoff thrust out a ham-like fist and shook Ed's hand, the marshal had all he could do to play his part.

For the next ten minutes it was business. Hoff sat behind his desk and spoke tersely in the way of a man who knows how to give orders: "We'll do it tomorrow night . . . the next morning, rather . . . around three, when the street quiets down. We'll break the lock in back and get everything set inside to

255

blow out the vault doors. I've got a light ore wagon with six salty bronchos that'll be driven down the street to the front doors ten minutes after we break in the back. You'll be ridin' that wagon alongside the driver, Ed. When the blast cuts loose, you're to hop off and cross the street and stand under the awning and keep everyone away from the front. If you have to cut down one or two, it don't matter. I want the way clear. I have nine men who can cart the gold out through the front doors and load it. Two minutes ought to be enough time. We go out the lower road, and, when the wagon starts, you're to go ahead down the walk and clear the way."

"And take whatever lead is flyin', I reckon." Ed's sarcasm was sharp-edged.

"I've thought of that. I'll put all nine men into the wagon. They'll have guns, and they'll use 'em. That ought to draw the fire away from you." Hoff hesitated, looking to the marshal for approval.

Ed nodded. "It sounds like an easy play. Only I'd a damn' sight rather be on the roof of the store across from the bank instead of ridin' the wagon. Why not put me up there to keep one wall clear and send another man onto the roof of the bank to sling lead under the awning on my side?"

Hoff considered a moment, then nodded. "That's better than my way. Miguel, here, said you'd have an idea or two."

Martínez smiled faintly. "My *amigo* Ed has been through these things before. Listen to him carefully."

"Another thing," Ed put in, indicating Martínez, "I'm in this to help out my partner here. But when I run the chance of lead poisonin', I don't work for nothin'. How much is there in it?"

"The bullion in the vaults is worth a hundred and fifty thousand. We've scared the mines into lettin' it pile up on 'em. Only a little gold has been taken out, and we've got most of that."

"But how much for me?" Ed insisted.

Hoff's look took on shrewdness. "There's the three of us, the driver, and the nine who load the wagon. That's a thirteen-way split. I get a third, the rest is even between you."

Ed shook his grizzled head, and the stare of his one eye seemed to bore into Hoff. "Then it's no deal. I get a tenth, or I don't even draw cards."

Perez Martínez purred: "Think again, *amigo*."

While Hoff was turning his glance from Ed to the Mexican, Ed gave Martínez a sly wink and said: "Miguel and I have the hard job. We'll have to fight our way out of town. You take your third and give each of us a tenth. Let the others split what's left between 'em. Don't make the mistake of ever over-payin' your understrappers, Hoff."

This sounded like sense, or so Hoff thought. At length he nodded slowly, considering the logic of the thing. But then he said: "Charlie will be sore. So will Apple Cheek."

"Give me the word and I'll cut 'em down as they come out of the bank," was Ed's cold-blooded offer.

The calm assurance of his manner struck home even to Spence Hoff. When he looked up at Ed, there was new respect showing in his glance. "I believe you'd do it."

"There'd be more for us," Ed drawled, and added: "Those two didn't make your play stick with me the other night."

The thought was intriguing Hoff. "They didn't," he breathed. Then abruptly he made a decision. He brought his fist down onto the desk top and growled: "You've called the deal, Ed. Get rid of those two for me and you can have their share. Apple Cheek's been gettin' ideas a little too big for him, anyway. He knows too much."

There were other details, and, before Ed left Hoff's office, he had to admit grudging admiration for the man's ability as a leader. Under any other circumstances he would have welcomed this man's brains and worked with him.

But when he did leave, Ed White found that he hated Spence Hoff as much as he had ever hated any man. Perez Martínez was a snake that could be stepped on, but Hoff was different. For twenty years the man had filed away the secret of Bob Packett's real identity, doubtless with the hope of some- day using it against him. Ed wondered if the saloon owner knew that Bob cared little about being exposed as an outlaw's son. Regardless of whether or not he knew, Hoff was a cunning enough man in other ways.

Before he turned in that night, Ed stopped in at the office.

"It's been a quiet day," he said to the sheriff, as he came in through the door.

"Yes," Bob answered laconically.

Ed saw that something was worrying his son. He sat down and filled his pipe, waiting for the other to speak.

Finally Bob muttered: "You're damned right it's been quiet . . . too damned quiet. Spence Hoff is gettin' ready for a play of some sort. I'd give every dollar to my name to know what it is."

"Would you?" Ed drawled. Then he drew his chair closer to the desk and told his story. "Hoff isn't even thinkin' about you in this," he said as he finished. "We can have him cold, just the two of us."

They stayed there another hour, planning what they would do. It was after midnight when Packett finally blew out his lamp and closed the office.

V

"PAY-OFF"

At eleven that night Ed met the sheriff in his office. "Time to be movin'," he said. "I had a look at the alley in back of Leonard's store today. You get over there now and shinny up that gutter pipe and wait. Keep your eye on the bank. I'll try and get there to side you before this thing begins."

"How about guns?" Bob asked. "I'm takin' a Winchester. You want one, too?"

Ed shook his head. "I do my smokin' with a plow handle."

Packett left a few minutes later, by the back office door. Ed, a nervousness strangely enough beginning to take hold of him, smoked out his pipe before he left the front way and crossed the street to the Mother

Lode. Inside, he made his way back to Hoff's office.

The saloon owner greeted him cordially. "Howdy, Ed. Have a cigar. The boys are ready. It's all over but the shootin'."

"One thing I forgot to ask you, Spence," Ed said familiarly. "When do Miguel and I meet you for the split?"

"Miguel knows. You ride out with him and you'll be with us before mornin'."

Ed nodded as though he were satisfied, although he was realizing that Hoff's plan was to see him dead long before morning. Miguel carried a knife at his belt, and Hoff was no man to lose a tenth of a one-hundred-and-fifty-thousand stake if he could find a way of keeping it.

Ed met Martínez at the bar an hour later. The Mexican edged in alongside him, ordered a tequila, and said softly without looking at Ed: "Shoot straight tonight, *amigo*. We have plenty *pesos* when we ride away."

The words had a double meaning that Ed White didn't miss. He said nothing, and a few moments later moved off into the crowd.

It was a long wait, and, standing alongside a faro lay-out, he kept an eye on Martínez and Charlie and Apple Cheek. He had sent Bob Packett to the roof of the store across from the bank because he didn't trust Spence Hoff. The man might make a try at the bank before the time he had set and leave his new partner, the marshal, out of it. But at two o'clock the Mother Lode was nearly empty, and Hoff himself was serving drinks, and all his men were there. So far, things had worked out as Hoff had explained it last night.

When the time came, at a quarter to three, Hoff singled out his men, and by either a look or a barely perceptible nod he sent them to their stations. Charlie and Apple Cheek, their guns swinging fin-like at their thighs, went out together. Ed had his last careful look at them, noting that Apple Cheek wore a light gray, flat-brimmed Stetson and that Charlie was outfitted in somber black. He would need to know that later.

Perez Martínez followed the pair, then others drifted casually out the doors. Ed, cautious, made his way down the hall and to a back door he had seen earlier that night. In the alley behind he turned right and walked on toward the rear of Leonard's store. He kept a close watch at his back, a time-developed wariness working keenly now.

It was an easy climb from the wood box at the back of the store to the roof seven feet above. Halfway to the front, he heard Bob's low challenge, and answered it in a muted voice. His sheriff son was hunkered down at a corner of the plank false front that was Leonard's garish attempt to make his place of business appear more imposing.

"They're on the way," Ed said. "You trot over to the other side and watch from there. And don't cut loose until I yell, no matter if I fire first. Maybe you can pull a board loose and belly down on the roof so you won't have to lean out the side." He was already applying his own advice, loosening a rotten board at eye level and breaking it off a foot or so inside the outer edge of the building's false front. This way, he could lie down and look through the opening, directly at the bank doors.

Now that the time was at hand, he felt really nervous for the first time in years. His confidence was still with him, yet he was now faced with the most important moment of his life, and he knew it. He scanned the street with an appraising eye, and one thing he saw satisfied him. The chimneys of the smelter at the edge of town were still blazing, and an occasional ore wagon lumbered past with its cargo of precious earth. Perhaps he would be lucky enough to find one or two close to the bank when he needed them to help block the street. He looked long and hard at the outline of the bank's roof. Martínez was not in sight across there.

Because there were other wagons in sight along the faintly lit street, he didn't see Hoff's three-team wagon until it was almost abreast the near corner of the bank. A second after he had seen and recognized it, the building under him trembled and a blast cut loose across the way that left his ears ringing. Windows burst outward from the front of the bank. A cloud of dust billowed lazily across the street, half obscuring the driver as he whipped up his teams and pulled even with the doors. Ed White reached for his gun.

There was a tense, ten-second wait. Then the first man ran out the sagging doors, staggering under the weight of a burlap-wrapped bar of bullion. He heaved it into the wagon bed and turned and ran back through the doors as another man emerged.

Ed raised his glance and saw the vague outline on the bank's roof. That would be Martínez. At that very instant Martínez fired, and from below shuttled up the choked cry of the bystander that the bullet had cut down. Martínez made a good target where he knelt up there, and it was a temptation to Ed to shoot him down. But he checked the impulse and, instead, sent a shot lancing down in front of a man running toward the bank along the opposite walk. The man stopped, turned, and ran, and others behind stopped and joined him as he went past them.

The walk over there was clear. Looking down at the wagon again, Ed saw four men carrying heavy loads out the doors. He recognized Apple Cheek and Charlie, but Spence Hoff was nowhere in sight. At that instant, Ed White realized that he wouldn't see Hoff down there tonight; the man was too smart to risk discovery.

"How about it, Ed?" Bob called across to him.

"Wait," was Ed's answer. As he spoke, he was lining his sights at Martínez, who now stood in plain sight on the roof opposite.

He squeezed the trigger, felt the solid buck of the weapon, and heard its hollow roar. Martínez arched his body and clawed at his chest, head snapped back and staring at the sky. Then, slowly and stiffly, he fell out across the coping of the roof and downwards toward the walk, turning over once before he crashed onto the wooden awning below.

Two men hurrying to the wagon in front

of the bank stopped, looked at Martínez's stiffening figure without recognizing him, and then went on about their work.

"Hold it, Bob!" Ed called in warning. They weren't through over there yet, and he wasn't ready.

Then he saw a loaded ore wagon coming slowly up the grade, headed for the smelter. The driver had heard the shots but was uninterested. This town had been hoorawed before and would probably be shot up again. When the wagon drew into range, Ed took careful aim at the on-wheeler and fired, saw the horse stumble. The driver, cursing, reined his team to one side and tried to turn the wagon around.

He was in that position, his wagon blocking the street, when the nine men across the way grouped in front of the bank doors and crossed the walk, guns out. Two of them wheeled to fire on down the street before they climbed into the wagon.

"Pick 'em off, Sheriff!" Ed yelled.

Charlie's black-shirted chest was dropping into his rear sight as Ed called to his son. He let his thumb slip off the hammer and, as the guns exploded, saw Charlie stumble backward and fall headlong out of the wagon.

Apple Cheek was next. But this killer had been bred to this kind of trouble and now whipped his glance upward at the store roof and swung both guns up in a blazing chant of gun thunder. Bullets splintered the boards above Ed's head, and one of them came through his small opening and took him full in the shoulder, spoiling his aim. Apple Cheek was shooting fast and accurately, with the precision of a man who lives by his guns. He had emptied one weapon and was crossing his .45s from hand to hand in the famous, smooth border-shift, and at that instant Bob Packett fired his first shot.

He had used the Winchester, and the steel-jacketed slug caught Apple Cheek with hands poised to catch his guns — caught him so that he staggered back away from the guns and let them clatter to the plank walk at his feet. Ed White fired then, wincing at the pain in his shoulder, and his bullet drove Apple Cheek on back so that he slid down along the brick wall of the bank's front, and rolled onto his face.

The others had vaulted into the wagon now, throwing themselves behind the plank sides of the bed. As the driver's whip cracked over the ears of the team, a man behind him rose on one knee and fired at the false front of Leonard's store, realizing finally where the danger lay.

But a hail of lead met him. Bob Packett

was levering shots with a deadly accuracy that made Ed White stop immediately and watch with a sudden pride and relief that his son had inherited his own shooting eye. The man on his knees in the wagon bed sprawled loosely over the side, stirring the dust as he hit the ground.

Ed looked to his side and saw Bob come to his feet and throw down the rifle and reach for the two guns at his thighs. Then Ed stood up, too, reloading as he rose. The teams down below were rearing, and Bob's first six-gun bullet knocked the driver out of his seat as he was tugging at the reins. The men that were left in the wagon, only a half dozen now, jumped over the sides and headed for a narrow opening between the bank and the adjoining building. As they lunged across the walk, two of them fell.

One of them managed to roll onto his back and see Ed White, leaning out from behind the false front of the store. He raised onto one elbow, took careful aim with his six-gun, and calmly shot Ed before he rolled over and died.

The slamming impact of that bullet caught Ed fully in the chest, and drove him back so that he lost his hold. He was off balance, and without the power to help himself he fell down and out.

The awning was ten feet below. He struck it on his wounded shoulder, and the pain of that jarring fall brought his breath soughing out of lungs already filling with blood. He rolled out across the awning and fell onto the street below.

He lay unmoving for seconds, not caring, thinking only that the secret of Bob Packett's parentage would die with him. But then he remembered Spence Hoff, and the package Martínez had given the saloon owner. The memory gave him the strength to stagger to his feet.

Ed reached the Mother Lode and half fell through the swinging doors. But as he felt his knees give way, he reached out and caught the panel on his left. He hung there, knees buckled under him, looking into the room.

Through a misty haze that blurred the sight of his one good eye, he looked along the bar and saw Spence Hoff talking with a hatless man whose right shoulder was matted with blood. One of Hoff's hardcases had escaped to bring the story back to his boss.

Then Hoff saw Ed. And with one sweep of his left arm pushed the man alongside out of his way. Hoff's right hand dipped in under the lapel of his coat and came out in a streaking draw that lined a short-barreled Colt chest-high at the outlaw.

Ed tried to raise his own gun. Hoff's first shot blasted outward at the saloon's walls, and his bullet jerked at Ed's body and broke his hold on the door. Ed fell, rolled over, and reached across with his left hand to grasp his other wrist and steady it.

Hoff shot again, and Ed's body slid an inch backwards along the floor from the bullet's impact, but still he kept his head off the floor and his gun gave one last throaty blast. Hoff stood there for a full three seconds, smiling, and then those few outside, who had had nerve enough to look in through the windows, saw the smear of red spreading slowly across the saloon owner's shirt front. All at once his stocky legs gave way under him, and he fell heavily. When they reached him, he was dead.

Four days later Ed White opened his one good eye and stared upward at a timbered ceiling. Vaguely he thought he remembered that ceiling. Then he was sure of it. He rolled his head to one side and saw the two men standing by the room's single window.

Yes, Cyrus Packett was standing there beside Bob. There was a look on their faces that banished the uneasiness that had been with him even in his delirium. Bob must have heard him move, for now he raised his glance, looked straight into Ed's eye, and took a step that put him alongside the bed.

"How is it, Ed?" he queried.

"It'd be a lot better if I could move," the outlaw answered.

"You'll move in a few days," Bob told him. "Only we're trying to find out what kept you alive. The sawbones dug four slugs out of your hide."

It took Ed a few moments to summon strength enough for words, to fight against that tired feeling that made him want to close his eyes and sleep. But finally he thought of something that made him ask: "Did I do much talkin' . . . while I was out?"

"A little," said Bob.

"Too much?"

Bob shook his head. "Just enough. From now on we're makin' this town toe the line. Only it ought to be the other way around. A man doesn't deserve a sheriff's badge when his father is wearin' only a marshal's."

So Bob knew. Ed smiled weakly, feeling strangely relieved as he drawled: "Don't forget, son, I'm drawin' three hundred and fifty a month. That's better'n sheriff's pay."

Lone Rider from Texas

Frank Blackwell edited Street & Smith's *Western Story Magazine* from its inception in 1919. He early attracted to the magazine Frederick Faust who wrote Western stories as Max Brand, George Owen Baxter, David Manning, among other *noms des plumes*. Blackwell also favored Western fiction by Ernest Haycox, Cherry Wilson, Robert J. Horton, Walt Coburn, and in the late 1930s introduced Luke Short and Peter Dawson into the pages of this magazine. Blackwell, in fact, had bought the first Peter Dawson story, "Gunsmoke Pledge," and published it in Street & Smith's *Complete Stories* (5/36). However, in 1938 he became involved in a power struggle at Street & Smith along with F. Orlin Tremaine, the editor of *Cowboy Stories* who had bought the third Peter Dawson story to be published, "Lawman of

Latigo Wells." This struggle resulted finally in the ouster of both Blackwell and Tremaine. *Cowboy Stories* was dropped from the Street & Smith roster of magazines. Blackwell was replaced by Jack Burr who would continue as editor until the magazine ceased publication in 1949. Burr genuinely liked the Peter Dawson stories, as did the magazine's many readers, and encouraged him to write more stories. Burr's editorial commitment was to a more mature orientation in Western fiction, stories likely to appeal more to adult readers than teenagers, and Peter Dawson was one of the authors he favored to accomplish this change in the magazine's target audience. Jon Glidden completed the story that follows in early July, 1938. It was submitted by his agent to Jack Burr on July 22, 1938 and purchased on August 21, 1938 for $171. The title was changed by the time it was published in the issue dated March 11, 1939 to "Lone Raider from Texas". In addition to publishing a great many Peter Dawson stories in *Western Story Magazine*, Jack Burr, in addition in the years 1941 through early 1943, serialized in the magazine's pages five full-length Peter Dawson novels subsequently published in book form by Dodd, Mead. The first of these, *The Crimson Horseshoe* (Dodd, Mead,

1941), won the Dodd, Mead Prize in 1941, an award co-sponsored by both the book publisher and Street & Smith Publications. For its appearance here, Jon Glidden's title for the story that follows has been restored along with the text of his original typescript.

I

"FLOOD TRAP"

When the first gray streamers of rain slanted down out of the black thunderheads that banked the low peaks of the Sentinels, Major Cyrus Dorn leaned out of the stagecoach window. "Get a move on, man!" he called up to the driver. "It's going to cost you your job if I'm not at the fort tonight."

"Doin' my best, sir!" the driver answered, his scowl belying the respect in his tone. But, knowing the major as he did, even that scowl and his obvious anger didn't keep him from putting the whip to his two teams. The road was rough, too rough for going this fast, but if it was to be the choice between pounding this Barlow-Sanderson to pieces or losing his job, he'd take the former.

Inside the coach the girl sitting the hard cushion opposite the major said: "That's no way to talk to him, Dad. He's going as fast as he can without shaking us to pieces."

Major Dorn growled something unintelligible into his bristly gray mustache and eyed the dark horizon to the west again. He was thinking of Dead Man's Wash, that wide and threatening arroyo four miles this side of Fort Reeder. Three hundred and sixty-odd days of the year its sandy bottom was dry as a bone. The other five days — it varied with the years, sometimes being six or seven — the arroyo was filled bank to bank with a raging torrent of clay-colored water foaming down off the slopes of the mountains. It was called Dead Man's Wash because it had claimed many lives, those of men and animals who misjudged the swiftness of the water or tried to outrace the oncoming flood.

The stage now gathered speed, rocking and swaying, the cushioning of the thoroughbraces doing little to break the impact of the iron tires against the ruts and the rocks.

Florence Dorn had a tight grip on a sling strap, yet her striped silk dress was nicely mussed in the next three minutes, and she finally had to remove her hat to save it from being crushed. "Do you have to do this, Father?" she asked. It was only when she was angry that she called him "Father."

"I do. Otherwise, we'll have to camp out

all night within sight of the fort," the major growled. His patience was at an end. The driver had loafed his teams all this hot day, all the miles from Gody, the way station where Dorn had gone to meet his daughter who was returning from four years of college in Kansas City. Bates, the post sutler, owned the stage. And if the major told Bates to fire this man, he'd be fired.

It happened fifteen minutes later, only seconds after the driver had booted home the brake and reined his teams at a walk down the steep slope and into the dry bed of Dead Man's Wash. A cracking of spokes sounded out from the left rear wheel, and the coach went down with an abrupt lurch, leaning precariously on the broken axle, jarring the major and his daughter so that for a moment they were both stunned.

The major picked himself off the floor and bawled: "Now what the hell have you done?"

As he was climbing stiffly out one sprung door, the driver answered meekly: "These last three miles shook her to pieces. Sorry, sir."

"Sorry, be damned. Drag this thing across to the other side."

"You won't make it," a voice called out from behind and above. "The water's less than half a mile above now. Listen to it."

Turning to face the direction out of which that voice had come, the major saw at the top of the high bank a tall rider astride a magnificent, straight-limbed claybank gelding. And from out of the distance droned the unmistakable low roar of the descending torrent.

"I'll thank you to mind your own business!" was the major's explosive retort. He turned, spoke sharply to the driver: "Get on with it!"

The driver, climbing down off his seat and still holding his reins, cautioned: "You and the lady had better walk on ahead, sir. I'm not answering for what'll happen."

"You leave that to me." The major made no move to get his daughter out of the stage, or to walk ahead himself. Instead, he arrogantly eyed the driver's efforts to get the teams started once more.

Florence Dorn looked out one window of the stage at that moment. The stranger on the trail above saw her for the first time. He must have instantly understood two things: first, that the major was a stubborn man; second, that the driver didn't have even a scant chance of dragging the disabled stage to the far bank, two hundred yards distant, in time to beat the flood.

Convinced of this, the rider's glance traveled along the near bank of the wash and finally settled on a slender, uprooted cottonwood stripped of most of its dead limbs. It seemed to be the thing he was looking for, for he called out: "Driver, have you got a rope?"

The driver, walking alongside his struggling teams, now fifty yards away, shot an angry answer back over his shoulder. "Sure I got a rope. But what we're needin' is a boat."

The claybank moved quickly down the slope, the rider smiling thinly at the driver's remark and unlashing a coiled length of rawhide hanging at the horn of his saddle. He reined the animal in toward the cottonwood, shaking out the loop of his reata. Throwing it deftly, he caught the top end of the slender straight tree, took a turn of the rawhide on the saddle horn, and eased the claybank into the pull. In thirty seconds' time he had dragged the tree the fifty yards out from the bank and alongside the stage.

As he swung out of the saddle, he said flatly: "Lay off that. Fetch your rope, if you want to get out of here."

The driver stopped the teams, eyed the rider stonily for an instant, and then reluctantly climbed up to lift his seat and take a coil of stout half-inch hemp from the box beneath.

Major Dorn was strangely silent. A moment ago he'd had his first close look at this stranger's lean face, and that single glance had prompted him to step out of sight behind the stage and lift the Colt Service .45 from the black holster belted about his thick waist. Now he stood there with it in his hand, hesitating at sight of the stranger's low-slung holster.

The rider kicked off the few remaining dead branches from the tree, dragging it in alongside the stage, and finally thrusting a third of its butt end in under the axle of the broken wheel. When it was in place, he lashed it firmly to the axle. The driver, his frown disappearing, took a hold on the front end of the long pole and lifted. As he lifted, the back end of the coach was raised out of the sand, the tree acting as a lever, the axle as a fulcrum.

"Tie to the brake arm," the stranger said as he came forward to help the driver. His words were flattened, crisp, for suddenly the distant mutter of the oncoming water increased in volume to an unmistakable roar.

The driver, as he climbed up onto the front wheel hub, took a quick look upstream. There, around a bend a scant two hundred yards away, foamed a three-foot high wall of water, rushing downward in a slow-moving and ponderous wave of destruction, and carrying before it small, uprooted trees, brush, and a few sizable boulders. That sight made the driver move in frantic haste, lashing the small end of the tree to the protruding arm of the brake.

Before he had finished tying the last knot, he called out stridently: "My God, Major, climb in!"

It was at this exact instant that Major Dorn stepped from behind the coach and called to the stranger: "Cruise, put up your hands!"

The tone of that voice, the mention of that name, caused the rider to whirl to face the blunt snout of the major's leveled .45.

Florence Dorn, who hadn't heard her father speak, called down: "Dad, let's go back before it's too late!"

"Unbuckle your gun and drop it," Dorn said, ignoring his daughter. "I'm taking you with me."

The stranger had the look of a man who might have acted differently under other circumstances. As it was, he quickly unbuckled his single shell belt and the holstered six-gun he wore low at his thigh and said, his sun-blackened face set in a grim smile: "You sure picked a hell of a time to make this kind of a play."

"You're Jim Cruise. Give me an excuse and I'll put a bullet through you."

Jim Cruise, the roar of the oncoming water growing, had no choice. He was first in the door, Dorn following immediately. Dorn's boot was barely on the step when the driver, half frantic, half amazed at what he'd seen happening below, swung his whip.

The first violent lurch of the stage threw the major hard against the frame of the door. For an instant his weapon was out of line. In that brief space of time Jim Cruise's fist whipped out and wrenched the heavy .45 away from him. The stage had gathered some speed, the teams at a slow and lunging run.

Florence Dorn stared in amazement at this strange rider, at her father whose face had now taken on an apoplectic flush of humiliation. She understood nothing of what had gone on. When Cruise abruptly tossed the weapon out the window, saying flatly — "We can settle our business without this." — she couldn't believe what she had seen or heard.

Cruise ignored the major once the weapon had arced out of view. He leaned out the window, called loudly above the increasing roar of the water: "Head downstream! Maybe you can outrun it." He glanced to one side and was relieved to see that his claybank was headed for the near bank on a line parallel with that of the stage.

The driver swung off to the right. The teams were now at a slogging run, dragging the improvised travois almost as easily as they had the wheel it replaced. And in this moment even Major Dorn forgot his anger as he eyed the rushing wall of water. His look toward it was as intent as was his daughter's.

The near bank of the arroyo seemed at times to be drawing away as quickly as the flood was overtaking the stage. But once Jim Cruise drawled to the girl: "He knows what he's doin'." His look and the tone of his voice eased the expression of terror that was beginning to show in her glance.

The last few seconds were the worst. For the past quarter minute the speed of the stage had kept the angry flood at its distance, a bare ten yards behind. But when the teams suddenly wheeled in toward the bank, the seething torrent raced down on them at a breathless speed.

For an interminable moment it looked as

though the water would crush in the side of the stage and drown them in its merciless grip. But all at once the stage's front wheels lifted. The menacing boil of water struck hard at the down-tilted back end, swept it a good three feet downstream, and then the teams pulled it clear onto dry, firm ground.

Jim Cruise's claybank stood twenty feet away, ears forward and obviously nervous at the awesome sound of the torrent. Cruise caught the major's eye and nodded toward his horse. "There's nothing to keep me now, is there, Major?"

Dorn's eyes were lighted by a cold fury. "I can't stop you. But sooner or later they'll kill you as they would any other wolf, Cruise."

"Who is this man, Dad?" the girl asked quickly.

"Jim Cruise, the outlaw we've been hunting. I told you about him this morning."

Florence Dorn's memory was evidently keen, for now her hazel eyes regarded this Jim Cruise with a look of mixed loathing and awe.

"There's nothing to keep me, but I think I'll ride on to Fort Reeder with you, Major," Cruise announced abruptly.

Dorn's expression changed from one of impotent rage to one of incredulity. "You'll

. . . you'll go on to the fort with me?" he gasped. "As my prisoner?"

"Why not?" Cruise lifted his wide shoulders in a brief shrug. He took a folded piece of paper out of a vest pocket and opened it up, handing it to the major.

It was a printed reward notice, with his name printed in big black letters across the top line. The reward of a thousand dollars was being offered by the United States War Department and would be paid to the person or persons delivering him, dead or alive, to the Commanding Officer, Major Cyrus Dorn, at Fort Reeder, New Mexico. The specific crime for which Cruise was wanted was listed as robbery of the post sutler's safe, the theft of two thousand dollars.

"Eleven days ago, down in Texas, a friend of mine sent that dodger to me in the mail. He's sheriff down there. I left that day and started up here."

"To give yourself up?" Dorn asked, a look of amazement still showing in his glance. For the moment, his arrogant bearing had left him.

"To tell you a few things about your sutler, Guy Bates. When I've finished, it'll be Bates and not me you want."

Florence Dorn had been looking over her father's shoulder, scanning the notice. When she looked up, her glance was puzzled. "But, Dad," she began, "I thought you. . . ."

"Florence," the major cut in, "you'll leave this matter to me." He looked once more at Cruise. "Am I to understand that you're willing to put yourself voluntarily under arrest?"

"The sooner the better."

Dorn's smile was enigmatic. He leaned out the window, called to the driver: "Put this man's horse on a lead rope and see how fast you can get us in to Fort Reeder. Will that rig hold up the back axle?"

The driver, down off his seat, came up to the door and looked in at Jim Cruise, a relieved smile on his tired face. "Sure, it'll hold. Stranger, if it hadn't been for you, we'd all be feedin' the buzzards this time tomorrow. That was close, too close."

"This man is Jim Cruise," the major said. "He's come in to give himself up."

Instantly the driver's smile vanished. He blinked stupidly, staring bug-eyed at Cruise. Then he swallowed as though trying to clear his throat of a fistful of cottonwood seed and muttered hoarsely: "Cruise. Givin' himself up. Never thought I'd live to see it."

He walked quickly over to catch the claybank. A minute later the stage was under way.

II

"ARREST"

At five-thirty that evening the Barlow-Sanderson rolled to a stop in front of Fort Reeder's post headquarters. Major Dorn, out the stagecoach door first on the pretense of wanting to aid his daughter in alighting, failed to give her a helping hand. Instead, he stepped away from the coach and called loudly: "Guard detail! Over here on the double."

Across the hard-packed parade ground a squad of eight armed soldiers under the command of a corporal, new sentries about to go on duty, wheeled and came on at a run.

When they came up, Dorn gestured toward the stage from which Jim Cruise was alighting. "I've brought in Jim Cruise," he said. "Corporal, you will put him in the jail and detail your men to guard it. You're responsible to me for the prisoner."

Cruise turned slowly to face Dorn, thinking his hearing had deceived him. "Couldn't I come into your office?" he queried. "I haven't a gun on me, and we can talk this over like gentlemen."

"I want a double complement of men stationed at the sentry posts tonight, Corporal," the major ordered, ignoring Cruise. "This man is dangerous and has dangerous men working with him. We're to take no chances on his men breaking him out of jail. Any stranger approaching the post tonight is to be challenged and shot if he refuses to identify himself."

As the squad stepped in to surround him, Jim Cruise said mockingly: "You go to a lot of trouble over a man wanted for stealin' two thousand dollars, Major."

Dorn laughed harshly. "Save your story for the hearing tomorrow, Cruise. For a man who's killed eight soldiers and stolen something amounting to fifty thousand dollars from the federal government, you're either a fool or making a play for bigger stakes. Maybe you gave yourself up on purpose, just to be inside the fort. Maybe your wild bunch is planning on raiding the post and stealing all our horses and guns. In that case, we'll be ready for them."

"But I'm alone," Cruise protested. "The only bunch I've ever had are the four men of my crew on my lay-out down in Texas. And what's this about killing eight men and stealing?"

"Take him away!" Dorn ordered curtly. Two of the soldiers took Cruise roughly by the arms, leading him across the parade ground toward the jail.

Jim Cruise looked back once at the stage, at Florence Dorn. What she saw in his gray-eyed glance troubled her, made her feel uncertain. But the next moment her father was reaching up to take her arm.

"We'll have to hurry, Florence," he said. "Bates is eating with us tonight, and you've got to look your prettiest. You're going to like Guy Bates."

As she climbed the steps and crossed the wide porch of post headquarters, catching the stiff salute of the two sentries posted at the door, Florence Dorn wondered what it was about Jim Cruise that made the story her father had told her that morning seem so utterly ridiculous and untrue.

Her first meal at Fort Reeder, her future home, was a trial for Florence Dorn. After the first few minutes with Guy Bates, she disliked the man, not passively, but with an intensity close to real hatred. There was more than one reason for this. Under any other circumstances she might have liked Bates casually, as she had liked other male acquaintances she had made in her four years at college in Kansas City. Guy Bates was tall, handsome even though his face was a trifle too full, too dark, and his manners were flawless. But his handshake, when he first met her, was a trifle too firm, and the stare his black eyes fixed on her was more than bold in its directness. Lastly, he was forty years old, nearly twice her age, old enough to be her father.

She could have forgiven all this and made herself like the man, but for her father's insinuations. His first remark, as he had stood out there in the hallway of the house with his arm familiarly about Bates's shoulder, introducing the sutler to his daughter, had been: "Florence, this is Guy Bates, my best friend. I hope he'll be yours, too."

That statement, with his obvious meaning, had brought back to her mind a dozen references her father had made to Bates in his infrequent letters and on their ride from Gody to Reeder. She saw now what had been planned between the two of them — her marriage to Bates. She remembered that her father had mentioned that Bates was the wealthiest post sutler in the territory. And Major Dorn had always put a little too much faith in a man's means, she knew all too well.

Just now trying to get down a mouthful of the rice pudding the major's housekeeper had prepared for dessert seemed to her an impossible task. Two hours ago she had been ravenously hungry. But with Bates across the table, staring so fixedly at her, she had lost the last trace of her appetite.

She had patiently sat through her father's recital of Jim Cruise's capture. She had even tried to point out that the outlaw had saved all their lives, only to be rebuked for the stand she took. Listening to the major's account of their escape from Dead Man's Wash, she realized suddenly that he was such an arrogant and boastful man it was difficult, if not impossible, for her any longer to respect him.

She was jerked rudely away from her thoughts when Bates said: "I wonder if his bunch will make another raid on the paymaster's ambulance?"

That morning her father had listed Jim Cruise's crimes. The theft of two thousand dollars from Bates's safe, four months ago, had been the original act that had made him an outlaw. But since then, on two different occasions, the paymaster's ambulance driving cross-country between territorial posts with a money chest packed with gold had been attacked, the guards killed, the gold stolen.

The last time Major Dorn had sent one of Bates's stages out to intercept the paymaster and transfer the gold to the stage for safekeeping, and the attack had come while the transfer was being made. The stage driver was the only man who had lived through that fight. He had been wounded in the shoulder but managed to get the stage back to Fort Reeder. He had positively identified Jim Cruise as the leader of the ten men who had made the attack and taken the money chest.

"They wouldn't dare make a try this time," was Major Dorn's answer to Bates's query of a moment ago. "Twenty troopers are riding down from Fort Taos, along with the paymaster. They're well-armed, and we've arranged to have the sides of the ambulance lined with sheet iron. In case of another raid, our men will lie behind something better than canvas to keep off the bullets. If Cruise's men attack, we'll kill every last one of them."

Bates's heavy dark brows had come up in surprise as he listened to Dorn's words. At length he chuckled softly and said: "Not a chance for them, then. Well, Major, I'm hoping to attend the hanging."

"The hanging?" Florence couldn't keep back the words.

"Certainly," her father said. "Jim Cruise will be hanged. We'll make an example of him."

Florence got up abruptly out of her chair, laying her napkin on the table. She walked around to where her father sat, leaned over, and dutifully kissed him on the forehead. Then, in a voice calmer than she realized she could command, she said: "I'm terribly tired, Dad. Will you excuse me?"

Major Dorn nodded, winked slyly at Guy Bates. "That'll give us a chance to go over those stores requisitions, won't it, Guy?"

Their laughter followed her out of the room and up the stairs. As she lighted the lamp on the washstand, she looked into the mirror above it to see that her face was crimson. Her father's remark was plain enough. Far from doing the trivial work of a quartermaster, Major Dorn had welcomed being alone with Guy Bates to discuss but one subject, his daughter.

Her father was going about the task of marrying her off with the same cold-blooded and ruthless lack of emotion he'd shown today in capturing the outlaw, Jim Cruise. *Could Jim Cruise be guilty of the things for which he stood accused?* Florence Dorn asked herself. He'd been obviously bewildered as he was led away from the stage by the guard. The girl remembered also his protests of the things her father had said when he was un-ceremoniously conducted to the jail.

A sudden resolve sent her to the door of her room to open it. Listening, she could hear her father's domineering voice echoing up the well of the stairway from a room farther back along the lower hallway. She guessed, rightly, that they had left the dining room and gone into the library. With this assurance, she stepped quickly to the wardrobe and took out a light woolen coat and pulled it on. Tiptoeing down the stairs, she pulled a silk scarf over her head and tied it under her chin.

It was a long walk down to the far end of the parade ground. Aside from the dim lights directly across the way at post headquarters and in the several small houses occupied by the married officers, the post was in total darkness. The barracks halfway the length of the long rectangle presented an obstacle she had to ignore. As she walked past the squad building, the sentry on duty saluted her smartly, and she bade him good evening.

Four minutes later she was at the far end of the parade ground, approaching the armed sentry who stood at the gate of the five-strand wire fence surrounding the well-isolated building that was the post's magazine, used for the storage of all explosives and ammunition. Alongside it, her father had told her, was the jail.

"Good evenin', miss," the sentry greeted her, saluting stiffly.

"I . . . I want to see the prisoner," she said, a trifle lamely she thought. "My father wants me to deliver a message."

"I'll be glad to take it in to him," the man said. He was the corporal who had commanded the sentry detail that had taken Jim Cruise away.

"But I was to deliver the message personally," Florence countered, a trace of her father's stubbornness rising up in her. Then, blithely, she added: "It may take me ten or fifteen minutes."

Corporal Kennedy, plainly torn between his duty and the authority behind this indirect order, finally gave way. "This way, Miss Dorn." He turned in at the gate and led her toward the low, single-windowed addition at the far end of the long building. He caught the salute of one of his men posted at the jail, unlocked the door, and threw it open.

"Miss Dorn is to be left alone with the prisoner," he told the sentry. Then, to the girl: "Just call if he gives you any trouble, miss."

III

"ESCAPE"

Before she quite realized it, Florence Dorn was standing inside the jail. At the last moment Corporal Kennedy had lighted a lantern and put it on the floor. In its meager light she could look across the small room and see Jim Cruise, lying on a pile of straw in the far corner.

When he saw who it was, he quickly rose to his feet. Then he smiled and gestured toward a thin covering of straw on the floor, obviously his bed. "That's the only seat I can offer you."

"I came to talk to you," she said, ignoring his words. Her glance went around the small room. It was bare of all furnishings but the pile of straw, a tin plate that must have held the prisoner's evening meal, and a large tub brimming with water.

He saw her looking at the tub. "It gets a little warm here in the daytime," he explained. "That's supposed to cool a man." Then, looking at her squarely: "So they've sent you to get a confession?"

His sureness was thinly veiled, and the light smile on his aquiline face was so bleak that she shuddered involuntarily. She said haltingly: "I came . . . that is, I wanted to know the truth. I don't believe what Father says about you." It was out before she realized it. She hadn't intended to be so outspoken.

His look changed subtly. It was no longer

hard and ungiving. His gray eyes lost their chill, and he drawled mildly: "Suppose you begin by tellin' me what they're sayin' about me. I can't get any of these guards to talk. What's this about killin' eight men and stealin' fifty thousand dollars?"

"You're to tell me."

"There's nothing to tell except that I rode up here to have it out with your old man about takin' that money from Bates. It was my money."

"Yours? Why did you take it, and why should you think it was your money?"

He didn't answer her for a long moment. He was eying her soberly as he took out a sack of Durham and shaped a cigarette. "Mind if I smoke?" he queried, and caught her answering nod. When he had lighted the quirly, he said: "You heard how I drove that trail herd up from Texas early in the summer?"

"Dad didn't mention it."

"That's how the whole thing began," he said. "Last winter I bid on a contract to supply Fort Reeder with a thousand head of prime beef. This last spring me and four of my crew spent a month pickin' those thousand critters, all prime and fit for the drive across the desert to the Pecos. We took it slow, brought the herd in to water in fine shape. From there on up here, it was easy. Good grass, plenty of water. It was the finest herd that ever hit this country. But Guy Bates didn't think so."

"What did he have to do with it?" Florence asked.

"He's post sutler. One of his jobs is to buy beef for the garrison and the Indians the government feeds in this country. It was his contract I signed. One of the requirements is that the sutler reserves the right of cutting out any poor beef, any critters below weight. He culled exactly half my herd, five hundred."

"But they were in good shape, you said."

Jim Cruise laughed softly. "They were, all but a few, maybe twenty. But that's one way any dishonest sutler can make easy money. He thought he'd made it with me. He bought five hundred at contract price. Then, when I was boilin' mad and ready to drive the culls away, he offered me half the contract price for 'em. It's easy to see how he was going to make a nice piece of change on the whole deal."

"By collecting the full amount from the government?"

Cruise's glance took on a touch of admiration. "That's it."

"So you got your money, anyway."

"I tried to see your father. Bates must have seen him first. Your father had me marched outside the post boundaries, wouldn't let me set foot inside again. That night I met Bates on his way to the tank town a couple of miles east of here. I stuck a cutter in his ribs and made him go into his store and open up his safe and pay off. There was a couple thousand more in gold I could have taken if it had been plain robbery."

The girl was silent a moment. "What about the rest?" she asked finally. "The two robberies of the paymaster's ambulance? Killing those eight soldiers?"

Jim Cruise hesitated. "You won't believe this, miss," he said slowly, "but I haven't set foot outside my home county in Texas in three months, not until I started up here eleven days ago."

"But. . . ." Florence Dorn caught herself before she voiced her doubt. Then, studying Jim Cruise's expression closely, she knew instantly that he was telling the truth. She had nothing to rely upon but her instinct. But it told her that this man was no killer, no thief, and she gave way to it. She told Jim Cruise as much as she knew, what her father had told her that morning on the ride out from the Gody way station.

When she had finished, Jim Cruise laughed grimly. "So they've made me eight times a murderer and with enough gold cached away somewhere to make me a rich man. Where did they think I found all the hardcases to make up my wild bunch?"

"Dad said you'd probably brought them up from Texas. He says they may try to hold up the paymaster's ambulance either to-morrow or the next day when it comes down from Fort Taos."

Jim Cruise stepped down to her. "Say that again. There's another payroll comin' through."

Florence nodded. At any other time the Texan would have been acutely aware of her beauty, although, if he was now, he didn't give any sign of it. She had drawn the scarf down about her shoulders, so that her tawny hair caught the lantern light and shone like spun gold. Her eyes, a deep hazel, regarded him with a softness that normally would have quickened the beat of his pulse. Seen that way she was beautiful, her pale oval face set in a look of bewilderment at the conviction that her father had imprisoned an inno-cent man.

"I'll have to get out of here," Cruise drawled at length.

Alarm edged into the girl's glance. "You

can't. I'll go home and see Dad and tell him the truth. But you can't try to break out."

"Your father's a mule in some ways," was Jim Cruise's blunt reminder. "He wouldn't let me talk last summer, and he won't listen to what you tell him." He nodded toward the side wall of the room. "What's that building alongside?"

"It's the magazine."

Jim's glance whipped up to meet hers once more. He laughed softly. "You mean there's powder, ammunition stored in there?"

"Yes. But what are you thinking of doing?"

He was smiling now broadly. "Never mind. All you have to do is to leave that lantern here when you go out. Tell the sentry anything you want . . . that I'm afraid of the dark, that I want to write the folks down in Texas and need light. Tell him anything so long as you make him leave the lantern in here. You'd better go now."

"Jim Cruise, I won't let you do it. Whatever it is, you can't be such a fool as to try to escape."

Something in the tone of her voice sobered him instantly. "You believe what I've told you?"

She nodded.

"Then go home and forget you've come here. Tomorrow, when I'm gone, have your father send a man over to Gody to telegraph Sheriff Len Grant at Rimrock, Texas. He can have all the proof he wants that I've been down there since early summer. And tell him to be careful how he spreads it around every time the paymaster's due."

All at once Florence Dorn caught a hint of the meaning behind his words. "You mean that it's Guy Bates . . . that he . . . ?"

Jim Cruise shook his head in a negative gesture. "I only mean what I say. The only thing I know against Guy Bates is that he tried to pull a forked play on me. He wasn't smart enough. But I wouldn't tag him with a thing like this unless I had proof."

"But you're sure he's the one?"

Cruise didn't answer. He nodded toward the door. "Here's wishin' you luck tomorrow mornin' when your father finds out where you were tonight." His easy smile took the edge off his words. "You'll help me if you wait until then to tell him."

A minute later, after he had countered her last protests, she went out. Through the locked door he heard her speak to the sentry. For five minutes, long after the sound of her light step on the gravel path had died out beyond the fenced-in enclosure around the magazine, he waited for the lock on the door to grate open again.

But after that long interval of silence he knew that whatever she had told the sentry had had its effect. They weren't coming in after the lantern.

He looked down at it, wondering if it would do. Then he glanced toward the side wall of the small room, muttering half aloud: "It's three feet thick if it's an inch."

He set to work immediately. First, he blew out the lantern, removed the hot glass globe by taking off his shirt and shielding his hands with the cloth. He unscrewed the cap from the base and went into the far corner to pour the coal oil into a deep crack in the hard-packed adobe floor. Next he took out the wick-holder and tossed it to one side. Then, with nothing but the lantern's bare frame, he inserted a boot between the two uprights of the frame, put his heel on the round base that had held the wick, and threw all his weight down on his boot.

The base of the lantern flattened slowly under his hundred and seventy pounds until at last, with the sharp edge outward, it was compressed to an inch thickness. When that was finished, he bent the two uprights of the lantern down until they formed a more acute angle with the base.

Dragging the full tub of water to the side wall was a more difficult job, since he didn't want to spill the water or make too much noise. But it was finally in place, and he had moved it noiselessly.

He sloshed water around the base of the wall and then tried the lantern, now a makeshift shovel, against it. Working slowly and as quietly as he could, he gouged out the wall's thin adobe plaster. Then, his hands feeling for the cracks between the brick-hard adobe slabs, he began loosening the dirt mortar in the cracks, softening it well with water before he used the spade lantern to dig it loose.

In an hour's time he dragged the first one-by-two-foot adobe brick from the base of the wall. The one above it came out in less than ten minutes. He enlarged the hole by taking out three more adobes. Then, his head and shoulders in the opening, he set to work at the inner tier of the thick wall.

He stopped once every twenty minutes to rest and smoke. Outside, he could faintly hear the sentry's regular pacing up and down the front length of the yard. Once he had to spend ten minutes quietly moving the mud and rubble from the front of the opening to give him more room.

It was three hours later, long past midnight, when his crude shovel went out from under his thrust and through the inner plaster of the wall. After that it was only a few minutes' work to enlarge the opening so that he could crawl through.

Standing upright in the pitch darkness of the magazine, Cruise was at first uncertain what to do. He knew that the magazine must be securely locked and barred, probably as tightly as the jail. He started walking, and after three steps stumbled awkwardly over a hard object. Feeling it, he dis-covered it to be a heavy wooden case — ammunition, he decided.

He walked on and, after groping about in the darkness for about five minutes, found what he wanted. It was a small, heavy keg. He felt along its top until his hand came in contact with a round plug. He drew out the plug, leaned over, and sniffed at the opening.

Black powder. He could recognize that odor anywhere. He picked up the keg and with difficulty lugged it back to his opening in the wall, probing it through ahead of him.

A quarter hour later he sat back and surveyed his work by the light of a match from the back wall of his jail. What he saw satisfied him. A mound of mud banked the foot of the steel door, which he had been careful to notice opened outward. Beneath that mound was upward of a quart measure of black powder. Out of a hole in the foot-high mound trailed a long grayish line of powder all the way to the pile of dirt and mud and adobe now banked in front of the opening into the magazine. The rest of the powder, what he hadn't used, was safely inside the magazine wall once more.

As the match flickered out, he reached for another. With it in his hand, he walked over to the break in the wall. It was closed now, although he'd saved enough mud and adobes to build a foot-high parapet as long as his body. He now lay down behind that low pile of dirt, and listened to the tread of the sentry's boots outside. As soon as it had receded into the distance, he leaned across and dropped the match into the line of powder, throwing himself to the floor as he let it go.

His last sight of the room was the streaking line of flame that leaped along the floor toward the door as the powder ignited. When the pounding blast of the concussion beat out, Jim's hands were over his ears and his head was low to the floor. The explosion came as an earthy pound that shook the building, compressing the air about Cruise as though a blanket of heavy sand had suddenly been thrown onto him.

On the heel of that concussion he was

coming up onto his knees, seeing the door as it went outward, torn off its hinges. He sprang for the opening, ran through it, and had a fleeting glimpse of the sentry through the billowy cloud of dust that shrouded the jail front. The sentry had been knocked to his knees and was now picking himself up, his rifle beyond his reach.

The darkness and the fog of dust raised by the explosion saved Jim Cruise's life. He was around the lower corner of the jail before the sentry called out to his startled companions beyond the enclosure, and he had climbed the tightly strung wire fence before the shouts announcing his escape sounded muffled from the inside of the jail.

The horse corrals lay a hundred yards in back of the magazine, well out into open country. Cruise knew that his escape was impossible without a horse, a good one. As he approached the corrals, he saw through the darkness the two dim shapes of the sentries. One was running toward the other, and, as Jim slowed his pace, he heard that man call out: "What the hell's happened, Bill?"

While they were standing there, looking off toward the magazine, Jim circled to the back of the corral, unseen. Back there was a picket line. One saddled horse, a chunky bay, was tethered to it. It was probably the mount of the sentry detail, whose duty would be to ride a periodical inspection in his platoon throughout the long night stand.

The bay shied nervously at his approach but didn't whicker. Jim was in the saddle in a scant ten seconds, headed away from the post, walking the bay north. Five minutes later, a safe distance away, he lifted the animal into a quick trot.

IV

"A STRANGE HOLD-UP"

Ten hours later, fifty miles to the north, Jim Cruise came down out of his uncomfortable McClellan saddle a mile short of a small group of adobe houses that was the first town he'd seen. He took saddle and bridle off the bay, threw them into a narrow, deep arroyo, and let the animal go, watching it long enough to be certain that it headed back toward Reeder, directly south. Then, afoot, he walked toward the town.

At the small horse corral that served as the native village's livery, he spoke in fluent Spanish to the Mexican owner. He explained that his horse had stepped into a hole while crossing the Río Grande five miles to the south. The horse had broken a leg.

307

In fairly good English, the man queried: "You shoot him?"

Jim shook his head, indicating his mud-soiled outfit. "He drowned. I damned near did, too. Lost my gun, saddle, the whole outfit." It so happened that in crossing the river his bay actually had stumbled and gone down, giving him a thorough soaking. It was none of the native's business that he'd managed to save the horse and himself.

The Mexican's nut-brown face was full of sympathy. He shrugged expressively. "The river, she bad."

"Can a man get from here to Taos by stage?"

"*Sí, patrón*. Tomorrow, the stage come through."

This was a bit of information Cruise had wanted to make sure of. "But I'll have to go on today. Can I buy a horse and saddle?"

The native shrugged again, this time expressing a doubt. "Me, I got only one saddle."

Looking out into the littered yard in back of the adobe house, Cruise saw a dilapidated buckboard. "How much for the rig and a team?" He could be thankful now that Corporal Kennedy's guard had left him his wallet even though they'd taken everything else out of his pockets.

"You bring 'em back?"

Jim nodded and was surprised to see that the man didn't for an instant doubt his word.

"How long you be away?" the native asked.

"Two, three days."

"Ten dollar."

In half an hour Cruise was again headed north, this time with a full meal under his belt and driving a fresh team of small, wiry horses. He had also managed the purchase of an old Colt .38 and a handful of shells. He was anxious to discover any sign of the paymaster's ambulance and its guard having passed along the road, and he inquired several times at houses along the road. But no one had seen it.

Twenty miles to the north, late that afternoon, Jim made out ahead a group of four buildings footing the face of a high ridge that followed the Río Grande. The corral with fine, well-fed horses in it told him at once that it was a stage station. He breathed a sigh of relief at that, for he had hoped to reach a station before meeting the paymaster.

After he had unhitched, fed, and watered the horses, he went into the main building. In there was one main room that evidently served as both kitchen and eating quarters. It was empty now save for a middle-aged woman who looked up from her work at the woodstove only long enough to nod him a greeting. Beyond, in a poorly lighted room, he could see a double row of bunks running along the back wall.

"Anyone through today?" he queried as he sat on the bench of the big slab table.

"You're the first," the woman told him.

The answer, strangely enough, didn't satisfy Cruise. "That's funny," he said. "I was to meet my outfit up here. There'd be ten of them. They're due in Taos tomorrow at sunup."

The woman shook her head. "Then they're goin' to be late. This is the only way in, and, unless they swam up the river, they couldn't miss passin' here."

That, to Jim Cruise, was the best guarantee that he had arrived in time. If the paymaster's ambulance was to be raided this trip, the bunch that would raid it weren't ahead of him.

His supper was already on the table when both he and the woman were roused by the sound of hoof thunder and the crunch of iron wheels echoing along the trail above the station. Cruise continued with his meal while the woman went to the door.

"Lord A'mighty," she complained. "Do you suppose I got to cook for that outfit?

There must be twenty of 'em. Soldiers, too." She bustled back to her stove, stoked up the fire, and began breaking eggs into a bowl. "Well, they got to take what I can give 'em. You'd think they'd let a body know."

The lieutenant in charge of the cavalry detachment was the first in. He was insistent on feeding his men and horses promptly and getting on. But when the woman told him firmly that it would take an hour to prepare a meal, and that they'd have to fork their own hay for the horses because her husband had gone to town, the lieutenant went out the door and called: "We'll spend the night here, Sergeant!"

After he had finished eating, Jim Cruise went out and leaned against a pole of the corral, watching the cavalrymen unsaddle and water their mounts. He even engaged one trooper in conversation, pointing out his buckboard and team. He was amused at the man's look of scorn as he inspected the shabby outfit. Later, when all but two of the soldiers went inside to eat, Cruise lingered outside. The sun had fallen behind the ridge across the river, and the quick dusk was already settling over this bottomland.

When the yard was cleared of the uniformed men, Cruise went inside, paid for his meal, and came back to the corral to get his team. He hitched, then sauntered over to the ambulance where the two soldiers who had been left outside were standing a listless guard.

"How's the road above?" he asked one of the pair, the one he had earlier showed his team and buckboard.

"Fair," the man answered, not interested in making conversation. It was obvious that he, a cavalryman, had little respect for a man who owned such poor horses.

Cruise made a point of looking intently into the darkened interior of the ambulance, which was nothing but a spring wagon with a canvas cover arched over its bed. "What you got in there?" he queried with an expression on his lean face that he hoped looked half-witted.

The other soldier nudged his partner. "Gold," he answered solemnly.

"Gold?" Cruise's gray eyes widened in mock amazement. "How much?"

"Thirty thousand."

Cruise whistled softly and looked impressed. "Ain't you afraid someone'll take it?"

The first guard laughed. He leaned his rifle against the ambulance's end gate and took the making's Jim Cruise offered him. "Yeah, we're scared to death," he chuckled.

He finished sifting tobacco out onto the wheat-straw paper, then offered his companion Cruise's tobacco, winking slyly at him. A private, he was enjoying this rare opportunity of impressing a stranger with his importance.

The second guard leaned his rifle alongside the other. It was while his eyes were lowered and his hands busy with the tobacco sack that Cruise brushed aside his vest and lifted the heavy Colt .38 from the waistband of his Levi's, drawling: "Either of you make a sound and they'll be leavin' you at the nearest cemetery."

It was so dark now that even this close, six feet away, he could barely make out the stupefied look that flashed into the two pairs of eyes that whipped up to stare at him. Slowly, hesitantly, the first guard raised his hands.

Cruise cocked the .38, the audible *click* of the hammer catch bringing the second soldier's hands up faster.

"Both of you turn around," Cruise rasped, emphasizing his words with a jerk of his weapon. They obeyed reluctantly.

He moved fast, once their backs were to him. Stepping in close behind the nearest, he raised his gun and whipped down a short, choppy blow that placed the weapon's barrel alongside the man's scalp at a point above his right ear. It was a practiced and effective bulldogging stroke. The man's face instantly went loose, his knees buckling to let him fall sideways to the ground.

His partner, hearing the sound as his friend's body hit the ground, whirled around. His mouth was open to call out, but it suddenly snapped shut as he stared into the bore of Cruise's weapon.

"Easy," Jim cautioned. "Be good and you'll only get hurt. Yell, and I'll let you have it square in the guts." He had known men in uniform who would ignore such advice, holding duty dearer than life. But this man's receding jaw, his weak blue eyes, proclaimed him as anything but brave. "Turn around again."

The man cringed visibly as he obeyed. An instant later his senses were wiped out under the impact of Jim Cruise's striking weapon.

Jim moved fast, needing what little light was left. What he was doing meant taking a big chance, but he considered it a secondary one. He pulled a bayonet from the scabbard of one of the unconscious men.

Then, leaving them where they lay in back of the ambulance, he ran to the corrals, to the lean-to alongside the nearest. There, placed neatly on the two long poles that ran down the sides of the lean-to, were nineteen saddles, all bearing the brass insignia of the United States cavalry. Nineteen bridles hung from the horns of the saddles. One by one, hurrying but making sure he did a thorough job, Jim Cruise slashed the bridles and the cinches of the saddles with the bayonet. Along one wall he found the harness for the ambulance team. He cut the leather of this, too, damaging it beyond repair.

It took him three minutes of feverish work to finish. Running back to the buckboard, he felt the hackles rise along his neck when he saw the stage station door swing open. A man in uniform, the lieutenant, stepped out, lighting a cigarette. He paused on the doorstep as someone called to him from inside. Then, incredibly, he turned without even a glance toward the ambulance and went in again.

Jim drove his team close in alongside the ambulance. Lifting himself up into the bed of the wagon, he felt around in the darkness. He found two small chests, one heavier than the other. Lifting the heavier one out, he pushed it into the small bed of the buckboard.

He was climbing up onto the seat of the buckboard when a call sounded out from the stage station: "Gifford, will you eat out there or come in for it?" As Jim picked up the reins, a heavy and ominous silence lengthened out. Then, louder: "Gifford! Baker! Where the hell are you?"

Jim slapped the reins across the backs of the team at that moment. The pair of under-size horses lunged into the harness; the buckboard started rolling.

Then, as the vehicle swung down into the road, a shot exploded from the direction of the stage station door. The bullet laid its whip of air along Jim Cruise's right cheek. The next instant he was crouched down in front of the seat, his perch narrow and precarious as the excited team broke into a run over the rocky road.

Someone shouted stridently: "Stop him! Get your rifles, men! Shoot to kill!" Mingled with those ominous words rang out a mutter of oaths and cries.

It was a full three seconds before the next shots came, a ragged volley of them. Those three seconds saved Jim Cruise's life, for by that time his buckboard was nothing but an indistinct shape sixty yards down the road. Most of the bullets droned above his head, probably aimed to catch a man sitting upright on the seat. A few thudded hollowly into the low sides of the buckboard's bed, while one evidently hit a brass fitting on the money chest, for it ricocheted into the darkness with a high whine.

For the next two minutes Jim listened for sounds of pursuit to take up that of the voices fading out behind him. But he heard nothing above the hoof thuds of his ponies and the rattle of the buckboard's iron tires against the hard-packed, rutty road.

Three miles farther on, the money chest set up a racket as it bounced in the bed over a rougher stretch of road. Jim reached back and pulled it in under the seat, taking off his belt to lash one of its leather handles to one of the iron footboard braces.

He had barely straightened in the seat from finishing this task when a wink of powder flame pinpointed the darkness not thirty yards ahead. A second later came the throaty blast of the gun. Tightening the reins, Cruise slowed the team.

"Hold it!" a voice called out loudly enough to be heard above the buckboard's rattle.

Jim Cruise's hand had fallen to the butt of the weapon thrust through his waistband before he made out the shapes of the group of riders through the darkness. A keen wariness warned him to lift his hand from his weapon and slouch carelessly forward in the seat, the team now at a standstill.

The first rider alongside the buckboard, a

squat shape in the saddle of a long-legged dun, muttered: "Hell, this ain't it."

"Ain't what?" Jim Cruise queried, leaning across to spit carelessly over the side into the road. "What you gents mean by shootin' at me?"

The others had reined in behind the first rider, farther away, making it apparent to Cruise that the man was their leader. He was close enough now so that his square, broken-nosed face could be plainly seen. That face was covered with a two-day growth of beard.

Ignoring Cruise's question, the rider wiped a match alight along the skirt of his saddle, held it out while he inspected first the driver of the buckboard, then the vehicle itself. The shadow of the seat and Jim Cruise's legs hid the money chest.

"Where you comin' from?" the leader snapped abruptly.

"Upcañon. I got a place up there."

"Where you goin'?" The man's voice grated curtly.

"To see a girl down below."

Someone in the knot of riders laughed and said: "I'll trade you places, stranger."

"Is there a stage station above?" queried the rider alongside.

"Four miles." Cruise's voice had taken on

an irritable ring. "You mighty near hit me with that slug, mister."

"Never mind that. I want to know about the stage station. Did you see anything as you came past? We thought we heard shots up there."

"Soldiers," Jim stated. "About twenty of 'em. A few down by the river shootin' at driftwood. There was one jasper there could hit a stick two times out of three. Shootin' a Forty-Five, too. I never did see such. . . ."

"How long had they been there?" the rider cut in impatiently.

Cruise shrugged his wide shoulders. "They passed my place about six. Likely as not, they're eatin' right now."

The rider wheeled his dun horse out from the buckboard, saying sharply to his men: "If we hurry, we'll surprise 'em." He cast a warning glance at Cruise. "You're to forget you saw us."

"I know a way to make him forget," one of the riders spoke up.

"Don't shoot, damn you, Bart!" the leader exploded. He swore at the man. Then: "Get your rig movin', stranger."

Cruise took his time about picking up the reins and getting his team under way again. For the next few seconds the muscles along his back crawled in expectation of a bullet's slamming into him. Then he ventured a look behind. The road was deserted.

V

"A LAST REQUEST"

There wasn't any way Jim Cruise could have avoided meeting Lieutenant McMurtry's detachment of ten cavalrymen from Fort Reeder. It was past noon of the next day, and he had succeeded nicely in circling the village where he'd hired the buckboard. Fort Reeder lay sixty miles to the south. He expected to be there by sunup tomorrow.

The team was at a walk, slogging up a steep grade in the faintly marked trail. Lieutenant McMurtry's detachment rode over the crest of the hill while the team was yet twenty yards short of it.

Corporal Kennedy was one of the ten riders. Kennedy let out a yell. "That's Cruise!"

Four seconds later Jim Cruise was staring into the bores of ten rifles. Cruise spoke to the lieutenant, pointing to the money chest under the seat. "Here's your payroll. Last night a dozen riders raided your men at a stage station up the Río Grande. I was there a half hour before and saved this for you."

McMurtry smiled smugly. "A damned likely story. Now, go ahead and tell me how one man could steal a paymaster's chest from a detachment of twenty soldiers?"

Cruise started to tell him, only started, for in half a minute McMurtry's laugh cut in sharply on his words. "You can't make it stick, Cruise." Then the lieutenant's face sobered. "You and your men probably did raid the paymaster at that stage station. We'll doubtless find you've murdered the whole lot. I was just plain lucky to run into you while you were making your getaway. But I'm damned if I understand why you'd head back this way." He nodded to Kennedy. "Cut one of those horses out of the harness and tie him onto it, corporal. And gag him. We can't listen to his talk all the way back to the post."

They rode all the rest of that day, stopping at dusk to light a fire and eat a hearty meal. McMurtry, a gentleman, didn't try to starve his prisoner. Cruise was taken off his horse, his arms and hands untied, and the gag taken from his mouth. He ate the same rations as the others, tinned beef, hardtack, and coffee.

Only once did anyone speak to him. As he was being lifted onto his horse once more, McMurtry came alongside and said: "The only thing I can't understand is why you dared come back this way."

"I was bringing the money to Major Dorn."

A laugh greeted this remark. "Better gag him again, Kennedy. He'll have *us* believing him if we aren't careful."

The lights of Fort Reeder winked across the distance at them shortly before one the next morning. Jim Cruise had caught brief snatches of sleep. He was exhausted after two sleepless nights, and only when the ropes had numbed his arms and legs did he waken to stir feebly and start his blood circulating again. He was thankful for the relief of being carried into the jail — he couldn't stand when they took him off his horse's bare back — and to be once more lying on the pile of straw that had served as a bed two nights ago. He was too tired to notice that the jail had been repaired, new plaster showing along the base of the wall adjoining the magazine and the door swinging on new hinges.

At seven the next morning Corporal Kennedy wakened him by sloshing half a pailful of water into his face. As Jim sat up, Kennedy growled: "Come along with me."

A short time later Major Dorn met them on the wide porch fronting headquarters.

He stood on the top step, a squat, neat shape with hands on hips, looking down at the prisoner. His grizzled face was flushed, and anger flared in his eyes.

"Corporal Kennedy, you are to hold your men ready to serve as a firing squad to execute the prisoner!" he barked. Then he turned to the two sentries, flanking the door. "Take him into my office."

Cruise was taken by each arm and unceremoniously ushered past the orderly's desk in the hallway and into a large office containing a desk and a long rectangular table with eight chairs arranged about its four sides. Four blue-uniformed men sat at the table. They rose as Dorn entered the room.

The major took the chair at the far end of the table. His voice, when he spoke, trembled with fury. "In my position as post commander I have the authority to hold any sort of investigation I think suits the circumstances. Is that understood, gentlemen?"

The officers agreed immediately.

"We'll dispense with the formalities and make this as brief as possible. You gentlemen understand the charges. The prisoner has committed robbery, murder on eight counts, and three nights ago endangered the lives of every man in this post by causing an explosion within the boundaries of the magazine. We don't know yet what has happened to the detachment riding guard on the paymaster. But we can be fairly certain that a few are dead. I ask that you find the prisoner guilty of willful murder and authorize me to order his execution at the hands of a firing squad."

"Has the prisoner anything to say?" asked a man wearing the shoulder bars of a captain.

Jim Cruise looked at Major Dorn. "Three nights ago I saw your daughter. Did she tell you about it?"

"I'm punishing her as she deserves." The major's manner was blunt, arrogant. "She will be confined to the house until I see fit to let her out."

"Did she ask you to wire that Texas sheriff?"

"She did. The idea is preposterous under the circumstances. You have furnished the evidence against yourself. You broke jail. You were captured with the paymaster's money chest in your possession. You aren't going to be brazen enough to still protest your innocence."

Jim Cruise had known minutes ago that talk was futile. He had never before faced a situation like this, one that left him so helpless. It had all started in his first dealings with Guy Bates. Lacking proof of the man's guilt in all this, he was at the same time convinced that Bates could furnish proof of his innocence, and he was just as convinced that the sutler would never do it.

That thought prompted him to look out the front office window and across the parade ground toward the sutler's two-story stone store. Even this early in the morning signs of activity showed across there. A three-team stage was waiting in front to start the morning trip to Gody, the driver busy loading his cargo into the boot. Three soldiers stood talking to him, a few more watching from the shade of the wide porch. A fine-looking dun horse stood at the hitch rail, down-headed as though. . . .

A dun horse! Jim Cruise was suddenly remembering the man on the dun who had stopped him on the stage road two nights ago, the man with the square, ugly face, the leader of those ten riders who had been so interested in what was happening at the stage station.

Cruise faced the table once more and drawled: "Has a condemned man the right to make a last request?"

"One that's reasonable," the major snapped.

"This is reasonable. If you'll look across there toward the store, you'll see a dun horse. I want the owner of that horse brought in here."

Dorn was frowning belligerently. "Why?"

"He's one of the bunch that raided the paymaster's ambulance two nights ago," Jim said. Then, to make sure he got action: "One of my wild bunch."

Dorn's portly frame lunged up out of the chair. "Cummings, get that man." One of the officers at the table rose quickly and ran to the door. Outside, his voice could be plainly heard calling out to Corporal Kennedy. In ten seconds Jim Cruise saw Kennedy and four of his men headed across the parade ground.

VI

"DOUBLE-CROSSER'S DOOM"

Florence Dorn, from the window of her bedroom, saw Corporal Kennedy and his men start across the parade ground. She had earlier seen Jim Cruise being taken to headquarters. She understood fully what was to happen to him.

She was a little awed at her feelings toward this Jim Cruise. Four days ago he had

been a complete stranger. Now he was anything but that. The morning after her visit
to the jail she and her father had argued violently over him, but she had found her father too stubborn a man to be reasoned
with. So that morning she had ridden the
two miles across to the town of Duty
without her father's knowledge. She had
paid a man over there twenty dollars to take
a telegram out to the way station at Gody,
promising him more upon his return, if he
brought an answer.

Just now she heard someone downstairs
at the front door, talking with her father's
housekeeper. She was a little annoyed at the
sound of their voices breaking into her
thoughts. But the next instant she heard the
woman call up: "Miss Florence! There's a
man here who wants to see you. He says it's
important."

Those words brought Florence Dorn up
out of her chair and across the room in
frantic haste. She ran down the stairs, seeing
that the man standing hat in hand at the
front door was the young 'puncher who'd
taken her message to Gody.

She was almost afraid to ask him the question in her mind, but finally she managed it.
"Was there a message?"

He grinned, nodded, and reached into his

Stetson to take a yellow envelope out of it. "There was, miss. I had to wait a whole day for it."

She snatched the envelope from his hand, hesitating only a moment before she tore it open. The delay in the answer meant only one thing to her — bad news. Nevertheless, she opened the blank and read the message:

Sheriff Grant away on fishing trip, but I can answer personally as to the whereabouts of James Cruise for past three months. He has been here in Rimrock since July Fourth when he won the turkey shoot. Glad to supply any further information.
Deputy U.S. Commissioner Waldron

From the despair brought on by the message's first sentence, Florence Dorn's hopes now surged alive. Before she had finished reading the words, she was already brushing past the stranger and going down the steps.

"How about the money, miss?" the 'puncher asked suddenly.

Florence turned, called to the housekeeper. "Get my purse out of the bedroom and give this man fifty dollars." And with that she was running out across the parade ground toward headquarters.

She was one of the first to see the paymaster's white-topped ambulance turn in at the main gates behind headquarters. Troopers rode on each side of the vehicle. One, the officer in command, she guessed, left his place at the head of the double line and turned in at the hitch rail in front of headquarters and climbed the steps. To one side of her, Corporal Kennedy's squad of men was coming back across the parade ground. Along with them were Guy Bates and a thick-set man outfitted in range clothes. Florence hurried, anxious to avoid meeting Bates.

As she approached her father's office door, the orderly on duty at his desk in the hallway said sharply: "You can't go in there, miss."

She ignored him, opening the door and going in before he could get out of his chair to stop her.

As she closed the door, she heard her father say: "Cruise, this finishes you. Three men were killed at the stage station the other night, four more wounded. The lieutenant recognizes you. I'd like to issue orders to have you drawn and quartered." Then he looked across at the door to ask who was interrupting, and his jaw fell open in amazement.

"Dad, I want you to read this." The girl

walked around to the major and handed him the telegram.

"Florence, you'll please leave," Dorn said, controlling his anger with obvious effort and throwing the yellow envelope onto the table before him. "I can't be disturbed now."

His daughter remained where she was, and said quietly: "Read it, Dad."

Not wanting to be made a fool of in the presence of his fellow officers, Dorn picked up the message and hastily scanned the typewritten lines. All at once something he read caught his attention. He reread the message. Then, holding it out to the officer on his right, he was about to speak when the door opened. Corporal Kennedy ushered in Guy Bates and a stranger.

Dorn must have sensed at that moment that this investigation was getting beyond his control. For days now he had worked himself into a passion of hatred around this outlaw, Jim Cruise. Now, with the undeniable evidence in Cruise's favor contained in the telegram, the major understood instantly that he was going to have to admit an error in judgment. He wanted to do so in the presence of as few people as possible.

That was his reason for reaching out to take the telegram away from the officer on his right before it had been read and saying crisply: "Something unforeseen has happened, gentlemen. If you'll be so good as to leave, I'll pursue this investigation privately." Then, faced with the astonished glances of all the men in uniform present, he told Corporal Kennedy: "You'll keep the room under strict guard . . . outside."

There was a thirty-second silence as the five officers and Kennedy and his men filed out.

Then, as the door closed, Dorn said irritably: "Get on with it, Cruise. You asked to have this man brought here. You know him?"

Jim Cruise stepped away from the table and alongside the window at the front wall. He eyed the rider of the dun with the hint of a smile easing the sharp angles of his lean face. "Tell him where you were night before last, stranger."

The man was about to speak when Guy Bates's protest interrupted him.

"Major Dorn, I want an explanation. This gentleman, a business associate of mine, was busy with me ten minutes ago when your men broke into my office. They insisted on bringing him over here. He's a private citizen, and you have no authority over him."

Dorn, somewhat taken aback by such an outburst from a man he had thought his friend, blustered: "Authority be damned. I'm commandant of this post."

"Ask Bates's friend where he was two nights ago, Major," Jim Cruise said.

Dorn didn't miss the look of fear that flashed into the stranger's smoky blue eyes. "Well, man, speak up."

"I'll answer for his whereabouts," Bates put in quickly. "He was with me at the hotel over in Duty two nights ago."

"There you have it, Cruise." The major shifted his hard glance to his prisoner. Abruptly he leaned over to bang his fist on the table. "I want it straight from the shoulder. If you've got something to say, say it."

Florence Dorn's low voice sounded from the far corner of the room. "You might read Jim Cruise that telegram, Dad."

The major shot her an angry look, but finally pointed to the telegram. "This is from a U.S. Deputy Commissioner. It says you haven't been out of Texas since early July, Cruise. What about it?"

"Ask Bates," came Cruise's easy drawl. "Two nights ago, right after I'd pulled out of the stage station with that paymaster's money chest, I met this stranger and ten other riders along the road. They stopped me, asked about the troops and where they were. He's one of the men that raided the stage station."

Dorn's glance whipped across to the stranger. Alongside, Guy Bates stood with eyes narrow-lidded now and most of the color drained out of his face. The major saw this, caught that look of guilt instantly.

"So you're mixed up in this, Bates." The major's voice was low, gruff. "So Jim Cruise's guess was right, after all."

A double-barreled Derringer slid down out of the sleeve of Bates's coat and into his hand. He whipped it up, lined it at Dorn.

"Back, all of you!" the sutler snarled. "If any of you makes a move, Dorn gets both barrels square in the guts."

Jim Cruise's high frame tensed, stopping his forward stride. Bates stood directly in front of him, at the end of the table opposite the major. The stranger, beyond Bates, reached in under his vest and lifted out a short-barreled Colt .45. "Play it right, Guy," he cautioned Bates.

Bates backed away from the table a step so that he could bring Cruise into his line of vision. Then, his face set in a mocking smile, he said: "You're leavin' here with us, Major. You're leavin' here with this cutter rammed into your ribs. And if anyone tries to stop us, they'll be layin' you in a nice soft six-foot bed of dirt and soundin' taps over you a day or two from now. Just step around here and let's be on our way."

The short silence was ended by Jim Cruise's soft drawl. "It was nice of you to bring that gun along, Miss Florence."

The girl was across the room, slightly behind Guy Bates. For an instant Bates's glance clung to Dorn, but then he shifted it, and turned his head toward the girl.

In that split second Jim Cruise lunged. Bates must have sensed what was coming, for his head whipped around and his Derringer swung toward Cruise. But it was beaten down a fraction of an instant later by Cruise's down-swinging fist. It whirled out of the sutler's hand and to the floor at his feet.

Bates dodged, so that Cruise's lunge only served to turn him completely around. "Get him, Dirk!" Bates shouted, and swung a fist at Cruise.

His blow never landed. Cruise caught the sutler's arm and twisted it, and Bates went to his knees. Then Cruise was on him, behind him, so that Dirk couldn't get in a shot. Cruise's right fist slashed down once, caught Bates a glancing blow on the head.

Florence Dorn saw Bates's hand flash out toward the fallen Derringer, and she cried: "The gun, Jim!"

Cruise heard her, rolled over, and his hand beat Bates's reach by a bare inch.

He swung the weapon up and around at Dirk. But he wasn't fast enough. Dirk's .45 blasted out a concussion that beat the air. Jim felt a breathtaking blow hit him at the left side of his chest. Fighting the blinding pain of it, he lined the Derringer and pulled both triggers. The buck of the gun whipped it out of his hand. He threw himself outward from Bates and into Dirk's legs.

As his shoulder hit the man's shins, a heavy blow struck his shoulder. The .45 abruptly hit the floor alongside his head. Something wet fell onto the back of his neck, and an instant later Dirk's heavy body dropped down onto him, driving the breath out of his lungs in a quick gasp.

As he struggled to get from under the weight of Dirk's heavy bulk and reach the fallen six-gun, he heard Major Dorn say: "It's all right, Cruise."

Glancing back over his shoulder, Jim Cruise saw Dorn's wide shape beyond the table, a service Colt in his fist lined at Guy Bates, who was picking himself up off the floor. Dirk didn't move. Wondering about that, Jim rolled over and pushed Dirk's weight away. He felt his shirt clinging wetly to his back. Once Dirk had been rolled over,

Jim Cruise immediately saw why he hadn't moved. The front of his vest and shirt was torn to ribbons. A gaping hole centered his chest where two shotgun charges from the Derringer had torn into him.

That sight was Jim Cruise's last before a red haze settled down before his eyes. He vaguely heard the shouts outside in the hallway, then voices nearer. Once he thought he heard Florence Dorn speak, and he tried vainly to make out her words. Then unconsciousness took its hold on him, and he wasn't aware of the hands that lifted him gently from the floor.

Hours later he opened his eyes to stare upward at a white ceiling. When he tried to take a deep breath, a pain like the stab of a knife got him low down at the left side of his chest.

"Better now?" a voice to one side of him queried.

Jim turned his head, saw a white-uniformed man standing alongside the bed. He nodded, realizing he must be in the post hospital and that this man was a doctor.

"Good enough to see someone?"

Again Jim Cruise nodded.

He watched the doctor go to the door of the room and open it. "Don't let him talk too much," he said to someone outside. "The bullet touched his left lung."

Then Florence was coming into the room, closing the door softly behind her. Jim Cruise couldn't take his glance away from her. As she stood now, the late afternoon light slanting in through the room's west window caught her tall figure and put dancing lights in her golden hair. Jim Cruise knew, without surprise, that he loved her.

She came over to stand alongside the bed and for a long moment didn't speak. Then, with utter frankness, she said: "I'll always love you for what you did today, Jim."

"Love is a strong word," was the embarrassed answer he made. He was wishing she hadn't said quite that. It was hard enough to see her standing there, a picture he would never forget, filling him with an indefinable longing.

"Not a strong enough word," she told him. "You saved Dad's life. Guy Bates has confessed. They found most of the money in his safe at his saloon in town."

Jim Cruise was silent for a good quarter minute. Somehow he didn't find it hard to meet this girl's amazingly direct hazel eyes. In them he read something that made him ask: "When I'm up off my back, would you ride down to Texas with me and look over a

337

fair-size ranch and a two-room log shack? It's up in the hills, alongside a trout stream."

"It could be out in the desert, ten miles from water, and I wouldn't mind," she said, as she leaned down and kissed him.

About the Author

Peter Dawson is the *nom de plume* used by Jonathan Hurff Glidden. He was born in Kewanee, Illinois, and was graduated from the University of Illinois with a degree in English literature. In his career as a Western writer he published sixteen Western novels and wrote over one hundred and twenty Western short novels and short stories for the magazine market. From the beginning he was a dedicated craftsman who revised and polished his fiction until it shone as a fine gem. His Peter Dawson novels are noted for their adept plotting, interesting and well-developed characters, their authentically researched historical backgrounds, and his stylistic flair. During the Second World War, Glidden served with the U.S. Strategic and Tactical Air Force in the United Kingdom. Later in 1950 he served for a time as Assistant to Chief of Station in Germany. After the war, his novels were frequently serialized in *The Saturday Evening Post*. Peter Dawson titles such as *Gunsmoke Graze*, *Royal Gorge*, and *Ruler of the Range* are generally conceded to be among his best titles, although he was an extremely consistent writer, and virtually all his fiction has retained its classic stature among readers of all generations. One of Jon Glidden's finest techniques was his ability, after the fashion of Dickens and Tolstoy, to tell his stories via a series of dramatic vignettes which focus on a wide assortment of different characters, all tending to develop their own lives, situations, and predicaments, while at the same time propelling the general plot of the story toward a suspenseful conclusion. He was no less gifted as a master of the short novel and short story. *Dark Riders of Doom* (Five Star Western, 1996) was the first collection of his Western short novels and stories to be published.

Additional Copyright Information: